William Hutchison

BEFORE
THE FACT

MACMILLAN

ACKNOWLEDGEMENTS

I would like to thank the following people for their time and expertise: Maître Dominique Coroller, barrister at Quimper; Jean-Marie Altieri, Commissaire of Police, Nice; Gerry Northam of BBC Radio; ex-Chief Inspector Tony Brightwell, of Bishop International; and Detective Inspector Terry Burke, of the Foreign Office Caribbean Task Force.

For Tom and Frances

First published 1997 by Macmillan

an imprint of Macmillan Publishers Ltd
25 Eccleston Place, London SW1W 9NF
and Basingstoke

Associated companies throughout the world

ISBN 0 333 66247 4

Copyright © William Hutchison 1997

The right of William Hutchison to be identified as the
author of this work has been asserted by him in accordance
with the Copyright, Designs and Patents Act 1988.

1 3 5 7 9 8 6 4 2

A CIP catalogue record for this book is available from
the British Library

Typeset by CentraCet Limited, Cambridge
Printed by Mackays of Chatham plc, Chatham, Kent

Chapter One

'I WANT TO SEE a lawyer.'

The thin-faced gendarme who drives breaks into a laugh, and says something unintelligible in his thick Niçois accent. Luccioni says: 'Did you understand that?'

'No.'

'He said you are two months early.' He pauses. 'In two months' time prisoners will have the right to see lawyers straight away. They are changing the law. But for now, precisely for forty-eight hours, you will talk to us.'

Forty-eight hours. Can I do that? Can I keep it up? Because if I can, I might have a chance. If I can get it right.

'The British consul?'

'No-no. Nobody.'

Suddenly I feel alone, and very daunted.

I am handcuffed to the younger of the two in the back, who wears a bandanna over his pigtail and looks like a drug dealer. The cuffs don't seem to bother him the way they bother me – cold, heavy.

Swinging in and out of the traffic boastfully, the squad car runs past the monumental conference centre that marks the limit of the smart coastal end of Nice. We leave behind now the rows of palms set in neat flower beds, the stately Empire apartment blocks, the Porsches and poodles. Then the older, also monumental Palais des Sports, a palace of the people. I am set apart from the morning crowds in the rain. It won't rain on my head, my upturned face.

Luccioni, small, melancholy, unsurprised, and impossible to read, turns in the front seat to face me.

'You must have lost control, huh?'

I don't answer.

'Maybe he said things to you that made you lose your temper?'

I don't speak. I have to be so careful of what I say. Everything hinges on what I now say in front of these four. *He confessed in the car. We all heard him.*

The squad car sweeps through a right turn; now we are in an area of high-rise blocks and wide streets, where children kick footballs around. Convenient, I suppose, that the police and their petty-criminal associates live in the same place. Not successful criminals – the ones I have come to know. They don't go back to where they were born. We turn again; a broad railway on the left, which opens out into stockyards, silent and empty in the rain. It seems to me that we are going round in circles, but perhaps I have lost my sense of direction. Between the towers I catch a glimpse of cliffs hemming in this grimy corner. This is the worst moment of my life.

'So perhaps it was passion, huh? You, the English – maybe you don't know? In France still it is considered a mitigating circumstance. Maybe four or five years in prison, if you plead guilty to that: or maybe you were not acting alone? Maybe you were just an accessory, in somebody else's plan – huh?'

Again I am silent, and he finally seems to lose interest.

'*Allez,*' he says to the thin, grim-faced gendarme, who turns again and this time drives straight.

We skirt a long high stone wall – at least three hundred yards – until we come to a gate. On the other side of the street is an open car park with some kind of gypsy encampment: old caravans and mobile homes with washing lines strung between them. That's it: my last glimpse of the world. I twist in my seat – I can't help it – and gaze through the rear windscreen at this dingy sight, longingly. Then we are inside the barracks of the *Police Nationale*.

We pull up. The young detective with the bandanna tugs my arm, and I slide across the back seat, out into the rain. Unlike the Nice any Englishman could imagine. There are twelve three-storey stone buildings arranged in four lines, solid and dull like platoons on a parade ground.

He pulls me to a gatehouse set near the high perimeter wall. A fat middle-aged sergeant with red hair and a huge, florid face stands up, pulls back the sliding glass window, and greets him. They exchange a few pleasantries in a bantering tone, and then he turns to me. *Nom?* I spell it for him. *Adresse? Age?* He fills in some more details. Offence?

Murder.

It isn't as I had expected: they're not cruel; quite business-like in fact. I could be a patient in a hospital.

'Come on,' the young one says, pulling at my arm again. I have been in a dream, my head bowed. Then I say to myself: *Concentrate. Everything depends on this.*

Luccioni, too, seems to be in a dream, standing at a small distance, staring out of the gate. But as we pass he falls into step beside me. We walk in silence until we reach the furthest building. It is different to the others: it has a basement, and all the ground-floor windows are blanked out behind their bars. In the middle, down a set of steps, is a metal door, painted a livid green. Luccioni himself presses the bell, and a spotlight switches itself on, so the wall-mounted camera can get a good picture. Then he turns to me.

'Of course, if you plead not guilty, then it would certainly be a charge of premeditated murder. And that is a question of life imprisonment. And because this was a very savage crime, that will mean thirty years. Think of it.'

He slowly descends the steps. A rattling in the lock, the door opening, the cuffs off, and I am pushed into a little lobby inside. Another sliding window on the right, the crash as the door is slammed, bars in front, shouting, and an echoing bang somewhere down a corridor. It is that noise, that prison noise that never stops, nothing to muffle it: shouts, shaking of keys, metal on metal.

I never thought of that: that they might accept a man-slaughter plea; that after three or four years I could be out. But I can't plead guilty. It's too late for that.

They remove the handcuffs, take the prints and the mug-shots, strip me, and bend me over. And a few minutes later, it seems, I am on a grey blanket in a small grey room, staring at a grey metal door, its tiny eye watching me.

If I can get it right, I can walk away from this. If I don't put a foot wrong.

I enjoyed taking drugs because nobody else in the regiment took them. When I was stoned, on leave, I added another string to my bow. This was a side of me my brother officers would never see.

I had a month's leave, and was spending the last fortnight of it in a villa near Marbella with a group of English people I hardly knew. I was there because I had started an affair with one of the women, the sister of an army acquaintance. I liked her group. Upper-class drop-outs with a penchant for drugs, they seemed to accept me, and I believed they were my friends. Later on, too late, I discovered that the English upper class doesn't do things that way.

My experiment with drugs produced its first unhappy result as follows. One evening I took some amphetamine sulphate, smoked hash and drank vodka. A little later we went to a very crowded bar, and I began to experience a kind of violent paranoia. I was absolutely convinced that certain other people in the bar were about to attack me, and this overwhelming sensation pushed me over the edge.

I was told afterwards that I injured three Spaniards, one of them badly enough for stitches. Glasses were smashed and some other damage done. We gave money to the owner and managed to mollify the injured Spaniards. My friends told them I was sick in the head.

I realized then that I was no pro when it came to drugs.

The experiment produced a second unhappy result. The girl I had been sleeping with was called the Honourable Lulu Messing. After the bar incident we argued, and she wouldn't give me any of her bed. I had broken some rule.

When I left, she gave me a parcel to give to her sister, a young married woman called the Honourable Mrs Graining Lensdorf. (No hyphen between the barrels. Let them sue.) The customs people opened it up at the airport. Inside was a wooden carving of an elephant. Inside that was a lot of hash.

When I came up for trial it was discovered that the Hon. Lulu Messing and her friends had set off on a transatlantic crossing by yacht, and were unavailable for comment. So I had acquired a fairly low opinion both of women and of the English gentry.

I served precisely two years, ten months and twelve days of a four-year sentence in a correctional institute near Barcelona. That's a long time when you're in a bunk not an armchair, twitching at the stink of bleach and bodies, worn out by the bright light, deafened by the continuous shouting and banging – the noise, the prison noise that never stops.

I remember coming out. Another kind of light, brighter and very rich, almost painful. It was a spring day with a strong breeze. I remember the blue of the sky, yellow of the sand. Spanish girls in the street, brushing long hair from their eyes.

Then there was a photographer, predictably, which made me furious.

Why a photographer? Because this affair had found its way into the tabloids, and I had become a very minor celebrity in Britain. The tabloids were interested because of my regiment – a smart one, the 7th/10th Hussars, home at that time to various titled people and a personable maharaja – and because I was a public schoolboy who had occasionally appeared in the social pages of *Tatler* and *Harpers and Queen*. Also because the Hon. Lulu Messing – daughter of a viscount who was more in the public eye than most (frequent trade-ins of wife) – was a name, not just an extra like me.

The bitch had a reputation to protect, so naturally she had blackened mine on the drinks-party circuit, turning my friends against me. They closed ranks, of course, as those people would against any outsider. *I never really trusted him; he was always a bit wide, wasn't he? Trying to blame it all on Lulu.* And in the *Sun*, where she gave an interview which I read months after its appearance. With it was a photograph of her sun-bathing at the villa near Marbella; in the public interest, no doubt, that she should be seen in her bikini. I could remember taking the picture. We had made love in the morning, a couple of hours earlier.

She even wrote me a letter saying how sorry she was. She asked me to understand that her father had made her say what she had said.

I was bitter.

I didn't want to stay in Spain. The sound of proletarian Spanish reminded me of the joint. But I couldn't face returning to England. I had no occupation now, no career. The army had been kind at the time of the trial. My commanding officer had written in commiseration, and the adjutant, more or less on his own time, had flown out to Spain to give a character reference. But there could be no question of being taken back. There had been enough publicity, and I knew that everywhere I went in

England, at every party, at every job interview, they'd say: 'Oh, you're *that* Johnny Denner. The one who said he was innocent, and tried to blame the whole thing on some aristocratic girl.'

I crossed the border into south-western France and hitched along the Mediterranean coast. My younger brother, who had become quite rich while I was inside, sent me some money – enough for me to hold out for a couple of months. I thought that I would spend the summer by the sea, lick my wounds, develop a plan. I eventually stopped in Béziers, a nice spot about seventy-five kilometres from the border, but there was no bartending or waiting work, which was what I needed to stop the gap.

Then a friendly restaurateur suggested that I try Cap d'Agde, a purpose-built resort on the nearby coast; the restaurants there might be recruiting seasonal labour.

That move put in front of my nose exactly what I needed: a big marina full of good-looking boats. I saw the masts from a mile away and thought: that will be my rehabilitation – time on a big boat. I love the sea. I love my own sense of balance with its force, through which my hand guides a vessel, the murmurs and shrugs of which I feel in the wheel. There I know what I'm doing; besides teaching me to ski and ride, the army qualified me an offshore yachtmaster. I could happily skipper any one of those sleek craft. So I made enquiries, called an old friend in the regiment to ask him to dig out the certificates, and set about finding work on land.

Without too much difficulty I got a bar job in a smart brasserie at the smart end of the marina. In some ways I regretted that I would be working in this concrete jungle and not among the old stone buildings and pollarded trees of Béziers or some other provincial town. But through the picture windows I could gaze at the forest of masts and rigging, gleaming white and grey, sharp as needles. When there was a breeze I heard the ringing, tuneless music, a little sad, of loose wire halyards slapping against aluminium masts. I could smell the salt, and it was enough for me.

I watched them for three months; perhaps it was just as well; I had a lot of bile to swallow. I had lost more than my career.

I watched the women, too. It's a good place to be, behind a bar: a safe place. A good barman has an edge over the clientele – something indefinable.

When I was in the army I was a rowdy: a banger of tables, a red-faced young man who roared and bawled when he was drunk, quick to take offence. People didn't like me very much and I didn't care. Prison had changed me. There I kept very quiet – because I was scared to death – apart from one fateful occasion early on, a fight in which I came off worse but proved that I wouldn't cooperate – you can guess.

I had the feeling now, standing quietly in my tiny kingdom, that I knew more than anyone around me, that I had seen things they would never see. It was peculiar; I would catch myself smiling a slight, enigmatic smile – the man who had gazed into the abyss. I was deliberate and guarded in what I said, and I didn't speak to people without a reason.

At the time I thought that this was a kind of self-possession, irony of a high order mixed in, and that I was being tough. Now I know that I was injured: the amputee who still feels an itch on his departed foot.

I wanted a woman; but not in any circumstances a whore – because I didn't merely want somewhere to put myself. I wanted a conquest. There was a woman called Sandrine who came into the restaurant quite often. She was an estate agent selling an apartment for Robert, the owner. She drank a pastis at the bar each time she came in; she usually had to wait a few minutes to see him.

She was about forty, very tanned, quite plump but shapely,

still, of course, stylish in simple monochrome suits scattered with gold costume jewellery, crimson lipstick and too much mascara. But she had lovely light blue eyes, a surprise against her dark, coarse, wavy hair: eyes that glittered in the sun like the opal she wore. And she had a good sense of humour, although it didn't always get her over that nervousness one can sense in women of a certain age.

On the second, or perhaps third, occasion we spoke I knew that Sandrine would be happy to have me. We talked about wine, and she mentioned a grower in Fitou (not far from there) who produced a wine so good I wouldn't credit it as a wine of the region. There was something in her eyes. We should drive up there one Saturday, I suggested.

I was guarded, I must admit, because – I know now – I was holding in such a rage about what had happened to me, and also about women, the two rages bundled up together and gnawing at each other. And I must also admit that what I really wanted was one of the little girls I saw in the marina, somewhere between sixteen and twenty, wide-eyed, firm-fleshed and indifferent, and so clean, so incredibly clean and unused, like a fresh orange sliced open, sunlight under water. I wanted to take that silk-skinned flesh in the dust, in the rubble, and fuck the hell out of it, and have the girl panting, soaked in sweat and dirt.

But I could hold in my rage, and I could see that sweets like that weren't for me. If Robert's brasserie had been in a cheaper line of business, the hundred-franc *prix fixe* for the tourist, or if I had been a windsurfing instructor, it would have been a piece of cake. But I worked six evenings a week, so there was little opportunity to meet girls in bars. I watched them during the day, wandering along with their boyfriends, all of them bronzed gnomes with ponytails.

The cashier at Robert's place was a demure, cool-headed brunette with deep, dark eyes and pale skin like marble.

Amazingly, given this Renaissance beauty, she was the local windsurfing champion. I made a play for her, took her out dancing one night, cooked her dinner on another, but it soon emerged that she was engaged to a young lawyer studying to be a ruler of the land at that bureaucrat's École Supérieur in Paris. At the time I was annoyed with her for flirting with me, although much more recently I realized that every woman, engaged, married or past caring, at least has the right to flirt.

And so back to Sandrine – once I had explored these other avenues and found them barred. Three or four weeks had passed, and she had been in on several occasions, usually during the day, and we had talked a little.

We drove down the coast to Fitou and then up into the dry hills behind. In all we must have tasted wines at six or seven producers, and when we got to Béziers, in time for some black coffee before dinner, we were laughing together. She had shown the sensitivity not to ask me about my past, which I regarded as the height of good manners, so I returned the compliment. She told me Robert's life story, hair-raising tales about her ex-husband, a man given to towering rages, anecdotes about idiotic English property buyers.

On our third date I cooked dinner for her, and it was then that I told her my story. Telling it – for the first time – was much harder than I thought. I almost cried because I felt so helpless and worthless; I felt such a strong sense of guilt. She said to me:

'You haven't been with a woman since then, have you?'

I shook my head, and she stretched out her arms. I held her head and I pushed my face into her hair as hard as I could, so that it really hurt me. Her rough, coarse hair; and there were tears in my eyes when I kissed her.

Three months later I had given up hope of skippering anything; the agencies I had tried had nothing to offer, and there seemed to be no way into the closed shop. Then I got my chance.

Horst Stacker strode into the brasserie late on a Friday afternoon. I think that everyone in the room must have looked up, briefly – the man made an impression. He was tall and loose-limbed, his blazer and chinos both slightly too short. It may have been his head that made him so striking: very large, a little chubby – a hint of the cherub – tanned and almost completely bald. Around the back and sides you could see a slight black stubble where he obviously shaved it. He had thick, coarse lips, a small, misshapen nose and protuberant eyes. This makes him sound grotesque, which is not accurate. Although each of his features was unusual, the whole was somehow compelling. It was no doubt in part his personality: he had the manner of a circus ringmaster, or a visiting US president charging down the steps of an aeroplane, bent on embracing someone.

He was an old acquaintance of Robert. On the first night of his visit they took a chunk out of the bar: Robert on cognac, Horst on kümmel. A professional charmer, I could see, watching him in action on his second evening. Robert had raised some capital by taking on a partner, a Parisian doctor. That weekend the doctor had come down to sail, and check nervously the progress of his investment. Horst went to work. At first he listened attentively and agreed with solemnity. As the drink flowed he began to tease and admonish. He took a mannerism and made a slightly piquant joke of it – a subtle form of flattery. Later he flattered the doctor further by disagreeing fervently with his political views.

It was all a little obvious, but Horst carried it off well. After their three pastis apiece they went to their table, father and son, a comedy duo, Horst's hand on the doctor's shoulder. There was something almost amorous about it.

I assumed – they were sitting at the bar but I only heard a little of their conversation, having some work to do in providing drinks for diners – I assumed that Horst was making a special effort on Robert's behalf. But later I saw that he approached every social encounter this way. The next day, and on days thereafter, he intermittently assailed me with his charm. 'I am interested in why a person such as you should be a *barman* here,' he said several times, with a grin in his big eyes – eyes like saucers. He had a habit of putting inordinate emphasis on certain words in each of his carefully constructed sentences. I was willing to be charmed. It turned out that Horst was kicking his heels here while his sixty-foot ketch was being repaired. His French skipper had run her into the harbour wall at Sète, and he had dismissed him. There might, Robert told me, be an opportunity . . . and I was holding my breath.

We had several after-dinner conversations. On the fourth or fifth occasion I told him something of the truth. He was sympathetic, and seemed to believe me.

Then the start of it, when Horst offered me a job. What clinched it was a day we spent together on a lively little fourteen-footer. Nominally Horst was skipper and I was his crew. He had a fair feel for it, but he lacked the confidence that comes with long experience. He was a weekend sailor, and unused to smaller craft.

It was a marvellous day to be out: bright sun, smooth sea, but a fresh force four to take us along at a lick. However, late in the afternoon, when we were some distance from the marina and about six miles from land, a savage little squall blew up. You could see the grey on the horizon darkening quite fast, and then the water in the middle distance ruffling. Horst was used to sixty feet of boat. I don't think he realized that the squall could be unpleasant for us in our light little racer. We had a discussion, almost an argument. He was delighted at the prospect of more wind, excited like a little boy, and wanted to keep all our sail up and run into shore before it. I knew that, if we did that, we would snap the mast, and I told him so. Eventually, and only just in time, he agreed to furl the jib down to a tiny patch and let me lower the mainsail. When the squall came and swept us along at eight or nine knots, he realized that I had been right, and he graciously acknowledged it, then and later back at the brasserie. As I poured the drinks he lavished compliments on my expertise.

The next day he invited me to have a look at his ketch, the *Margherita*. It was custom-built to extravagant standards, far more luxuriously than anything I had sailed. It was very seaworthy too: everything solid, well placed, dependable. The cabin was done out in dark red hardwood, brass and hide, the recessed lights glinting on the shelf edgings and the trimmings round the seats. The table, polished to a glaze, would host a nice dinner party for ten.

While we went round the boat, and I looked at the essentials – rigging, instrumentation and so on – I repeated to myself, rather childishly I admit: *Please ask me to skipper this lovely boat. Go on, ask me, for God's sake.*

After dinner he popped the question, and I jumped at the chance. He could have offered me a salary of dried lentils. My only small regret was that I wouldn't be able to say goodbye to Sandrine; Horst had already squared things with Robert, and wanted to sail the next morning. So sail we did.

Most of the time there were just three of us on board: Philippe, a quiet, almost taciturn young Frenchman, his fiancée Isabelle and myself. Their companionship suited me quite well. Philippe was waiting to do a postgraduate qualification in marine biology, and could explain all kinds of things about the sea and what lived in it. Isabelle was bright and honest. I won't talk much about them. Towards the end of the summer they gradually fell out, and the engagement was called off.

On the boat I savoured a freedom greater than any I had known since childhood, and I still relished some of the everyday things I had missed in prison, the food and drink as much as anything else. One evening in a restaurant in Italy, eating on my own, I had a dish of calves' liver in butter and sage. It almost made me cry, that liver, absurd as this may sound; it took me back to a little Italian restaurant in the Pimlico Road in which I used to develop my prospects with uninhibited girls.

On the boat I had plenty of time to think about what I had lost. My education would have opened to me most doors in the establishment, most of the oak-panelled doors on which most English people care to knock. I could have continued as the dashing officer, and perhaps floated up to the general staff. I could have obtained a soft job in the City and pulled in a six-figure salary. An even softer option would have been the gentlemanly sale of houses, land, wine, antiques – all the jobs reserved for people like me. All the jobs closed to people with drug convictions.

For much of the summer Horst was too busy to join us, occupied, so he told me, with the raising of capital for a number of film projects which would be shot in Eastern Europe. Sometimes he would bring business associates. Usually they were pretty short on table manners, but they doubtless made it up in boardroom skills.

In September we went to Corsica and collected him in Bastia. Then we circled the island. After that we headed for Antibes, where the boat was to be laid up for the winter. The idyll was almost over, and my recovery – it seemed to me – almost complete.

On the last hot, rich night we anchored off Saint-Florent. I cooked the dinner, and the four of us ate together. Then Philippe and Isabelle disappeared, and Horst and I drank kümmel on deck. I pictured myself standing in the marina at Antibes, my suitcases at my feet but no ideas.

'What do you *do*, Horst? What do you really do?'

'I am a consultant. Really that would be the best term to describe my occupation. I facilitate meetings between people, I make introductions, I raise money for projects that interest me; if they really interest me, I might even *invest*, although that is rare. You see, Johnny, one of my true areas of expertise is in the emerging and developing markets in Eastern Europe and the former Soviet Union. There is incredible unreleased *energy* there, you know – and people over here, they look at the place and see the smokestack industries falling to pieces and the grim-faced people and the corrupt bureaucrats, and they *throw* up their hands and say: we can't do business there. They don't know how to deal with this; they don't know how to deal with these people. I help with that.'

'OK, then,' I asked him, 'how would you offer a bribe?'

'You might be discussing a matter, and you might say: "I can see what the obstacle is here. It is quite impossible to resolve our problem in a discussion in this little office. I would recommend some time in the *mountains*, away from these pressures. Is there anywhere you could suggest?"'

We laughed.

'Or: "Of course, we understand that some payments may have to be made to officials who expect this kind of thing, and we would at least like to ask somebody trustworthy to administer and supervise the matter."'

'Of course,' I said, 'they'd be horrified if anyone suggested *they* themselves might accept a bribe.'

'Of course. How much do you think these *officials* might require?'

'At least a hundred thousand,' I replied, archly.

'That's too much. Do you not think that they might be persuaded to accept less?'

'They are very unreasonable, I'm afraid.'

'But they have more reasonable associates, perhaps?'

'There's a lawyer in Dickens who has an imaginary partner who's incredibly severe, and whenever an employee asks for anything he says: "Of course, I'd be happy to oblige – but my partner would never allow it."'

'It is also like the man who goes to the doctor and says: "My friend has a venereal disease."'

'Oh, really? Show me.'

'That is just what you *don't* say.'

'You don't say.' I filled our glasses. 'I shouldn't be doing this. A kümmel hangover is pretty well the only thing in this world that can make me seasick.'

'Here's to your hangover, Johnny,' he said, and he raised his glass. A good man; we had become friends.

He sat upright suddenly, as if just waking up, and said:

'Now, listen, you have done a really superb job, I mean it, a really *superb* job, and you know it makes me think that next year I want to get the boat in March, for example, and not May. So I want you to skipper her again, you know.'

'Well. In principle I'd love it. It's been great for me, Horst. It's really restored me. But I don't know where I'm going to be in March.'

'Where do you want to be? You're going to go back to England?'

'I don't think so. I'm afraid my celebrity status might make life a little difficult. I'm not really a celebrity, but what happened to me is well enough known for somebody to remember and tell everyone else.'

'And your claims of innocence? They made no difference?'

I laughed. 'If anything, my claims of innocence earned *more* publicity, because this girl Lulu Messing was a gossip-column figure – much more than me; I was always on the fringes. She defended her reputation in public. Anyway, you know what people are like with claims of innocence. Unless they're family or really close to you, they say no smoke without fire.'

He spoke about a similar thing that had once happened to him. At school a boy had given him a flick-knife, with the pretence that the gift was a mark of respect. It had been used the day before to injure another boy. When the authorities discovered it, Horst took the blame.

'That must have been a rough school,' I said.

Horst laughed uproariously.

'No, no, it was a *very* expensive private school.'

He laughed again, then turned the conversation back to me.

'But why don't you stay the winter in Antibes?'

'I would, Horst, but – it's one thing finding a seasonal job in April. In September they'll be laying people off.'

He gave a long 'Ye-e-s,' leaning back in his chair and closing his eyes for a second.

'But *you* have something to offer that these assorted' – he waved his hand and wrinkled his face in disgust – 'beachbums and Italians and Filipinos and people like this don't have. You are an *upper-class Englishman*.' He sat up again, then whispered: 'I mean, this is a very valuable commodity, Johnny.'

'To whom?'

He laughed again.

'To who-o-o-m! I like that. The *Americans*! That's whom. In Florida there are many upper-class *Englishmen* working as butlers. But they are paid so well. It is such a status symbol, you see. It is much better than having a Mercedes *car*, for example. And there are many Americans in Cannes, Nice, Antibes.'

'A butler,' I said, raising my eyebrows, laughing a little. A servant. In a sense I was Horst's servant. But a yacht's skipper isn't a servant to its owner, any more than a sergeant is to a young officer, or a skiing instructor to a tourist. We know what we're doing, we're experts, and our masters are under our protection, and when necessary they have to obey us. It's also the only way to follow an expensive vocation. Domestic service is by comparison a despicable occupation. And yet . . . if I found such a job in that part of the world, it would allow me to return to the *Margherita* not much more than six months later. And if not the *Margherita*, something similar.

'I know a number of these kind of people myself. So I could make some enquiries, if this interests you.'

After a moment I replied: 'Can I think about it during tomorrow, Horst, and tell you in the evening? I am grateful, but I'm just not sure yet what I want to do.'

The following afternoon I thanked him and asked him to follow up his leads.

Five days later I was on deck in the marina at Antibes, polishing a pair of old brown brogues I hadn't worn since before my time in prison, spit-and-polishing them until they glinted in the sun. That would be among my duties as a butler, no doubt. In this respect the parade ground is not a bad schooling for domestic service. These shoes – which I had had sent to Cap d'Agde, along with various other articles of clothing – had powerful associations for me, like many of the things I had grown up with but hadn't seen for ages – since before prison. When I left my public school my father walked me down Jermyn Street. These had been among the purchases that day. They had never quite fitted, in fact, but they had never worn out.

Later that day I was due at the house of an American lawyer named Marenkian, acquaintance and business associate of Horst.

I laid out an almost new pair of cream cotton trousers, a belt of woven leather, a striped summer shirt from Lewin, a woven silk tie from Turnbull and Asser, my regimental blazer. (This last didn't carry any insignia; it was simply the regulation item supplied at great expense by Huntsman. It was capable of keeping the Catterick wind out, and thus far too heavy for Antibes, but I had nothing else and assumed that I was expected to be smart and very English.)

This is what Horst told me about these people. 'John Marenkian is an American lawyer who works sometimes here and sometimes in the States. He helps these expatriate Americans to evade tax, and he also advises Europeans on investing into the States, which has been useful to me in start-up finance for films   which is what I really like to do, you know. Yes, we have dealings, and you might see me occasionally when you are working there. He has a grown-up son and a daughter – I don't know if they are there. I think he will like you, because he is a smart New England person who will enjoy a *smart* English army officer in his house. A delightful old farmhouse near the old town of Valbonne – do you know this? Ah, it's very nice, a small place in the hills about fifteen kilometres from here. Very difficult to get one of those in this area now. Very useful to be a lawyer to get one, and more useful to have a lot of money – and he has both. So, good luck, Johnny. I hope you get on well.'

Chapter Two

I PASSED MANY places along the way that could have housed rich Americans: Californian haciendas in prominent places to enjoy the view and make a statement; that's what I expected of these people. But the Marenkian place turned out to be quite hard to find, and I had to ask for it twice. It was down a rutted byway (*rutted*, on the Côte d'Azur!), behind a high white wall about sixty yards long, with flat black metal gates set into it at the far end. There was an entry phone with a camera beside the gates, so I got out, buzzed, and stood selfconsciously as the little red light beneath the lens illuminated. At the crackle on the speaker I said, 'Johnny Denner,' and got back into the rental car. With a slight shudder the gates opened.

'Deeply-to-die-for,' I heard an estate agent say once; he must have been referring to the Marenkian place. A gravel drive curved up a slight incline to a big Provençal farmhouse, built of the pale sand-coloured stone of the region, its roof, four or five tiles thick, projecting over the windows of the upper floor. Along the front ran a raised terrace, shaded by tall parasol pines. On the left was an open outbuilding, providing a cool space with deep sofas and armchairs at one end and a large wooden dining table in the centre. Beyond it the ground sloped down to a wooded hollow in which, I found out later, the tennis court was set. To the right of the house was a circular paved area, from which a set of steps led down into another hollow. At the end of these lay the swimming pool, with its own outbuildings. The overwhelming impression was one of calm: patches of bright sunlight on the walls of the house, its shutters closed; pools of shade in the grounds; beds of acacia and oleander. In front of the house was a rich green lawn. Maintaining a lawn in that climate is something that requires effort.

I walked up to the terrace and put my head around one of the sliding glass doors at the centre of the façade. They opened on to a cool living room, at least forty feet, with a wide fireplace at each end. In the middle was an arrangement of four sofas and four armchairs around two rosewood coffee tables, all resting on a thirty-foot Chinese rug, which in turn rested on polished terracotta tiles. Everything was as big as it could be: a lacquered tray that must have been four feet long, table lamps that much in height, cast-iron candlesticks that came up to my nose. Not everything was in good taste. Guarding the entrance to the sofa enclave were four emerald-green lions on their haunches; by the set of steps leading into the hallway a bronze mastiff, its collar studded with semi-precious stones. The room was impeccably tidy: no sign of personal possessions, not a book in sight. It had, in fact, a strange air of desertion, as if nobody lived there – the air of a hotel apartment or the reception area of a luxurious office suite.

After I had stood there a couple of minutes, making this decor analysis, one of the doors off the hall opened and a very tall man aged about fifty stepped down to greet me.

'Mr Denner?' he said. 'I'm John Marenkian.'

He had the slow, measured speech of a senator or a law-school professor; relaxed control. His hand was gnarled, heavily veined, strong, but it gripped gently. His head was long, with high cheekbones, topped with straight, steely-grey hair combed across. His nose was thick, his ears swollen, Adam's apple prominent. He was impeccably groomed, as you might expect of a wealthy East Coast American: a pale blue shirt in sea-island cotton, crisp and clean as new over his suntanned neck, grey trousers with a sharp crease. His eyes were penetrating; deep-set and dark under thick black eyebrows.

'Come down to my office,' he said, and we walked down a narrow asphalt path under the trees to the left of the main garden.

'I have a small building out in the grounds, and I can commute to work in the mornings. Gives me some peace and quiet.'

The small building was a low, flat-roofed affair made mainly of glass and steel to what looked like a very exacting specification. Marenkian reached into his pocket and pulled out a credit-card key, which he swiped through the protruding lock.

The interior was in sharp contrast to the modernism of the structure: Afghan rugs, deep leather armchairs, a wooden desk with the glow of old age. The bright light of outside was here filtered to a silent grey; the air was conditioned.

He talked about the staff, and what he now required.

'The arrangement is not so satisfactory as it once was. Our cook is no longer with us, so we need someone to look after the three of us that way, the three of us being myself, my daughter, and my son. I'd also like someone who can drive us when it's necessary. Monsieur Pierre, the gardener, used to perform this service, but he's getting a little old now for the way the roads are. We have a maid, whom you'll meet, who lives in Valbonne. She does the domestic work six days a week. So for you it would be driving and cooking, and a certain amount of handiwork around the place. Tell me a little more of your experience.'

I underplayed education and the army so that he wouldn't wonder why I was applying for this lowly domestic job, and skipped altogether my stay with the government of Spain. I knew that I would be able to fulfil his requirements, and I put on the best performance I could, because I had already decided

I would take the job if it was offered. The house was just out of the Nice–Antibes conurbation, private and luxurious; the work would be fairly easy. And on first appearances Marenkian seemed as though he would be a sympathetic employer. This would be a good place to mark time until the spring.

We went back to the house, and he showed me the bedroom and bathroom on offer to me, the kitchen, utility rooms, cellar. Then he wanted me to meet his children, partly, I assumed, so that they too could vet me.

We stepped outside, into that wonderful, enveloping warmth. I caught a slight smell of sun cream. Then, as we reached the steps down to the pool – one could see a corner of it from the top: a pane of acrylic blue past the deep green foliage – a woman I assumed to be the maid came out of the house. She was olive-skinned, slim and flexible like a dancer, not pretty but graceful, her hair tied back severely. It seems there was an urgent telephone call for him. He asked me to wait, and went back inside. She followed him, giving me a little smile over her shoulder, *coquine*.

I waited in the sunlight for a little while, sunlight on the greenery sharp and rich, bright as a freshly cut lime. Then I took a couple of steps down to see more of the pool, and stood there in the shade, the hum of the pump in my ears, the smell of chlorine.

She was lying on a divan at the far end of the pool when I first saw her: still as and glossy as a photograph. She was like a ripe fruit, a peach, skin golden velvet. She would put every bitch on the Promenade des Anglais to shame. And every dog on heat. I examined her in detail. Perhaps there was *one* little imperfection: a slight heaviness in the thighs.

I could have gone on staring at her all day, but the boy was doing something that distracted me for a moment.

To the left of the pool was a fairly high wall, retaining the bank of flower beds and shrubs above. The boy – man, I should say; probably about twenty-five years old – was wearing jeans, cowboy boots and sunglasses, no shirt. He was very powerfully built, like a college athlete, big shouldered, smooth skinned. He sat on the paving, back against the wall, a beer by his side; and in his hand, his hand resting on his knee, he held what was unmistakably a gun which he levelled at something across the pool.

At the point where his gun seemed to be aimed was a red object around which a small swarm of flies was buzzing. It was a piece of raw meat, nailed to a short post stuck into the earth of the flower bed. There was a click-spit, and on the left of the meat a blue feathered dart hung. The flies scattered, then returned.

The girl had got up, removed her sunglasses, and now stood on the diving board. I had been wrong: there was no imperfection at all. Her figure was a dream: shapely legs, slender wrists and ankles, a flat stomach, and breasts just a little larger than they should have been. It appeared that neither had seen me.

The boy reloaded his air pistol and rested it once more on his knee. Then the girl spoke, with the long-suffering irritation of a sister.

'Hey, Bruno, cut it out, huh?'

He cocked his head slightly but said nothing. Then he fired again, and this time missed.

'I said cut it out.'

'You're putting me off,' he drawled.

'I wanna swim, fuck,' she said, aggressively. In curious contrast to her extreme good looks, she had a rasping voice, in a low register but without depth. That kind of language is never very attractive in a young lady, either. Bruno reloaded the pistol, and she put her hands on her hips and said, 'Bruno!'

Then she looked up, saw me, and stared for a second. He caught the line of her gaze and looked up at me, too.

And so, as if caught eavesdropping, and feeling a little

guilty for it, although the exchange I describe had only occupied a few seconds, I walked down the steps to join them.

The girl, indifferent, dived into the pool. She wore a one-piece swimsuit with black and bright yellow zebra stripes. Flashes of it underwater, like an exotic fish, made me struggle to remember the exact shape of her torso.

Bruno stood up as I reached the bottom of the steps, and he said, a little truculently, 'Yeah, can I help you?'

The girl surfaced with a splash, her bronze hair darkened and flat.

I turned to Bruno, 'I'm seeing Mr Marenkian about a job here. He had to go in and take a phone-call.'

'Oh, right. You're, uh . . . ?'

'Johnny Denner.'

'I'm Bruno Marenkian. That's my sister Natalie.' With a wave of his arm to indicate her.

I smiled in acknowledgement. Bruno looked down at his air pistol and the little pile of lurid feathered darts.

Marenkian reappeared, Natalie got out of the pool, and we passed a few moments in desultory conversation, they standing either side of him, under his wing, he joking heavy-handedly to draw attention away from their sullenness.

Let me describe them a little more.

I said that Bruno was fit. He was big, too, like the lampshades and porcelain lions. He stood a good two inches above me, and I'm six-two. And at a guess he had a good stone on me, and I'm fourteen. He had his father's dark eyes, but much lighter eyebrows, which somehow accentuated their sharpness. The rest of his face was monumental: a big shapeless nose, a great jaw like a boxing glove. Later I realized that his head was unusually large even for a frame as substantial as his.

But as for Natalie . . . as for Natalie – she was a dream come true, an advertising fantasy. Her hair, wet then, I later saw was fine and thick, burnished. Her skin was the shade of dark honey. Her eyes, under thick arching eyebrows, were deep and brown. Her lips were full, her cheeks and chin delicately curved. I tried very hard not to stare at her nipples, which stood out under the wet Lycra, or the dimple of her navel. About twenty-three years of age.

I had a small triumph when Marenkian introduced them both and explained my provenance. Just after she said: 'Pleased to meet you,' her eyes very briefly, perhaps involuntarily, swept me up and down. Well, well.

Marenkian and I went back to his study. He named generous terms, and I accepted them without question. It was an ideal job, although I think that even then I suspected that Bruno might be trouble. Three days later I had said goodbye to Horst – on the last night we drank a powerful quantity of kümmel – and moved into the Marenkian household.

Claudine, the maid, was quite shy and formal to begin with, and not at all *coquine*. She was single, aged about thirty-five. She was terrified of what I might do to the family's food, not because I was a man but because I was English, and it's well known in France that no English man or woman can cook. The first day she came up with a little joke that she repeated at intervals for the next week: 'Ah, you English – you boil everything!' It's true, I told her, that an Englishman who can cook is uncommon; but so is a Frenchman with a sense of humour. It allayed her fears, though, that my grandmother had been *une bourgignonne*. The French set aside their regional rivalries to acknowledge the supremacy of Burgundian cuisine. On the fourth day or so I persuaded her to take home with her a left-over portion of *sauté de veau*, and the next morning she was cautiously complimentary, which is as much as I could have hoped for from anyone of her nationality. This small, sinuous woman appeared every day on a fairly powerful motorbike, which I thought said something positive about her character. I started to wonder whether we might not, with a bit of luck, end up in bed. She had good legs.

Monsieur Larribault, the gardener, addressed with respect by all – including Marenkian – as Monsieur Pierre, was aged at least seventy, tall, stooped, almost completely bald, bespectacled, and somewhat deaf. He arrived three days a week in a beige Citroën mini-van that seemed to struggle even with the shallow gradient of the drive. It was immensely difficult to hold any kind of conversation with Monsieur Pierre. His local accent was so strong that even I, with more than adequate French, could make out no more than one sentence in three. When I spoke to him, he would affect an inability to comprehend me any more than I could him, shaking his head slowly and hopelessly, muttering that he couldn't understand. My employer told me, laughing, that Monsieur Pierre had been tending the garden longer than Marenkian had owned the house, and that he himself had never been able to communicate with him. He had decided long ago not to try, but to let the old man get on with it, because he did a fine job without instruction. Monsieur Pierre's isolation from human communion in the Marenkian household must have been self-imposed. After all, instructions can hardly be followed if they have not, strictly speaking, been received.

During that first week I got to know the lie of the land: where to buy good food, hardware, chemicals for the pool. Claudine was helpful, although her choices were not always to my liking. It was nice to be able to run things on a seemingly unlimited budget, when in doubt to buy the most expensive cuts of meat, the best charcuterie. There was a household charge-card and chequebook, and I simply had to keep the receipts and some record of what was spent weekly.

I saw something on my second day there that shocked me a little. Natalie was away with friends, her father told me. It was a hot afternoon, and I was upstairs in my room, finishing my unpacking, and alone in the house. Bruno and Marenkian had gone out separately, and both cars were absent. Then I heard another car in the drive, and I walked out into the corridor to have a look. It was an Alfa Spider, and it so happened that it had drawn up directly below my window. A dark-haired man in a polo shirt and jeans was driving; Natalie was in the passenger seat. They cut the engine and sat for a moment, talking; I could hear the murmur of their voices.

I must confess that I stayed there watching, because from there I had a direct view of Natalie's slender, shapely legs. She wore a black skirt too short to polish one's sunglasses on, and what I could see, looking straight down into the cockpit, was a feast for the eyes.

They must have assumed, seeing that neither car was there, that there was nobody else in the house. The man leaned over to kiss her, and a moment later ran his hand between her legs. I watched. They must have spent the previous night together. She thrust her pelvis forward, her legs squeezing his heavily veined forearm. The little skirt rode up until I could see the heel of his palm.

I swivelled away from the window and leaned against the wall, my throat dry. I didn't dare look again, and a minute later the car drove away. A few minutes later I heard her go down to the pool; heard the splash of her dive.

I settled into a routine. At about seven I got up and shortly thereafter went into Valbonne to fetch bread and brioches. Claudine could have brought them when she came at eight, but I enjoyed the empty roads in the morning shade, the dark shadows and piercing light in the square, its old stone solid and clean, the asphalt just sprayed. I liked the smile of the middle-aged *boulangère*.

Marenkian was at the table punctually at eight, and took Fortnum's English breakfast blend with his brioche, skimmed the *Herald Tribune* and retreated into his office. I would get him a *Financial Times* later in the morning. Natalie and Bruno would appear some time after eleven, Natalie usually before Bruno. Neither ate breakfast very often; for the most part they went straight to the pool and stayed there. The Côte d'Azur sometimes gets cold in October, I was told, but we seemed to be having an Indian summer, and it was as hot as in July.

At about midday I would go down and ask what they wanted to drink; then, and at half-hourly intervals until two, when I served lunch, for Natalie endless Pepsis, for Bruno stiff Ricards with ice and a little water. She had a vast repertoire of swimsuits, some two-piece, some one-piece. Sometimes, not often, she went topless. People claim there's nothing erotic in this, but that is not always true. When I stood over her with a drink I was badly disturbed.

She and I got on well. I joked feebly with her about her abundance of swimwear. Did she keep her collection in a warehouse? In the cellar? Was she going to marry a dictator? But between Bruno and me there was a slight, unmistakable tension. He lay there with his Walkman, playing American redneck rock at loud volume. You could hear the lyrics scratching through the headphones: women from hell, bottles of bourbon. Rock. Rock you Tonite – Rock the Nation – Rock this City. Irritating proletarian music.

He had an air of aggression. Always a little tense in the morning, he didn't seem to calm down until after his second drink. I had a feeling, as I did my bit of honest flirting with Natalie, that he was watching me from behind his sunglasses. Was he protective of his little sister? Or even jealous of her? Because she was certainly a flirt; she flirted back at me. His look, when I caught it, held something aggrieved in it, as though I had injured him.

I wasn't encouraged by what happened a day or two later. I went to his room one afternoon to check whether the insect repellents, little plastic packages with a cake of poison that you plug into the mains, needed switching. I had the refills in my hand. As it happened, it wasn't necessary.

The room was tidy, doubtless at the hand of Claudine. I had a quick look in the cupboards and the bathroom. I don't know why, I was developing a servant's curiosity, and I had an interest in Bruno, a desire to understand him. On his bathroom shelf stood two brown bottles bearing the rubric: THE TABLETS. It reminded me of childhood, and struck me as curiously old-fashioned.

Then there was the padding of bare feet down the landing outside, and I felt a touch guilty, knowing that he was going to surprise me in his room, although there was no reason I shouldn't be there. So I went back to the insect repellent and changed the cake just the same. I was putting it back in the wall as he came in. He stood there and looked at me sullenly, calculating.

'Hi, Bruno,' I said.

He continued to stare.

'What are you doing in here?'

'I'm changing the insecticide plug.'

He shook his head decisively.

'No . . . I mean – what are you *really* doing?'

I laughed politely and said:

'That's what I'm doing,' but a sort of curling grimace was spreading over his face.

Then he thrust his head forward and said, 'Listen, man. Just fuck off. Don't let me find you in my room again, OK?' He started to walk towards me and I thought: *What the hell is this?* 'OK?' he shouted, enraged.

'Sure, Bruno. No problem.' I slipped past him and through the door, and for the moment I was within his reach I thought I was in trouble. But words had been enough for him.

I must admit I was shaken; that kind of aggression in the

home of my millionaire employer. A fifteen-stone bundle of nerves. I was curious, though: what could make him so sensitive about his room, his privacy? Had his outburst been meaningless, pathological? Or did he really, as they say, have something to hide?

Later I gossiped with Claudine, of course, but she only had opinions.

'What about the children?'

'*Ouff*,' she said, one of those French grunts that can indicate a variety of emotions, in this case disapproval. '*Ils ne sont pas méchants.*' They're harmless enough, I suppose is the way that would translate. Faint praise.

'You see, Johnny, it is often like this when the father is very civilized and he gives too much to his children. Often' – and here she stopped sweeping and leaned on her brush – 'it is because there is no mother, and the father gives too much to his children to compensate. Hm?'

That pearl of wisdom safely delivered, she resumed her work.

'What about the mother?'

She stopped again.

'Nothing is known about the mother. Nothing.' She repeated the *rien* dramatically, as they do.

'Not a good topic of conversation, then?'

'That is certain.'

The next day I approached the pool again, trying again not to ogle Natalie.

'Would you like a drink?'

She took her sunglasses off and sat up in the divan.

'Hi,' she said brightly. I kept my eyes on hers, forcing them away from her body. I had seen it once; I knew what it looked like – why did I need to see it again? She curled and stretched, which made my attempt more difficult. But her face was enough of a feast. It was refreshing that she didn't have that American apple-pie look. With her dark eyebrows and darker eyes, she looked Spanish or Portuguese, Brazilian perhaps. With a name like Marenkian? Armenian? A typical American cocktail.

'Uh – a little early for me,' she continued. 'Dad says you play good tennis.'

'That's what I told him.'

'Did you tell the truth?'

'I suppose so.'

'OK. Wanna take me on?' She raised her eyebrows and curled down in the divan again. It was outrageous. I could hardly control myself. I imagined having my teeth drilled.

'Sure. Any time.'

'Late this afternoon?'

'Fine. Let me know when you're ready. Perhaps Bruno would like to play?' He was sitting a few yards away, in his world of rock.

'I don't think so,' she said simply.

I asked Bruno whether he would like a drink. He was in a subdued mood.

'What's the time?'

'Five past twelve.'

'Oh, sure. I'll have a Ricard.'

'Right.'

I was just turning to go when he whispered my name, beckoning.

I leaned down, and he said, quietly so that Natalie wouldn't hear, 'Uh, Johnny, listen. I'm sorry I was – uh – kinda rude yesterday. See, I have this problem about privacy. I get strung up about it.'

'Oh, don't worry at all, Bruno. I quite understand. Don't worry about it.'

But I was being proud and insincere, and my manner of accepting his apology – as though I was just doing my job –

made that plain. Something in his strange, disjointed way of speaking had convinced me that he too was insincere. That the day before he had shown his true colours.

Later Natalie and I played tennis. She was a good, aggressive player, with the solid strokes that come from early coaching. She liked to serve and volley, unusual in a woman, and it stood her in good stead: she won the first set. I was determined, though, not to let her beat me, and I made the effort to take the second and third. By the end of it we were both exhausted, so that when we shook hands, firmly, her flesh was wet against mine. She looked up at me as if a little shocked, and it seemed to me that her body was drawn to mine.

After dinner something happened, and not very clearly for me, because I had already gone upstairs. It was a humid, close evening, and there was some kind of tension in the air as I served drinks and then food. From the kitchen I could only guess at what was said: there were long silences, punctuated by the low rumble of Marenkian's grave, measured voice, occasional short bursts of frivolity from Natalie – and nothing from Bruno. I discovered the beginnings of the grim pleasure a servant might take in the troubles of his employers.

When I served coffee Bruno was looking aggrieved and truculent. By my estimate he had drunk about a bottle of red wine at dinner, after the customary procession of Ricards. I thought: *I bet he's a nasty drunk, a violent drunk.*

Natalie sat between them, pretty as you please, smiling. She didn't acknowledge me in any way as I poured her coffee, and I read something into this. Marenkian was his usual calm, civilized self, although he was looking tired. When I had finished pouring he said:

'Thank you, Johnny. I don't think we'll be needing anything more tonight.'

'Thank you, Mr Marenkian. Good night, everybody.'

Half an hour later, from my room at the other end of the house, I heard the shouting start. This time nothing from Natalie. Still the calm rumble of Marenkian's voice. And shouting, roaring almost, from Bruno. I was tempted to go down, but thought better of it. For one thing, I might provide a target for his mysterious rage.

Then there sounded a different voice, and I thought that the house had a new arrival. But the new arrival was Marenkian shouting – a shouting that had real edge to it, that made Bruno's sound like the bawling of a child.

After that everything was quiet.

It turned out a day later that I would have good reason to be interested in the development of my relationship with Bruno.

I was seeing Marenkian regularly. I was his domestic servant after all, and it was up to me to discover the tastes and routines of my employer. He was an unusual man. What was it about him? Like Bruno's, his small dark eyes seemed opaque, polished stones. His movements had something automatic, slightly stilted about them, as though he had needed to learn again how to walk and gesture after a stroke. Yet he seemed strong and athletic for his age, and I had seen, when he took a lesson with a young French coach, that he was a good tennis player. I wondered whether he had been born in poverty, whether that might be why he wore his manner with slight unease, like a tight-fitting coat.

He was conscientious with me: he would ask me how I was finding everything, whether I liked the work and the perks. I did like them. It was true that the quiet and comfort of the place suited me very well, and the money I would earn over the winter would mostly go into the bank, to join what Horst had paid me for the skippering. By the spring I would have a good ten thousand pounds, perhaps more. For the first time in my life, for some reason, I had acquired a strong, almost over-whelming desire to have some money in the bank.

'I didn't make it clear, Johnny, that this building' – he was referring to his office in the grounds – 'is looked after exclusively by Claudine. As you can see, there are a great many papers in here, and we try to keep them all in a certain order.' He waved his arm mechanically to indicate the many piles of documents arranged on the low cupboards that skirted the room.

'That's fine.'

'It's not that I would wish to cast any doubt on your discretion, Johnny. I hope you understand that. It's simply better if we can give an undertaking to our clients that no one but myself has any contact with material relating to their cases. Claudine's English is not good, and besides, I've known her for some years now.'

'I understand that perfectly. No problem.'

'In fact,' he went on, 'there is a house rule, which everyone is aware of, that no one should enter this office without my say-so. I'd like you to help me enforce that, Johnny.' I laughed to myself. Help enforce that – a nice way of putting it.

He got up and wandered around the room, seeming a little distracted.

'Now, I wonder if I could ask you to take on an . . . informal duty. Bruno and Natalie are both fond of the nightlife, as they should be at their age. Now Bruno can be a little . . . a little wild sometimes. Nothing too serious, of course, but he does sometimes drive back from Nice or Cannes very late at night when he's had too much to drink, and I find this disturbing. To be frank with you, Johnny, last year he had a bit of trouble with the gendarmerie. He is in fact under medication, and he shouldn't drive while taking it. What I want to ask you to do, Johnny, is to drive Bruno in and out of Nice, Cannes, wherever, as the occasion calls for it – and, of course, when it doesn't interfere with your other duties. I know this'll cut into your evenings sometimes, but I would greatly appreciate it. And this will be reflected in a monthly bonus.'

'No problem at all.'

'Good.'

At Bruno's age I had been left on my own, nobody to mollycoddle me. Not that my father would have had the resources or the inclination, had he been alive. In any normal family Bruno would have behaved or got busted.

'There is another aspect to this. I'd like you to keep me posted on where you're going and where you've been. Sometimes I need to get in touch urgently. And, to be completely frank' – he looked me straight in the eye – 'I want to know who Bruno sees.'

That was strange, and it struck me as a little underhand that this term of engagement was only mentioned once I was safely installed in the house. But I didn't have any strong enough objection to make, so I agreed to play the spy.

'Finally, Johnny, a word about my clients. I'm not sure how much you know about my business, but let me just explain one thing. I deal primarily with matters of the law relating to taxation and investment, offshore and inwards and outwards of the US, both corporate and private. Therefore quite often the kind of information I hold on my clients' behalf is of an extremely confidential and sensitive nature – the kind of information that interests the IRS, for example, and no one is friends with the IRS. So there may sometimes be other parties attempting to acquire information on the affairs of my clients, I'm afraid.'

'I see.'

'It's not very ethical that people should try to do this, but they do. That's the way of the world. I'm sure you can understand that.'

'Of course.'

'What I'm saying, Johnny, is that my clients are very sensitive about confidentiality – and so am I. When they're here, I would ask you not to stay in the room longer than you need. If for some reason anyone tries to ask you questions about these matters, please just let me know. These people have a right to confidentiality.'

'I will let you know, and I will certainly not breathe a word myself.'

'Good. Oh – even down to the identity of my visitors here. We meet down here for privacy rather than self-indulgence.'

'Certainly. You can rely on me.'

Chapter Three

'DRIVE ME INTO Antibes and back? Bullshit, man. Think I need a goddam bodyguard?'

'It is simply a question of the driving. *You* know the score.'

'Listen, I've told you there isn't gonna be a repeat of last year. Believe it, OK?'

'Wouldn't it just be easier to take advantage of the chauffeur service? I certainly would.'

'Well, I certainly wouldn't.'

'Come on, Bruno.'

'No way. No way. *You* can be driven where the hell you want, but *I* drive myself.'

I was standing quite near them trying not to be noticed. The exchange went on a little longer, in the same monotonous way. Finally, when Bruno really started to lose his temper, Marenkian seemed to decide it wasn't worth it, and gave in.

He said, 'I don't want another episode with the police, Bruno. I will be very angry if there's another episode with the police. OK?'

I guessed that Bruno must realize this plan would constitute a not very subtle form of supervision. For my part, I was relieved, because I had no desire to play nanny.

But Marenkian was more stubborn than that. The next day the conversation resumed awkwardly. Marenkian summoned the pair of us into his office, and we stood in front of his desk like a couple of employees of a big corporation who were about to receive a carpeting for some administrative error.

'Now, listen,' he said. 'I've gotten you in here together so we can get this straight – and get it straight now. Johnny is going to drive you.'

It seemed to me tactless that the matter was being discussed in my presence, but there wasn't much I could do to object.

'Oh,' Bruno said. 'Really?'

'In the evenings.'

Bruno's face soured. 'We need to talk about this.'

'There's no need to talk. It's decided. Just let Johnny know when you plan to leave. Give him some notice.'

I sympathized with Bruno, and I was surprised at Marenkian. It seemed like the ruse of a weakling, having a third party in the room to head off the confrontation. It would only delay it, if I knew Bruno.

'We'll talk about it,' Bruno said. The thinness of his self-control was evident: his chin thrust out, his eyes narrowed.

'Just let Johnny know what time you're going out tonight.'

'I'm not going out tonight.'

'I thought you were going into town.'

'No, I'm not going out. I've changed my plan.'

Marenkian raised his eyebrows and shrugged.

Bruno turned and started for the door, saying over his shoulder, his arm waving behind him, 'We'll talk about this.'

It was expressive body language, not lost on his father, who didn't reply.

When the boy had gone Marenkian said to me: 'It is difficult, but it has to be done. He started a fight with a Frenchman who turned out to be a lawyer, and who I had to settle with out of court. Then three months off the road, drink driving charge. Don't worry. I'll talk to him again.'

'OK,' I said, and left him.

It was by chance that I heard part of the sequel to their

conversation. I suppose I was eavesdropping, though unintentionally. I was upstairs and they were outside, but the house doors were open, and the terracotta floors and echoing stone walls carried their voices.

'So why talk about it in front of Johnny?'

'I didn't think that would cause you any problem. As you said, having a chauffeur is quite a luxury.'

'You know he isn't just gonna drive me, right? He's gonna be there, huh, next to me, everywhere I go.'

'And you know why.'

'No, I don't know why. I don't know why I can't have friends.'

'You *can* have friends, Bruno,' his father said, sympathy and sincerity in his voice. 'There are just some people you *can't* see.'

'Why?'

'Because they want to attach themselves to this family. Because they want to make our business their business.'

'That's what you say, but it's not true. I have friends of my own, people who are nothing to do with you or your friends, and you can't accept that.'

They walked further into the garden and I could no longer hear.

The next day I started driving him.

Perhaps he was a little embarrassed that the first trip we took together was to his psychotherapist. On the way there he gazed out of the window with a distracted, almost nervous air.

'You probably wonder why I'm seeing a shrink,' he said.

'Well' – I paused, a little surprised – 'I've never been to one myself, so I don't really know the ins and outs of it.'

'Yeah.'

'Of course, you Americans are very keen on psychoanalysis, aren't you?' This was my way of being diplomatic. 'You'd be considered quite unusual in New York if you didn't have an analyst, wouldn't you?'

'I wouldn't say that, but there's plenty of people who've got one. You should try it.'

'I probably should.'

'It's good for me,' he said absently, then looked out of the window at the Baie des Anges. A mistral was blowing, it seemed a little rough, and there was the odd whitecap on the deep, rich turquoise. Everything looked fresh, crisp and clean: the sea, the sharp rocky outcrops on either side of the auto-route, the lawns and flower beds as we got nearer the town.

Then the centre of Nice. I wasn't long in recalling its drawbacks. The place reminded me of a garish film set, perhaps a long-disused one that they kept up as a tourist attraction. The illusion was fostered by the old casino on the Promenade des Anglais; all of it had been demolished save the façade, which was held up by a structure of girders behind. Then the cakemaker's rococo of the hotels and apartment blocks, the elaborate dress of the middle-aged females, the showroom polish on the cars, the greased suntan of men in lemon-yellow polo shirts. Even the green of the grass – livid PGA green, sprinkled for two hours a day – looked as if it had been spray-painted on. On the beach young women with superb bodies, topless; on the Promenade ageing ones with too much make-up and toy dogs; on the shaded terraces of the hotels the old and faded. Endless clothes shops and rows of over-priced cafés. The glitter of the Baie des Anges.

But nowhere in the real world *is* like a Hollywood film set; there is always something behind the façade. You might think that the extras who crowd the Promenade are the rich, but you would be mistaken. The real rich are behind wide blank gates and whitewashed walls. Like the Marenkians.

We rich drove straight through, and then up the hill to Cimiez, a vast cul-de-sac behind the coastal strip, the place where Nice once kept its money. The street climbs to Regina, queen mother of fading apartment buildings, two hundred yards long and seven or eight storeys high: a fat old woman draped in petticoats, falling to pieces in her slumber. And everything behind that building – part of which is a geriatric hospital – seems to sleep as the sun bakes it, especially in the afternoon when the streets are wrapped in silence; and it seems as though the pine needles on the pavement have been sprinkled to deaden your footfalls, as they used to be when someone in the house was dying. Bright haze, drawn shutters, the bleached grey of the road.

The office-cum-residence of his psychotherapist was an avant-garde design from the Thirties. It was a house to suit a German intellectual: rectangular with curved edges, large flat stretches of white wall into which were set square metal-framed windows. Whoever built it had wanted no truck with the easy pleasures of the Mediterranean; some cold northern misfit.

One of the gateposts bore a little brass plaque, announcing the presence within of M. SCHENCK. No indication of his profession.

As I pulled up, Bruno said: 'Can you come in? Max wants to meet you.'

I had been expecting something like a surgery, with a reception area and a white counter behind which a starchy nurse might sit, but there was nothing of that kind. Bruno rang the bell, then opened the door and stepped in without waiting for a reply. I followed him into a small, dark hallway lined with gloomy old engravings of the Alps, which resembled fat stalag-mites, beneath which tiny humans on donkeys struggled against extreme weather conditions. There were doors in all three walls.

The one directly in front of us opened, and a stocky middle-aged man stepped out, light shining from behind him.

'Hello, Bruno,' he said warmly, and shook him by the hand. 'Why don't you go in and make yourself comfortable.'

Bruno said, 'Sure,' and shambled through the open door which the psychotherapist then shut behind him. Bruno, in that brief moment, had seemed absolutely submissive; his usual surly aggression had evaporated and now he was bright and eager to please, like a dog who has found his master.

Schenck, who now faced me, was not a giant like the Marenkian men. He probably measured a mere six feet, but he had a barrel-like torso, cylindrical and a little stout. His suntanned face was topped with hair that was still almost black – just a fleck or two of grey around the temples. The effect of his powerful physique was quite peculiar; he was as contrary to the stereotype of a psychotherapist as anyone could be. Instead he looked as though he might have spent his life – he seemed about fifty, but was probably five years older – performing some demanding physical task like farming or cultivating vines, rather than questioning neurotics in a book-lined study. And yet his eyes betrayed him; they were hooded, under angular brows. The eyes of a mandarin, they betrayed his intelligence.

I took an irrational dislike to him – a dislike which became rational after we had talked for a minute. He motioned me to a hall chair, and I sat. He smiled. 'So, Mr—?'

'Denner.'

'Mr Denner. An Englishman, huh? And you've been working for the Marenkians for two weeks?'

'That's right.'

'Uh-huh. And – how did you come by the job?'

Who are you? I thought. *Who the hell are you to sit me down and question me?*

'I applied.'

He smiled, irritated.

'Look, I don't want to put you out by asking you a lot of questions – but it's very important for me to know Bruno's ongoing circumstances in detail. I am his doctor, and it could be a lot of help to me in encouraging him to get well again.'

'Sure,' I said, suddenly feeling that I had been unreasonable, although I still didn't quite see how *my* background could have any bearing on Bruno's mental health.

'I'd like you tell me what your duties are in relation to Bruno.'

Ah, straight to the point. Should I or should I not tell?

'I drive him. Well, really I'm the butler. I look after the whole family.'

'Bruno tells me that you've been asked to spy on him – for his father.'

'Well, not exactly.'

'What are you telling me? Is this in Bruno's imagination or not? That's what I want to know.'

'It's not entirely in Bruno's imagination. Mr Marenkian asked me to drive Bruno – since Bruno's taking medication at the moment – and he asked me to keep an eye on him.'

'So he didn't ask you to spy on him?'

'Well, not exactly. Look, this puts me in a very difficult position, and I think that if you want to know about Mr Marenkian's orders to me you should ask him.'

He looked at me in a beady way and said: 'I have asked him.'

I thought: *This is ridiculous – what are you trying to say?* 'Well, Dr Schenck, I think I'd better be going.'

'Do you have any idea how dangerous Bruno is?'

I gaped at him for a moment.

'I – haven't had the impression that Bruno was particularly dangerous.'

'Ah, but he is. That is one reason I am treating him. He has a record and a history of violence. Serious violence. It has taken a lot of influence on the part of Mr Marenkian to keep Bruno out of jail. He perhaps hasn't asked you yet to supervise

Bruno with the – closeness that he needs. But you can be sure that he will.'

'I see,' I said, curious again. I wanted to know what I'd be letting myself in for.

'What kind of violence?'

'I too have a duty of confidentiality. Oh yes, I admire your loyalty to your employer, particularly when it's such a new employer. But I can't speak about that. I'm doing you the favour of giving you a warning, basically. Have you ever been involved in – security work?'

'Not precisely. I was trained to kill people by the British Army.'

'Oh – the British Army,' he said archly, facetiously. 'What about – more on a street level? Have you been employed by anyone in Mr Marenkian's line of business?'

There he went again.

'No, I've never worked for a lawyer before.'

He burst, for a second, into a mirthless laugh, and I felt pleased, I must admit. I was being obstructive and deliberately obtuse.

'With your talent for evasiveness, you would make a good lawyer yourself. Now, listen to me,' he continued, and his tone changed altogether.

And I took notice, because there was a real strength in his self-possession. He didn't point a finger or wave an arm, and his thick hands hung by his sides, completely at ease.

'After these sessions, get him home quickly, and then to bed. He should not be encouraged to talk. He will have done enough of that.'

'I see.'

'Don't provoke Bruno, ever. You know – don't argue with him.'

'I—' I started to protest that I had no intention of doing any such thing.

He held up two fingers, like a saint, and said: 'No, don't bother to say it. I can see, because I understand these things, that you are a person who has some difficulty with authority. So don't say anything.'

My temperature rose about fifty degrees; if I didn't already have a problem with authority, he was giving me one with his bullshit.

'Bruno will be difficult sometimes. He will cause problems for you. His father has asked you to spy on him, hasn't he?'

'I gave you my view on that.'

'He will lie to you. He may attack you. That is because he is not well. You, on the other hand, are paid to look after him. So don't react when he provokes you, don't believe what he tells you, and don't talk to him after these sessions with me.' Schenck paused, fixing me with his eye.

'Particularly one thing. Don't talk to anyone else about Bruno's affairs – including his family. Understand?'

The man was outrageous.

'OK.'

'Good,' he said, and moved towards the door.

As he went, I said very childishly, pointing to the stalagmites, 'I wouldn't fancy skiing down those.'

He glanced at them, then at me, and said, 'I have skied many of these mountains. It is very exhilarating. You should try it. Goodbye.'

'I'll see you later.'

'Wait outside for him. Goodbye.'

Fuming, I took the car down the hill. There didn't seem to be any bars in Cimiez, and I needed a drink. Near the Palais des Sports I found somewhere native and cheap, a small place with a few tables down one side of the room and a battered chrome bar along the other. There were five or six customers: a brassy middle-aged couple, two Arabs, a young Frenchman in a brown leather jacket and alligator cowboy boots. I propped up the bar, drank three beers, and made a little conversation with the small, bright-eyed proprietor.

Unusually for his kind, he was genial and talkative, and that cheered me up a little. Here, perhaps, was a sort of local, somewhere I could go every week while Bruno submitted himself – and hopefully responded – to treatment.

It became quite a day for confrontations. I had come out of the bar and was on my way back to the car when I heard a dreaded voice: 'Hey, Johnny!'

And there was an idiotic-looking Englishman, lanky, with a purple-striped shirt too small for him; and with him a short thick girl with a Marks and Spencer hairband and a string of pearls.

'Hey, Johnny.' He charged over to me, grinning. To the best of my knowledge I had never seen him in my life.

'What are you doing down here? We met at the Cresta Run Ball years ago. I hit you with an ice cube.'

'Right. Hi.' I gave them the thinnest of smiles.

'Darling, this is the Johnny – oh, what's your name?'

'Denner.'

'You spent three years in a Spanish clink, didn't you? He got the stuff planted on him by Lulu whatsit – remember, darling? You in exile down here, then?'

I felt angry suddenly.

'Listen,' I said to him. 'Why don't you just shove it up your arse?'

I turned on my heel, his protests fading in my ear as I started to put some distance between us.

'Well, well. Oh dear. Sorry I spoke . . .'

Ten minutes later Bruno came out of Schenck's door with a dazed, almost beatific smile, got into the Range Rover and leaned back heavily against the door. I followed instructions, and didn't open any conversation with him. So we passed the return journey in silence, and as soon as we got to the house he went to bed. I didn't see him again that day.

I saw Schenck again not much later, when Marenkian invited him to lunch along with an American client. I was beginning to develop my eavesdropping skills. A servant eavesdrops because the world of his employer is his only world, and yet in that world he counts for nothing. So he watches, and listens, and stores knowledge. And the Marenkians' world was not lacking in interest.

The prospective client was a little short of five feet, and had the kind of overdeveloped nose and ears you normally associate with Disney dwarves and garden gnomes. He wore a candy-striped polo shirt and vermilion trousers, and he shifted every few seconds with sudden, sharp movements like a cartoon bird, and he even spoke like a cartoon character, hard and exaggerated, as if struggling to suppress some incredible energy. Schenck sat with his legs crossed, weighty and silent.

'So, let's get it straight, right,' the small man whined. 'You telling me in Liberia there's no entry for the law, period?'

'That's absolutely true,' Marenkian replied. 'For example, if someone were on the run for a killing and they got to Liberia, they'd be absolutely safe.'

'No extradition.'

'None at all. But would you want to spend the rest of your days in Liberia? You'd have to be desperate.'

'Your days would be few, huh?'

'Maybe. I can tell you one thing about Monrovia, though. I heard this from a man I met at a convention recently. At the worst stage of the civil war, when there had been a complete breakdown of the rule of law, it was still always possible to obtain Black Label.'

'Hey-hey, I'll drink to that. But that's gotta be true every-where, right? Where there's life?'

I put a plate of canapés I had made on the table between them.

'So you've got companies there?'

'I have a couple of dormant shells Monrovia-registered. As it happens, it's not usually necessary. Where possible I prefer to keep things accessible. It's only at the end of the line that you sometimes need to be *inaccessible*.'

'Say again?'

'If, for example, you want anonymity at the end of the chain. If the Liechtenstein company is owned by an Andorran company, owned by a Panamanian company, owned by a Liechtenstein company, an investigator would have to do a great deal of work to track those four steps. Particularly if I break the chain with nominees.'

I put their drinks down in front of them and then, regret-tably, had to leave the room.

'But if you want to be particularly cautious . . .' Marenkian continued, as I went back to the kitchen. I was almost tempted to stand by the door and listen, but I had their lunch to cook.

The phone rang about twenty minutes later, and Marenkian excused himself to take the call. And so Schenck was left with the little man, and I bustled around the lunch table which I had already laid inside.

'Yeah,' the little man said in his tight nasal drawl, 'Azerbai-jan, right – place like that. It doesn't have to be there, you know, but it could be there, right? You get the guy over from there, the fuc— the minister of, industry, right, or the secretary of trade' – he waved his arms in frustration at the obvious effort it cost him not to swear – 'and they've got the mining concessions, and the concessions to build the chemical plants, right? You don't have any of this stupid public safety shit,

right? Pump the fucking poison right out into the fucking river'
– he laughed – 'and obviously the corporations are gonna put
up some introduction money, and some money for the planning
consents. They meet the minister, right – hey' – and he leaned
towards Schenck, confidentially – 'and then you disappear,
right, with your proceeds. And this Ivan Shitski, he's never
gonna be seen again.' He laughed his braying laugh.

'Presumably,' Schenck said, and he seemed immeasurably
patrician beside the New Yorker, 'the minister does not need
to be a minister at all.'

'You got it, Max. You got it. You get any old schmoozer
with a beard from there, right, and he's the fucking minister.
Who the fuck's gonna know different?'

'Tell me, how convincing are your actors usually?'

'Gotta tell you they're not actually that convincing.'

'This is good, because when you do meet politicians they
often astonish you by their stupidity and the very open nature
of their dishonesty.'

'Can I get you another drink?' I asked the little man.

'Sure, sure. Scotch on the rocks.' Then he turned to me.
'So where'd the old Johnny Marioli pick you up, huh? Tell you,
the guy here before was crapolo, right. But *you*,' he said,
putting on an affected voice, which he did so well I had to
laugh, 'exude class.'

'Thank you.'

'I'm sure you're glad to be told that, Johnny,' Schenck said
ironically.

'Always accept a compliment gracefully, my nanny told
me.'

'His nanny,' the little man sneered. 'His fucking nanny –
get outta here. Hey, you stick around here, you could do well.
It's a good place to be. See, although I'm Johnny Palloni's
client, right, he is a very useful man to a businessman. You

know he's dual-qualified? You know that? OK, so any fuck can be dual-qualified, but he uses that – any country in the world, he's got the connections, right? Even knows old Max, right? So he can get his head shrunk.' And he laughed again.

And I must admit I laughed too. Not because what he said was funny.

I then got a lofty order from Schenck, mixed and brought them their drinks. And wondered a little at the peculiarities of this household, and of the first I had seen of Marenkian's client base.

Not quite our class, dear.

A somewhat larger-scale client entertainment was planned, and I would be playing a central role, under the gentle supervision of Natalie. We had a meeting about a week before the day.

She had put on a pair of brass-rimmed spectacles, so that she looked like a very pretty student – although there was a touch of Janis Joplin as soon as she looked at you.

'So, if you're gonna be a *real* butler,' she said after we had discussed the hiring of servants, timings, car parking and various other administrative details, 'you'll need a butler's costume. Something to make you *look* like a butler. Something to make you look distinguished.'

'So you're telling me I don't look distinguished enough?'

'You would plan to wear that rather – strange – blazer of yours.'

'Strange? That's a Huntsman blazer.'

'Well, it may be good hunting, honey, but it looks like an old coat.'

I laughed. 'Huntsman is the best tailor in Savile Row, and hence in the world.'

'Johnny, it's three inches thick. It looks as if you could stand it upright on the floor.'

'That's how the best clothes are supposed to look.'

'For impoverished Brits who buy a new jacket every generation.'

'That's right.'

'Anyhow, there's not the time for you to buy. Hire something in Nice – then we'll get you fitted for one.'

'Happily, miss.'

She leaned back in her chair.

'What are we gonna give these people to eat?'

'The usual things.'

'OK, so – uh – bits of pizza, maybe? Nuts for sure and, uh, little crackers. Listen, you may think this is incredibly stupid of me, but I just don't know what people eat on these occasions.'

'Oh, I can give you the range, I think. Devils-on-horseback – which are prunes wrapped in bacon; angels-on-horseback – liver wrapped in bacon; satay – we could have chicken, prawn if you like – with a peanut sauce. Do you think we could get a French butcher to make small sausages?'

'I doubt it.'

'We could try. Then vol-au-vents with a prawn filling.'

'And chicken,' she said, looking up from the paper.

'Melon wrapped in Parma ham.'

'Mmm. That's one thing *I* could handle.'

'Gambas cooked in garlic. Rolls of bread and soft cheese, and ham. You know, when you make a little thing like a Swiss roll.'

'This is your true talent coming out here, isn't it?'

'In my few years on this earth I've been to so many drinks parties where they serve this kind of thing, and weddings, I could recite the list in my sleep. We're very conventional in England, so it's practically always the same. Asparagus tips on puff pastry.'

'How about filo pastry?'

'How about filo pastry? How could we forget? Ricotta in

filo pastry. Chopped mushrooms. Oh – salad tomatoes scooped out and filled with prawn cocktail.'

We both laughed, I don't quite know why – just at the ridiculous plenty of it, I suppose. It wasn't until later, as I was getting ready for bed, that I was struck by, marvelled at, the complete ease I had with her and she with me. We seemed to think in the same way. And this discomfort I felt – that persisted the more I tried to ignore it – in being a servant, in being at the beck and call of these Americans, I felt nothing of when I was with her. I felt as though we could have been friends for a long time.

I was hoodwinking myself, of course, because what was really growing in me was a thirst for her, a longing that was with me all the time. As we talked my eye would stray for a moment to her hand, a strand of her hair, her forearm; a strained sweep across her torso, hidden in dark blue silk, or her supple golden thighs brushing against the hem of the short skirt. It's hard to describe this: my glimpses were like glints on the surface of the water, knowing that below there was far more than I could imagine, and yet catching an intimation of it, some music on the threshold of hearing. Oh yes, I waxed lyrical – much more than this dull prose suggests.

'So who are the guests? What is our consumer group?'

'Very choosy, Johnny. Very rich, you'll be amazed to hear. They're my father's clients – pretty much all of them. Rich men who are accustomed to being fed and watered well. Although, actually that doesn't stop a lot of them from being very greedy. You'll probably notice it: although they're often being fed like that, this kind of greedy look comes into their eyes when they see a tray of prawns or something, and they grab at it.'

'Really? Sounds charming.'

'Oh, it is. You'll love it.'

'Who are they?' I said, and I sounded abrupt to myself. 'These – I mean – what do your father's clients do?'

She paused, took her glasses off, looked at me.

'They're businessmen.'

'Ah – so no doctors and dentists, eh? Why an American lawyer, though – in France?'

'Oh, he doesn't deal with, uh, local law, or law-enforcement. He manages people's affairs. High-net-worth individuals who need somebody who can have a total overview of their affairs, who can manage investment matters for them, tax affairs, how they structure things.'

'Right.'

'Johnny.' Marenkian had put his head round the door, and I jumped up.

'Mr Marenkian.'

'I need you to go to the airport and pick up some clients.'

'Right you are.'

He gave me instructions and I went.

Chapter Four

WITH A GREAT rush of phone-calls, orders, payments and the whipping in of our dim-witted assistants, the drinks party came round. Natalie appeared in the kitchen late: a sex kitten in a little black cocktail dress, of course, but also the soul of efficiency. The most difficult part of my job was to keep my eyes off her pert rump and pay attention to her instructions. Because I couldn't look at her without picturing that thrust of her pelvis in the car. She had been so turned on.

She showed a certain respect – it made me smile – for her distinguished butler. Should we serve the devils-on-horseback before or after the prawn satay; should we continue to put cognac in the champagne cocktails once the guests were rosy? She even upbraided me for not taking my position seriously enough. At the beginning of the party I took a plate of food around, and when I got back to the kitchen she said:

'Johnny, you're the butler, and the butler doesn't take trays around, right?'

'If you insist, miss.'

'Don't "miss" me. Leave the trays to Claudine and her cousin.' Claudine and her cousin (the local butcher's wife) were both dressed in the regulation black skirts and stockings with little white lace aprons, and their uniforms lent a certain old-world charm to the occasion.

For much of the early evening, while the silky pink dusk turned to blue and the guests' babble hung in the air, I wandered among them topping up glasses with champagne, occasionally taking lead crystal tumblers into the house and filling them with ice and Scotch, vodka and, in one surprising case, Wild Turkey. I needn't have worried that Marenkian wouldn't keep it, though in the cellar were a mere three bottles as compared to the twenty or so of preferred tipples like Black Label or Stolichnaya.

Cars rolled up the drive. I was reminded of Horst's jibe about Mercedes cars. To merely meet the requirement here, it seemed you had to be at the top of the production range; to stand out you needed one of the unusual ones with an engine twice the normal size. I could thank God, as I watched them arrive, that I didn't take any of it seriously; but they certainly did. Sitting in state in the back seats (almost all of them had chauffeurs), they wore the impassive expressions of old-style Eastern Bloc leaders, power sitting heavily on their well-covered shoulders. Perhaps I'm exaggerating, now that I know the kind of people they were.

Marenkian went to meet them with a dignified enthusiasm, lavishing a particular courtesy on the wives. The wives! Some of them looked practically embalmed, with their leathery skin and their hair so heavily permed that it looked as though you could chisel it off in chunks. The wives gravitated together as if by magnetic force – though doubtless more by the force of realization that in their husbands' eyes they served no purpose other than to preserve the proper decorum. I watched them, and they seemed to me proud, brittle, and perhaps a little frightened. My observation was sharpening.

Heavyweights gathered together like bears: bears with a market to make. They had a curious ability to ignore everything peripheral. Those who look around themselves are sensitive and poor, whereas these had seen it all before. Or perhaps they all had plans in which their surroundings didn't figure. I missed the manners of the English middle class, the wives who smile effusively and say, 'Thank-you so-o-o much,' even if they never mean it. These men shoved their glasses in my direction without even troubling to look at me, and said, 'Scutch.'

I began to see how the company was mixed. Some were bourgeois kingpins; they sipped their kir royales and talked about food. I overheard part of a very earnest conversation about where in the world one could obtain the best *tarte tatin*. The entire world.

Others, the 'Scutch' drinkers for example, were altogether rougher under their expensive suits, and these had tarts with them. Perhaps they were builders made good. I asked Claudine, and she screwed up her eyes.

'That one, I think,' she said, looking at the only slim man in the group, and handsome with it, his long dark hair swept back, 'is the mayor of . . . I'm not sure where, who is a client of Monsieur Marenkian; and this one is the *président-directeur général* of the company which builds a lot of the roads here – and possibly also the autoroute, but I am not sure. And the other two I don't know.'

I smiled. Those builders had made very good. What's more, I am ashamed to say, I felt a certain warmth that at least these were successful yobs, influential yobs. There it is. It's not that I was pretending to despise them. I just couldn't quite manage it.

One of them, of course, was Horst, holding court to a large group who laughed at his bad jokes. For the moment he just nodded at me. I was impressed.

At about eight thirty I went, at Marenkian's request, to clear the drive of cars. People, he said, would go on arriving throughout the evening, and some would be coming in while others were departing. Half a dozen vehicles blocked the access, each with its young chauffeur leaning against the bonnet or boot, admiring his feet or setting the thrust of his pelvis a little more accurately. I exaggerate – I don't remember them all, but that's what the first looked like.

I went up to him and said, in a casual, friendly way, in French: 'Could you move the car out into the road, please?'

He just gave me a brief, bored, insolent glance and then gazed away.

'Ah, excuse me. I said, could you move the car out into the road, please? We've got other people coming and we need the space.'

'*Va te faire foutre*,' he said. I looked round at the other drivers, hoping that I had had the bad luck to pick a maverick, but they all looked surly or gazed back at me in a bored sort of way.

'I can't believe this,' I said.

He rounded on me and hissed in my face, in English, this time. 'I said fuck off, you bastard.'

I backed off – I was the butler, after all – and I was very slightly amused by his calling me a bastard, an insult no Englishman would use to your face (it's migrated to headlines in women's magazines: *Is your man a bastard?*).

I went back into the house, shaken but not stirred, with a vague idea of seeking out Marenkian, although I was sure he wouldn't want to be bothered by a trifle like this.

But in the hall I bumped into Bruno and, thinking it might be just the job to cheer him up, I said: 'Bruno, you know your father doesn't want the drive clogged up with cars? Well, I can't seem to get any of these chauffeurs to move.'

'Oh, right,' he said. 'That's predictable.'

He went out of the front door, and I followed. He swung down the steps two at a time, the Riviera cowboy, then at the bottom looked at me as if to confirm that the young Frenchman on the convertible Mercedes was the culprit. I nodded, and he strode up, shouting as he went.

'Hey, you. Move the car.' He waved his arm. Marvellous. He would have made a great policeman.

The young Frenchman stood up and said, in a surly sort of way, 'Monsieur Ablondi does not want his car moved.'

I saw Bruno's hackles rise.

'Just move the fucking car,' he growled, and then, there being no sign of cooperation from the chauffeur, he pushed him hard on the shoulders.

'Move it,' he shouted, and the chauffeur, looking at him with loathing – like a whipped cur, as they would have said – got into the car, started it up, caused it to jerk forward once, twice, the wheels spinning. Bruno turned to the others and shouted: 'You too. *Vite!*'

They moved.

I grinned at him.

'Well done, Bruno. You showed him who was boss.'

'Don't worry, man.'

'Do you mind if I call on you again?'

'Leave it with me. I'll stick around for a little while.'

'Hey, thanks very much.'

Horst charged up to me on my way back through, and we chatted for a while.

'Good to see you, Horst. How are you?'

'Busy networking at this *celebrity* party.'

'You'd better not waste your time on me, then.'

'But you are my *skipper*. You are the most important person for me to network. Tell me how you are finding life at the Marenkian household.'

'It's fine. Easy enough.'

'Not too easy, I hope. I will want you to skipper for me again in March.'

'Well.'

'Some doubt? Oh dear.'

'You might have to match their salary.'

'Oh, if it is only a question of *price*, Johnny, then we all have that. And what do you do with your day?'

'I cook, look after the swimming pool, go shopping, drive Bruno around.'

'Oh, Bruno is here? Of course. And what else?'

'Sorry?'

'What else do you *do*? This surely does not take up your whole day?'

'Fix things, serve drinks, play some tennis.'

'And you must be kept on your toes entertaining the *associates* of John Marenkian?'

'There's a certain amount of business entertaining.'

'Oh, really. Tell me, have the Agostinis been here? They are such old friends of mine. You know, Marenkian and I have many friends in common.'

'I don't know. I don't get introduced.'

He laughed.

'Of course. They are all so rich and important, Mr Marenkian would not introduce them to a servant. Even one as charming as you, Johnny, who has been to public school.' And he laughed again. 'Do you not find this irritating?'

'Not at all. I have no desire to meet them. I'm sure you must understand, Horst, that when you come from my sort of background in England it's very easy to look down on almost anybody.'

'Ha-ha-ha, how wonderful.'

'Particularly unsavoury foreigners.'

'Oh yes, particularly unsavoury foreigners. But are you saying that there are *unsavoury* people at the Château Marenkian? How upsetting. Can you bring yourself to hand cups of tea to these unsavoury people?'

'With immense difficulty. But these unsavoury people are probably among the friends you and Marenkian have in common.'

'Well, they may be. Tell me some of their names.'

'Horst, you're interrogating me.'

He laughed again. 'Ah, Johnny, well, this is true. I am interested, I must admit. And you, of course, are being the model employee, very discreet, and one would not expect anything else.'

'I'm actually not in the least bit discreet. But tell me,' I said, lowering my voice, 'what's your involvement with Marenkian?'

Horst drew a little nearer and spoke quietly.

'He is a partner of mine in a deal to establish a chain of amusement arcades on the beautiful island of Majorca. Do you know, I don't really trust him. I have some reason to believe that he may be involved with the competition in this deal, you see. Although it may not be Marenkian himself. It may be the wild son, or even the daughter.'

'Well,' I said, and I had a laugh in my voice, but I took a good look round to make sure nobody was listening, 'I think you can count Bruno out as a business rival. He's under medication, under the supervision of some weird shrink. I think he's getting more raving mad by the day. I should know. I'm supposed to be his bodyguard.'

'You?' Horst said incredulously.

'Yes, absolutely.'

'And why should he need a bodyguard?'

'Well – Marenkian wants to keep tabs on what he's up to.'

'Really? Why?'

'Because he has the idea that some of Bruno's friends have ulterior motives – and those who do are banned. Bruno's not allowed to see them.'

'And who are these people?'

'I don't know yet. I haven't met any of them.'

'And do we know what ulterior motives they may have?'

'No, we do not. Presumably he just thinks they're scroungers.

It has to be said that rich layabouts do attract scroungers, spongers, flies on a piece of shit, you know.'

'Well, I'm so glad you've made friends with him.'

'He is a waster – Bruno, I mean. You couldn't say that of his father, who works every hour that the devil sends, particularly at night for some reason.'

'Oh, that's quite simple. He does quite a lot of dealings on the markets – obscure places, sometimes. He is not brewing potions.'

'Ah, I'm glad to be reassured on that point.'

'Does Bruno not work with his father? I thought he worked with his father.'

'No, he doesn't seem to. He doesn't seem to be doing anything except going mad.'

Horst laughed. 'You have a cruelty in your character, you know that?'

'So would you, Horst, if you were a domestic servant. And speaking of domestic service, I'd better do some.'

'I'm going now, anyway. We'll have some lunch when I'm in town next, huh?'

'OK, sir,' I said, and we shook hands.

Natalie was in the kitchen when I returned, and I told her about the incident with the cars.

She laughed. 'Bruno hates his French contemporaries,' she said languidly, then took a pull on a joint, which amazed me.

'That's a shame if you happen to live in France.'

'He wouldn't live here if he didn't have to.' She handed me the joint.

'Really?'

'So *you* couldn't get those chauffeurs to move?'

'I didn't really think I was going to get so much resistance. Why are they so surly?' I ignored her imputation.

She curled her lip for a moment, and in that moment looked remarkably French herself.

'It could be because they wouldn't want to obey someone else's bodyguard. Who was it?'

'Ablondi.'

'Ablondi wouldn't obey my father. Why should his bodyguard obey my father's bodyguard?'

'Bodyguard? How ridiculous. They're not all bodyguards, are they?'

'Yeah, more or less.'

'Do these people really need them?'

'There were kidnappings in the Seventies and Eighties, and there's more crime here than there used to be – street crime. But really those men are just a fashion accessory. But you're not a bodyguard, right?'

'Right,' I said, handing her back the joint. It was strong.

'So what *are* you? What would you call yourself?'

'The chef, perhaps.'

She laughed.

'Uh-ho, no; I don't think so. The skivvy?'

'The major-domo?'

'The slave?'

I smiled. 'That sounds good to me.' I held her eye. 'People can do what they like with slaves.'

She met my gaze, laughed, then said laughing: 'Uh-oh, eye contact.'

Claudine rushed in with a tray, sniffed loudly, muttered in French, then said to me: 'We need some more champagne.'

She turned her back on Natalie, who sauntered out. And I suddenly felt just a little bit bad-tempered.

An hour or so later the composition of the party was shifting, and the older dignitaries were leaving. I took a bottle round again; there wasn't much else to do, and it allowed me to see what was going on. Two sixty-year-olds with Marenkian, watching the girls hungrily – and what a quantity of girls there was, all in their mid-twenties. A good age, I thought, for a whore: ten or more years' experience behind her but still quite firm. And that's what they were by the looks of them. A forty-year-old with cropped grey hair was sitting on the wall explaining something to a sad, olive-skinned waif. I caught a glimpse of the dark areola of her breast brushing against the inside of her leather jerkin. Two balding men, mid-forties, hairy chests and bellies, were shouting their laughter at the tipsy Barbie dolls standing with them. Another doll, this one at the end of her shelf life, was sitting alone in the high-backed chair near the front door, drunk but waving away my offer of another glass.

Around the coffee table sat Natalie, Bruno and their contemporaries – eight young men, four girls – snorting coke, laughing. A fast kind of lawyer, my employer, I thought to myself. Sleaze is one thing, and semi-pro girls, but here was cocaine on the coffee table and nobody bats an eye. Bruno glowered. In his lightweight lumberjack shirt, Wranglers and baseball boots he looked totally out of place: a sharecropper gatecrashing the mansion on the hill. He swigged from his glass, and I saw the bottle of Wild Turkey I had opened earlier. He'd need the coke just to stay awake; there was about a finger left. I wondered what these slick Italians made of him: a redneck out of his depth.

I watched Natalie banter with the young man who sat next to her, and I wondered whether he had been the guy in the Alfa Spider. I decided not. With each jibe or joke – they spoke in Italian, Natalie quite fluently – he insinuated himself towards her, and she in turn parried and pushed him back, laughing. I could see that he had never slept with her.

I saw the man with the grey hair leading the waif away by the arm, the ageing doll finally getting a chance to argue with her husband. I went and sat in the kitchen with Claudine, her cousin and the waiters, reading a book and occasionally sending one of them out with a couple of bottles, seeing a guest out, calling a taxi, emptying ashtrays.

Suddenly it was three in the morning, and I felt stale and empty, and as sober as I had ever been. And I started having regrets, as one does at that time of night. I had suffered a huge setback, my first career ruined, and I was at a severe disadvantage in that farmyard of a country that raised me. So I should have been trying to claw myself back into its favour, somehow. But I realized what a forlorn hope that was; I had blotted my copybook for good. Whenever I thought about going back there, I had visions of old men like my commanders, mouldering in their folds of Harris tweed, their faces like stale suet stained with red berry juice, dismissing me in a word. *He was a wrong 'un, and we always knew it.* Even my mother was gone now, her cottage, the Wolverhampton twang she never really got rid of. My mother was the sort of woman who did the sewing for people like the Honourable Lulu Messing, and some things never change – not in England.

You may wonder, therefore, about my meteoric rise, my Harry Flashman place among those cavalry grandees. It was thanks to my father, head of the French Department at my middle-ranking public school. I would never have attended that school, or any other public school, were it not that my father paid only a small percentage of the normal fees. And I was never allowed to forget it by my father, who reminded me of it every time my work slipped behind, or I misbehaved. I misbehaved, I admit, a lot, and the poor man must have suffered. *Denner, you really must bring up your children properly!* 'Johnny,' he used to say, 'don't you know how lucky you are? Your education here will open up so many doors to you. We could never afford to send you here were I not a member of staff.'

The other boys always had a certain sneer at the back of their eyes. No matter how rind my viles, no matter how polished my shoes, no matter absolutely of the gentry the cut of my corduroys, I would never be allowed to forget that I was teacher's son, there on a discount, the boy whose mother had Wolverhampton in her voice.

The bloody snobs. I thought of them every time I thought of going back to England and trying something else. Down here nobody knew better.

There was a lot of noise in the drive. The young Italians were heading off, Natalie with them, but not Bruno. I saw them into their cars. Marenkian having disappeared to his office, that left only the laughing fatties and their dolls. I went back into the kitchen. I wanted to tell the hired help they could go, but there was a business meeting the next day and everything had to be cleared up, yet clearly nothing could be done until the last guests had left.

Half an hour later it sounded as if by some miracle they might have gone. I went round the house and could hear or see nobody. Another of the perspectives you become used to as a servant: the burnt-out ends of other people's pleasures; the desolation of those dawns – not wishing to be too dramatic about it. This one had a particular sting, however. I opened the door to the den and there, on one of the sofas, was one of the fat men screwing one of the dolls. He was hunched over her, his tiny furry buttocks pumping quite fast. She opened her eyes, if they had ever been closed, and saw me. She seemed quite unconcerned, and very detached. Another servant. His friend was slumped, asleep, on the other sofa.

I shut the door and went back to the kitchen. I doubted he would make it, considering the quantity of Scotch I had poured for him. I told the servants they could clean up everywhere except the den, then went and made some fresh coffee. It was already light.

The other doll, the one who had been with the sleeping fatty, came in and asked me sulkily to order a taxi, which I did. Then I asked her if she'd like a cup of coffee, which she took.

We didn't speak; she thought I was an inferior because I was serving her coffee, and I thought she was a slut.

(Although here, perhaps, I was wrong. Most of us, in our weakness, want to hang on to people who have status, who command respect, and what commands more respect than money flaunted? If you're some doll without a brain, what could be better than a man with great thick forearms and a wad of high-denomination notes who knows how to spend it, who's known in the restaurants? Isn't that the ultimate aim of most human endeavour, to be known in the restaurants?)

By the time her taxi came, the others had appeared, the men both looking bad-tempered and businesslike, the sofa doll glancing at me slyly with a smile, as if to tell me I could be next. Can you imagine?

They left, and I discovered that I had been unfair to the fat man. He *had* made it – and left something on the sofa for me to clean up. I didn't feel I could ask anyone else to do that.

When I went to bed, Marenkian was still working.

Chapter Five

IF I CAN GET it right, I can still walk away from this. If I don't put a foot wrong.

'Why?'

He keeps at it, keeps repeating the question, although I sense that he isn't much interested in the answer.

'Why this . . . savagery?'

And I stay silent, because I know if I put a foot wrong I won't have a chance. But that if every step is just right, I might make it.

'Here is the pathologist's report,' the other one says. 'It is unbelievable, you know – really disgusting. Uh, Michel? You've read it?'

The one with the bandanna says something in French I don't catch, while his colleague shuffles casually through the document on his lap, feet up on the desk. In the silence I shift again on the little low stool, trying to get comfortable. Maybe I can rest my hand on my knee; that way the edge of the handcuff won't cut into my wrist.

'In excess of twenty blows were delivered to the facial area.'

Then he looks up.

'The face looked like an old bit of fruit that someone had kicked around the street. You could hardly see his nose or his eyes.'

'It was beaten to a pulp.'

I bow my head.

'I mean . . .' the one who has been reading the report shouts suddenly, throwing the file down on the desk in front of him, 'I mean, why didn't you just kill him quickly? You hated him, we know that, you wanted him dead – why didn't you just kill him quickly? Why did you have to torture him?'

Still I am silent. Then the one in the bandanna stands up and says:

'OK, monsieur. Let me tell you what they will hear first in court: the forensic evidence. Your fingerprints were found in the house. You had no business in that house, no reason for being there. You had never been there at any time other than the time of the murder. Your thumbprint on the socket wrench that was used on him, the socket wrench that smashed his face up. The socket wrench we found buried near the swimming pool. Who else buried it? Huh? Who else?'

Then he leans towards me, and half whispers: 'Do you know what the jury will see? They'll see these photographs first. How do you think they'll feel? Do you think any of them will vomit?'

He throws a set of about a dozen large photographs in my lap, and I pick them up. Michel was right; his face looks like a watermelon that has been kicked around in the dust and left for a few days: a mess of red, purple, blue, and yellow, his eyes closed up, black and bulbous, one end of his upper lip split right open.

'Then they'll see the socket wrench, with dried blood all over it. The one with your thumbprint on it. And the expert witness will tell them about that.'

I say nothing, just shake my head.

'Then your T-shirt, the one you came back with at the end of the day, with the bloodstain matching the victim's blood group on it, the one you tried to burn – but not quite thoroughly enough, did you? The way your knuckles were broken because you gave him your fists too, didn't you?'

He too is beginning to get angry.

'Didn't you?'

They look at each other, then shrug, and Michel picks up the phone and calls for a turnkey. After a few minutes he comes, removes the handcuffs from the ring in the wall and leads me by them down to the cell block, and the big door slams shut, and I sit staring at its chipped grey paint work, thinking. Tomorrow there'll be another conversation like this, and the next day. But if I can get it right I can still walk away from this.

If I don't put a foot wrong.

Natalie and I played tennis again a couple of days after the party, and she almost beat me.

'That was a good game,' she said, 'although I'm not really sure you're up to my standard.'

I laughed. 'Your standard in what?'

'Very funny. My standard in tennis.'

'You appear to have a high opinion of your standard, particularly considering you've just been beaten.'

'Yeah, but you know, Johnny, that the result of the match doesn't necessarily reflect the quality of the participants.'

'Often true, I'm sure. Life isn't fair.'

'I mean, the strength of your game is your determination not to be beaten. Would you agree with that?'

'I hang in there.'

'My technique is better than yours.'

'That's true.'

'I'm probably a little bit fitter.'

'I doubt that, Natalie, from what I've seen of your lifestyle. You're talking to a clean-living ocean skipper and part-time butler here. Whereas I'm talking to a Riviera party girl.'

She snorted. 'A Riviera party girl? What the fuck is that?'

Then she covered her mouth. 'Uh, excuse me,' she said, wide-eyed. 'I have got the most *foul* tongue.'

'Don't worry,' I said. 'I've heard worse.' And I smiled, and thought: *But never from sweeter lips.*

We had reached the steps of the terrace.

'Listen,' she said. 'I'm thirsty. How about you get us both a beer and we'll go drink them by the pool?'

'Sure.'

We lounged in the sun with the complete relaxation that follows exertion.

'Do you live down here permanently?'

'I have been for – about two years. I came here to work.'

'So what went right?'

She looked at me. 'Believe me, I'd rather be working right now. You can get very bored doing this kind of thing.'

'A lot of people don't mind.'

'*Some* people don't mind. Ladies who lunch, and ladies who shop, and girls with rich daddies or rich uncles. Women who don't have any ambition except to gratify themselves – and their men.'

'Actually I've sometimes wondered what motivates some of the women you see down here. What motivates a young woman to marry some old, rich man—?'

She surprised me by looking slightly taken aback by my question. 'Why not?' she said. 'The men you're talking about are often very successful in their fields, they're experienced, charismatic. They may be getting old – but they're winners. And if you're gonna attach yourself to a man – well, a lot of people like to attach themselves to a winner. People have money because they're winners. It's simple. If you're aged forty and you haven't got any money, you're a loser. You might be a nice guy, but you're a loser.'

By then I'd be rich, without any doubt.

'Let's put it in male terms,' she said, 'because this isn't just to do with marriage, right – or even sex. The guy at college who has that ability and force and charisma, everybody wants to be his friend, right?'

'That's true. But people can actually be mistaken about that, can't they? I knew a guy at Sandhurst who was just like that,' I said, and added, in answer to her wrinkled brow, 'It's the English equivalent of West Point. He was incredibly popular, he had a real magnetism, but it didn't come through. He was caught stealing.'

'Oh, sure, and I guess people fail in less spectacular ways, over longer periods of time. What about you?' she said suddenly. 'What about the British Army?'

The implication threw me. I was a good liar, but not when it came to this. I was just about to go into the routine: the military life didn't suit me, my desire to travel – life on the ocean wave and so on. But on an impulse I told her the truth. I suppose I knew she wouldn't be shocked.

'Well, I could bullshit you, Natalie, but I won't. But I've got to ask you not to say anything about this, because your father doesn't know.'

'OK.'

'I was still in the army, and I was on leave in Spain, and somebody asked me to take a parcel back to England for them. And I got stopped at customs, and inside the parcel was a lot of hash. And that put paid to my army career.'

'Shit, what an asshole, whoever asked you to take the parcel through. I mean, presumably it wasn't a stranger.'

'It was a girl.'

She opened her eyes wide and took a deep breath.

'You mean – a *girl*?'

I nodded.

'Jesus, Johnny.'

'Not very nice of her, I know. But perhaps she thought

there wasn't much risk. But enough of that. You, we take it, are not in the market for a sugar daddy.'

'That's right.'

'Not – if you'll excuse me saying so – that you really need one.'

'And what does *that* mean?' She looked slightly annoyed at my disarming frankness.

'Just that you seem to have a great life here. Everything you could want.'

'No, no, *no*. I don't have everything I want. I have the things that a lot of other people might want. Particularly the things rich people have and poor people always want. Things we don't really care about. Or maybe we take them for granted. Swimming pools and cars, nightclubs and chic restaurants and designer labels. You know, I'd give all that up tomorrow in exchange for a chance to have my own adventure. To make my own mark.'

I liked her sense of independence. She didn't want her daddy's money, and she didn't want another man to step into his shoes. Although I'd believe that stuff about giving it up tomorrow when I saw it.

'You see, my father is a businessman in a highly competitive field, and he's grooming my brother for the succession, and I don't see why I shouldn't be a businessman. I have the ideas and I have the energy, and the balls – not literally – and I'd give all this up to have the chance.' She sounded deadly serious.

'Why can't you be? Can't you be groomed for the succession too?'

She smiled. 'Not exactly so easy in his business. The thing is ...' she struggled a moment for the sense, 'it's partly my father, who has old-fashioned ideas about the place of women. It's partly the nature of the business he's in.'

'Which is?'

Again she frowned. 'I would say investment advice is the

most accurate description. I mean, he's an attorney, and he's also qualified as an accountant, and he can do a lot of different things, but mainly he advises people on how to invest large sums of capital. Actually, if we're honest about it – which he is not – on how to conceal them. Rich men store their money away, and my father does it for them.'

'What, directly? You mean he actually takes possession of the money like a banker?'

'In a sense. We're not talking about cash, Johnny. Convertible bonds, bearer shares, various kinds of mechanisms the tax people can't read.'

'Ah.'

'You see, this is the way it's going. There's a flight of capital from the old onshore bases out into the ether. You know what I mean? Untraceable bundles floating around the world, down the wires, touching down here and there, unpredictably. And anonymously, so that no one can ever say: "Johnny Denner, you bad boy, we've just found several million of yours in Manila, liable to state and federal tax." So you give your several million to my father. And he puts it into this company, which is owned by that company in Grenada, which in turn belongs to another company, which is owned by a dead man in Anguilla who, it so happens, entered into a contract with my father making him sole executor, and this contract is in a safe somewhere else – you know what I mean.'

'Blimey,' I said. I hadn't quite understood what on previous occasions I had overheard.

'But maybe you've seen the flaw here.'

I hadn't, so I just raised my eyebrows in what I hoped was an intelligent way.

'Trust,' she said.

'Trust?' I wondered what kind she was referring to. Most of my friends had one.

'You see,' she went on with the slightest trace of impatience, as if I were being a little bit slow, 'say you've given your several million to my father. The whole idea of giving it to him is that there should be no documentary evidence of the existence of the money. Because the transaction is gonna be of somewhat dubious legality, in any case, and because you wouldn't be coming to my father if you didn't want to conceal it.'

'I see what you mean. I don't want to go back to him and say, "I think I'll just withdraw a little of that several million, John," and he says, "What several million was that, Johnny? I'm afraid I don't recall."'

'Or if he's not discreet. Your business associate you ripped off to get the money has been told you've got it, or the authorities in the City of London, whatever.'

'And they won't trust a woman.'

'That's about it. Sure, it's not quite as simple as that. There's a kind of freemasonry about this. It takes years – this is what my father says – it takes years to build up a special kind of trust between men. Who can you trust in this world? Your family? That's why the goddam Italians are so successful. But sometimes you have to go outside those groups of family and friends and villages and all that shit. I admit my father is good at cultivating that trust. And it helps that he has twenty years behind him now, and he's never defaulted or ripped anyone off. And that is his asset. That's what he'll hand on to Bruno.'

I wanted to say something intelligent. 'So there must always be an element of force – of compulsion. Perhaps that's what makes it a man's world, at least to some extent. In the normal world – above the surface, in the legal world – a contract exists as something that has a force behind it ultimately, and if someone defaults you can take them to court and make them pay. And in your father's world? What happens there?'

She nodded slowly, knowingly, a slight smile on her lips.

'Oh yeah. There's a force behind it, ultimately. But it's much better for everybody if that force can remain unused.'

So my little probe had turned up another hint about her father's world. *The man is a gangster,* I marvelled to myself. With all his East Coast ways and his high-tech office and his old-world courtesy, he's nothing more than a gangster. Or nothing less, I should perhaps say.

She said, 'How about lunch?' and I looked at my watch. It was ten past one.

'Cripes, he'll kill me—'

I hared up the steps and back to the house.

Chapter Six

'TONIGHT YOU'RE gonna meet Nico Mammalio and Sally,' Bruno said, his voice rich with irritation, contempt even. Then he imitated my English accent: 'So that you can give an accurate report to my father, you know – I'm just making things easier for you, telling you who you're gonna see. Sally's bringing a friend, who I might take somewhere and fuck while you're sitting in the car. You won't wanna be there and watch, though, will you? Jerk off?'

He stared at me, perhaps hoping for some response. I didn't oblige. He reminded me of an Englishman I had known in prison: the only other Englishman there, in for a much more serious drug-running offence, who thought he was an artist, or perhaps a saint. He used to put his fingers up to his forehead in a gesture of extreme concentration and say, his voice slurred from years of acid, *'I've got this story, know what I mean, and it's begging me to write it, right. It's begging me – it's inside me. It's about this big man, right, and he's a strong man, and he's too big for the world, right. So the world just crushes him, man. Just crushes him.'*

I thought that maybe that wasn't a bad basis for a story, until I read his seven-page draft. It was drivel. Bruno reminded me of him. People like that are on another planet, and there are more and more of them about. He was convinced someone had it in for him. Someone was preventing him from expressing himself.

Bruno leaned against the door, persevering with his attempt at wit. Was a servant obliged to laugh at his employer's son's witticisms? Not in my book.

'I think Daddy is going to get you to give me swimming lessons soon, Johnny. And then maybe you'll do a birthday party for me and my friends, and we'll have peanut butter and jelly sandwiches.'

I smiled, and he changed back.

'My father is – kind of outta touch about things, you know? He lives his life in conference rooms.'

'I can imagine.'

We passed a building made of a substance looking like translucent toothpaste.

'Whereas I just – you know – I live in the twentieth century. Why do you think you have to trail around after me?'

'I don't really know, Bruno. Your father says you shouldn't drive.'

'Yeah, well that's bullshit. Come on, *what* did he tell you?'

'He really didn't tell me very much.'

'OK,' he said, his tone a little more serious. 'Well, *I'll* tell you. What he thinks is that I'm gonna get stoned out of my mind. He thinks that I'm in danger of becoming a drug addict, right?'

'Are you?'

'Hey. I do some coke, right? Who doesn't? You do coke?'

'I have done.'

'He thinks I'm gonna do so much coke I'm gonna take a ride on the underside of a bus, or kick a wino's face in, or go in the fucking sea and drown.'

He burst out laughing.

'Yeah, I'm gonna do the coke, right, but I'm not gonna drown. *You* think I'm gonna drown. *You* the lifeguard?'

'I hope not.'

'No, sincerely, you know what I'm saying,' he continued in

an impatient whine. 'I don't want some guy who works for my dad with me when I'm out with my friends trying to have a good time. You dig?'

You dig. Was there a revival in psychedelic slang?

'Bruno, I just have to follow your father's instructions. He pays my salary. This is what he's asked me to do.'

'Huh-huh-huh. How about when you're with me you do what *I* say?'

'You don't pay my salary.'

'You like coke? I'll get you a gram of coke a week.'

I shook my head.

'Sorry, Bruno. Can't do it.'

'Aw, come on.'

'I can't. I have to follow instructions.'

'Fuck,' he shouted. 'Waste of fucking time.'

There was a pause, then I said, 'Listen, I'm not gonna cramp your style. You can do anything you like. You can take that ride on the underside of a bus, OK?'

'No, come along, man, join the party, you know. Only don't expect to have a good time.'

We parked in the underground car park next to the Meridien. We walked up the steps into that bright, crystalline Niçois light, intense from the blinding glitter of the sea. For a moment, as I stepped up from below, there was no colour; just layers, it seemed, of dazzling monochrome reflection. Then my eyes adjusted to the brightness. The Promenade des Anglais was bustling with aimless walkers, cyclists, old women and juicy young girls; a couple of coaches pouring Italians into the hotel; shiny, dusty saloon cars arguing with their horns, the drivers making wild gestures, everyone hot and bothered.

'What time is it?' Bruno said, then, 'Time to start drinking.' We walked up to the Place Masséna and then a bit further, to the kind of bar I would avoid like the plague. I don't know how whoever had built it had got away with it. Intruding in an elegant arcade of matching shop fronts, all high-arched windows and fussy cornices, it was a slab of smoked plate-glass, a gob of spit in your face. It's called brutalism, I believe, although this was brutal in an effete sort of way, like a homosexual in a hard hat. The black letters on the glass announced the name of the place: *Nefertiti*. Not very original.

'This was done by Nils Hennigen,' I thought Bruno said. I must have looked at him blankly, because he continued, 'He's the world-class designer right now. His company's called Hennigma. He did the Ice Lounge.'

'Oh, right.'

'I met him. I'm an investor in this place. He's a very unassuming guy.'

I could imagine that a Scandinavian had designed it; it was monochrome and antiseptic, tone on tone of grey in brushed metal, steel cable and pipe-work constructions that looked rather like scaffolding. A depressing sort of place.

'Bruno, how you doing?' the manager asked.

'Fine, Michel, fine. This is my new bodyguard, Johnny.'

He glanced at me and I nodded.

'You made someone angry, huh?'

'Too many people, Michel. Maybe they're gonna get me.'

'I'll deal with them, Bruno,' I said.

'You will, huh? With what?'

'See these?' I said, and I held my hands up. 'Killing machines.'

'Killing machines,' he growled – and we both jumped back in some approximation of a martial-arts stance, and laughed. It was one of those silly moments that help you get on better.

'Hey, Michel, set up a bottle of fucking pastis.' When it came, Bruno downed one without water, refilled with a double, water and ice, and turned outwards from the bar – we were sitting on bar stools – to look at the clientele. It was the after-office stage of the evening; standing near the bar were a couple of groups of men in those soft, floppy suits the continentals wear. At a table near the door was a very old-fashioned and elderly woman on her own, dressed in black. She looked to me like a reproach or a protest, and I wondered what she was doing there.

'Bruno, mate,' said a hard, slightly slurred London voice behind us, and we both turned round.

'Hey, Phil. How you doing?'

'Good, man, good. I'm one of the good guys.' Then he chanted, tunelessly, as he swung a bar stool round: '"Something for your mi-i-ind".' He tapped the pastis bottle on the counter and a barman put a glass in front of him, and he poured. 'How you going, Bruno, man?' He bobbed up and down in his chair, nodding his head to an unheard beat and twisting his glass.

'I'm under supervision.' Bruno glanced at me. 'This is my supervisor.'

'Oh, yeah?' Phil said, and gazed at me for a moment with glazed eyes, his mouth open like a fish. 'You qualified?' Then he laughed a silly, squealing, stoned sort of laugh.

'The name's Johnny,' I said, and immediately felt pompous, stiff, and old.

'"Something for your mi-i-ind",' he chanted again, then turned away. So did Bruno, and I was left on my own, listening to their almost completely banal conversation.

'Yeah, I went to a fucking club last night. I tell you, man, the clubs here are such fucking shit, you know what I mean, and the music is such fucking shit and all, I don't know what I'm gonna do. Why have you gotta live down here, then?'

'You know why, man.'

'I don't fucking know.'

'You do.'

'I don't.'

'I told you.'

'No, you didn't.'

'Yes, I did.'

'No, you didn't.'

'Listen, man, I told you but you were right out of it, yeah, just like you are now, and if I tell you again now, you'll just forget it again.'

'Well, that's good. So, like when you're with me, you've always got something to talk about. Because I've always forgotten what you told me before. Know what I mean?' Then he laughed his squealing laugh again, and chanted, '"Something for your mi-i-ind."'

'It was the condition the court made when I was busted, right? That I had to live here with the old man.'

'Oh, yeah,' Phil said, narrowing his eyes. 'Yeah, I remember.' He was small and wiry, his neck and jaw knotted with sinew, chin dotted with dark stubble. His black hair stood on end, and he had curiously bulbous brown eyes.

'You know something?' he said. 'Goldfish and that – possibly all fish – have got very small memories, right, which is why they never get bored. So they go round this bowl, right, and every time they go round it's like they're seeing it for the first time, know what I mean, and they're going "Wo-o-ow, man, look at that fucking glass!"'

That really set him off, and he laughed hysterically for a few minutes. Then he brought himself back to earth with: '"Something for your mi-i-ind."'

And Bruno said, for about the third time, 'What are you on, man?'

'No, no, wait,' Phil said, holding his hand up while he got his breath back. 'Seriously, listen. Imagine if . . . every time you saw the sea, right, you saw it for the first time . . . or the stars? Like you had never seen them before? Fucking hell, man.'

I was astonished by him, I must admit – astonished by the

conversation. And although I know that on paper it seems remarkably banal and immature, it was actually very attractive: conversation without inhibition, experimental conversation, conversation of today. It did have a certain wit, it seemed to me.

'So that's where you're headed?' Bruno said. 'You know, I always wondered if you had *any* kind of ambition, and now I see this is it. You're aiming for a total memory loss, right?' They laughed. 'I'd say you're doing well.' They laughed again. 'Go on, man, wipe the slate clean!'

That finished Phil off, and he was slapping the bar for five minutes.

Then Bruno disappeared and I was left with Phil. We sat in silence for about five minutes, then Bruno came back and there was more of the kind of conversation they had been having before, except that Bruno now seemed to enter into the spirit of it even more, and I wondered whether he had snorted a line of coke in the lavatory.

A little later two more people turned up, and the bottle of pastis started to look sad. I had been drinking a little more than I had intended – drink-drive enforcement in France doesn't seem to have a very high priority – and Bruno and Phil had been punishing it.

The newcomers were American. The man was in his early thirties, wiry and sallow, with heavy eyelids and lips. He had the look of a shagged-out guitarist, someone who's pounded smelly old rock venues for years and paid the price. Whereas his girlfriend with shiny, long brown hair and freckles on her cheeks looked like the daughter of a wealthy farmer, just back from roaming the orchards in the morning dew. She could have been in a shampoo commercial.

'Hey, Nico, man,' said Phil, swinging on his bar stool.

'Hello, Phil. You been drinking too much coffee again,

huh?' Nico said this adenoidally, with an admirable coldness, and then turned slightly away, cutting Phil dead. An arrogant customer, evidently – but he had presence.

His girlfriend said, 'Hi, Phil,' very sweetly, and kissed him on the cheek.

I was amused by that. Perhaps I had had too much to drink, but it seemed to me that she was going around after Nico cleaning up his mess, and that her politeness to Phil reflected no particular affection – merely a desire to do a service for her arrogant boyfriend.

I was introduced again, this time as the chauffeur, and Nico looked at Bruno and said in a sad, bored sort of way, 'You're drinking with your chauffeur?'

Then he turned to me. 'Terrible when your employer has got no friends, so you have to go drinking with him. This in your contract?'

'Yeah, there are some special clauses.'

'Make sure you get the extra pay. Danger money.'

I got stools for them while they finished the pastis and ordered a fresh bottle, then resumed my place on the sidelines and lost interest in their conversation for a while.

A little later the peculiar part of the evening began.

Phil said. 'What, *that* casino? We going up there? Oh, yeah.'

'Think they're gonna let him in? State he's in?' Nico said contemptuously.

'They'll let him in if I tell them.'

'Have you told Johnny about this?' Nico said.

Bruno shook his head.

'Yeah, go on, tell him,' Sally said.

Bruno grimaced and patted the bar with the palms of his hands. He was not at all sure he wanted to tell me.

'This is a strange kind of gambling we do sometimes in a private club.'

'Yeah, it's fucking strange, man,' Phil said. 'Strangest I've seen.'

'But maybe Bruno doesn't want to tell you about it.'

There was a pause, while they all looked at Bruno. Then he said, 'Come on, let's go.'

He slid off his stool and walked out without looking back. Michel stood at the other side of the bar, waiting to be paid. Nico looked at Phil in a nonchalant sort of way and went, Sally following, and Phil dug into his pocket. It interested me in an idle sort of way that there was such an obvious pecking order here, one that was reasserted with such regularity. It interested me too that Bruno, who had until then seemed to me one of life's underdogs, was the undisputed leader of this little pack. Nico quite clearly deferred to him, and Nico was obviously no pushover. Bruno seemed to possess a strength of character that I hadn't seen. Back at the house he was in his father's shadow, and he was darkened by it.

Then again, I thought as I walked behind them through the dark, crowded evening streets, watching Nico talking earnestly to Bruno, chopping the air with short movements of his hand, while Phil listened quietly to Sally . . . then again, it could be that these people were the kind of hangers-on, spongers, that always gravitate towards very rich people. I wasn't yet sure whether the Marenkians fell into the category of *very rich* as it is defined on the Côte d'Azur, but they couldn't be far off it, given what I had already seen of their resources.

Bruno shouted, 'Hey, Johnny!' and waved for me to catch them up – which I did.

'Yeah, listen, I gotta tell you about this place, right. My father is one of the owners of this casino, right, and sometimes they need to balance the books, OK?'

'Do me a favour,' Nico said.

'Hey, shut up, Nico. They need to balance the books, and it suits them that we should go and make a loss there.'

I was astonished: Marenkian's *wealth*!

'I think you'll have to count me out of that, Bruno.'

'No, no, we don't lose *our* money. We lose the casino's money, yeah? They can show a bigger profit.'

I couldn't really get my mind round it; didn't, in fact, even try. Partly because, to my amazement, we stopped there and then – in a leafy boulevard behind the busy part by the Promenade – and Bruno pulled from his pocket a wad of dirty five-hundred-franc notes you could have used as a doorstop. He handed six notes to each of us and kept the rest. Like conspirators, which I suppose we were, we pocketed the money in unison.

'Uh,' Sally said, 'it'll be sad to say goodbye to you,' and kissed hers before putting it away in her little bag.

'Sally, make sure you *do* say goodbye to it, OK? Bruno said. 'Every cent.'

'And don't kiss it,' Nico added, 'if you value your lips.'

'Come on, you know last time was an accident,' she told Bruno. 'I'll get rid of it.'

'Yeah.'

'Lose it *all*, Johnny. OK?'

'Every penny, Bruno.'

'"Something for your mi-i-ind,"' Phil chanted, and laughed. Bruno rounded on him and said:

'Listen, Phil, keep it down, right? Or go home.'

'Sure, Bruno. I'm down anyway. You won't know I'm there, man.'

And the entrance was just a few yards away: a small illuminated door between an antiquarian bookshop and a place that sold extremely upmarket lingerie. Bruno pressed the button next to the brass plate that gave the club's name in elegant letters: REYNARD. The door buzzed and we went in.

On the way down the stairs Phil chanted, '"Something for your mind"' – which caused the reptilian doorman to wrinkle his nicotined lip in disgust, and Bruno and Sally to hiss in unison, 'Shut up, you asshole.'

I had imagined it in the old, opulent Edwardian style, with gilt and chandeliers and acres of patterned carpet. Or at least on the grand scale of the Las Vegas enterprises. I was disappointed. The room was not much bigger than the average bar, coloured a deep crimson on ceiling, carpets and walls. Everywhere but the two tables – roulette and blackjack – was in shadow; a leather-quilted door swung shut behind us, blacking out the light from the stairs. There was a faint glow – I saw when I got my bearings – behind a tiny, scruffy bar at the far end. The place had a down-at-heel air, as if it had had nothing spent on it for years. It reminded me of the Seventies, of cheap materials that look cheap, Fablon and Kitchen Queen, of nothing being clean.

Except, of course, for the glorious felt of the table, rich and impeccable. Under the light it was the deepest green imaginable, and the black and red of its markings had the preciseness of incisions. What did the rest of the room matter? The hungry, dried-out people gazing silently at the clicking and fall of the ball couldn't care; they weren't even drinking. I could see immediately, even with my limited experience, that this was a serious gambler's club. Some of the punters were placing only small stakes, but that was probably because they had been cleaned out and were struggling back, or were playing the long game and had some secret strategy. Some of them pushed larger stacks of chips, but with a modest, businesslike air as though they weren't betting at all but performing some complex technical operation in a laboratory, an operation they were none the less highly skilled in. It was obviously nothing to them.

Most were solitary, and none met the others' eyes. No one had a wife or girlfriend stacking the chips for good luck.

Our party, therefore, was conspicuous. We were like wedding guests who had accidentally gatecrashed a funeral.

The gamblers sized us up with the briefest of disinterested glances.

Amateurs.

Phil, Bruno and Nico went for the blackjack table, which until their arrival had been deserted, and a croupier appeared there to relieve them of their chips. I decided to play roulette, partly to be away from them and partly because, I must admit, I lacked the confidence to expose myself on the blackjack table, where you actually have to play a game under the eyes of others. On the roulette table you can lurk in the background like a beggar and furtively get your chips on just before the wheel spins. Nobody notices what you do unless, of course, you make a big win – then you don't have to be furtive any more, and you can glow in their envy. Sally stood behind Nico and gave him her chips, much to Bruno's annoyance.

Three thousand francs was not that much money and, while I knew I *had* to lose it, I wanted to keep it long enough to match the length of their stay in the casino. Perhaps Bruno and Co. would go through their share almost instantly; perhaps they would eke it out. I kept an eye on them.

For a while I played a cautious sort of game – the kind of game I would play with my own money. I bet on red and black, odd and even, and increasingly the columns, where I seemed to be quite lucky. Over half an hour or so, my three thousand became just over ten and I glowed with excitement, forgetting completely that I'd have to lose it again.

The blackjack table was quite near and I could see roughly what was going on. Phil had taken a bad-tempered tumble and was almost cleaned out, which didn't surprise me, given the state he was in. Nico and Bruno were clearly old hands, and were playing calm, controlled games.

My game was becoming quite exciting. Of the last five spins of the wheel I had won four, and I now had about fifteen thousand francs. I had been doing well enough to earn the odd resentful glance from the other gamblers, who played meticulously, most of them filling little columns with a record of the winning numbers. I couldn't get it through my head that I was supposed to be losing. I tried to stifle the high I was feeling: You idiot – *lose*! So, with a little subtlety because I assumed Bruno wouldn't want me to show an obvious suicidal tendency, I started to play the numbers as well as the columns.

I had dropped about five thousand, and that rather slowly, because my good luck on the columns refused to go away; therefore I was down to ten. So I decided to up my stake a little. Two thousand on seventeen. I lost, and felt good about it – down to eight thousand. There was no buzz, none of that joy of winning on a number in roulette when thirty-five times your stake comes back, but it was satisfactory. I looked back over to the blackjack table. Things had changed a little over there, much to my surprise. Nico was out of the game, and was sitting in a corner near the bar, talking earnestly to Sally. Phil was almost dancing; now he had a medium-sized pile of chips. But Bruno only had a few left, and I guessed that when those were gone we would leave.

Four thousand on twenty-three. I bet on the most ugly numbers, the numbers that couldn't possibly come up. I was down to four thousand now, and I could see Bruno talking to Phil, telling him, no doubt, to hurry up and get rid of his chips. Two thousand again, on seventeen.

Then minor disaster struck, sending a shiver through my stomach. Seventeen came up, and seventy-two thousand francs in chips was pushed across the table at me.

One or two of the other players looked at me with slightly shocked, disapproving expressions. After a second I realized why this was: my face was sour at the misfortune of winning. So I checked the oaths that were ready to spring to my lips, gritted my teeth, and left the chips where they were. Four months' salary on the spin of the wheel. Doubtless the other players thought I was insane. The wheel spun; the little ivory globe rattled into place. Number eight, thank God. I breathed a sigh of relief, put my two remaining chips on black, and lost. And now, showing a little more presence of mind and shamming great disappointment, my head cast down, I turned away from the table.

Sally had been standing behind me. She said, 'That was a shot. Pity you lost.'

'For all the good it would have done me to win.'

'Least you had some fun.'

'It was strange, hoping to lose.'

'There could be a lesson in it.'

'Really? What do you think the lesson might be?'

'Oh-ho,' she said, laughing slightly, 'you don't expect me to have that figured out, do you?'

Nico came up and swept her off, Bruno behind him, then Phil. We were leaving.

I stood back to let Bruno and Phil past me, but Bruno waved me on, at the same time gripping Phil by the arm. Curious, I turned back as I went up the stairs, although I felt I could already guess what was going to happen. And, sure enough, Phil pulled from his pocket three chips – five-thousands, I guessed – and then, on further prompting, another. Bruno had caught him red-handed.

I went up to the street, stood and stretched, and took deep breaths of the cool, balmy air.

Sally turned to me and said, 'Phil taking some chips with him, huh?'

'It looks like it.'

'That guy is an asshole.'

I felt rather embarrassed that their Englishman was such a poor example.

'Well,' I said apologetically, 'I suppose it was a temptation.'

'Oh, it's not that exactly,' she said in that crisp drawl that Natalie also used. 'He could never have cashed them in – if he had *tried* to cash them in.' She laughed and looked at Nico, who was listening with his usual studious expression.

'What do *you* think?'

'That it's all bullshit,' he said after a moment, and I got the impression that he thought she was being indiscreet. '*Pas devant les domestiques*', he might have said, had he spoken French.

She shrugged and put on a childish voice. 'Some big men would have come out from a backroom and asked him where he got them from, and why he was cashing them.'

'Bullshit, honey. He woulda played with them. Even Phil isn't that stupid.'

Bruno and Phil then came out, and we walked quietly back to the car park. Phil looked at his feet, and Bruno looked far away. Again he had shown his authority.

On the drive back we talked about gambling and exchanged one or two exaggerations.

Then Bruno said, 'So what you think of Nico and Sally?'

'They seem nice. Interesting mix as a couple.'

'How d'you mean?'

'Well, she seems like a country girl, whereas he's very much someone from the city.'

'Yeah but the country girl bit is expensive cosmetics and what she was born with. She was brought up in a fifteen-room apartment on Park Avenue. Maybe what you mean also is she's a Wasp and he's Italian?'

'Yes, perhaps it is.'

He sighed.

'Listen, I gotta tell you that my father doesn't like me seeing them, you know that? I mean he doesn't give a fuck about that low-life thief Phil, right, but come to Nico it's no way. You know, I'd appreciate it – what I mean is – he's gonna ask you about this evening and who I went out with, and I'd appreciate it a lot, Johnny, if you'd say it was just you, me, and Phil.'

So Phil had his uses.

I didn't have to think much about Bruno's request; the small omission seemed the least I could do after what had turned out to be fun. And I suppose I thought that I might in some way become a friend of these people. Sally, at any rate, seemed to like me.

I suppose I was lonely. I must have been, to have started thinking like that.

Chapter Seven

MARENKIAN'S FEET had hardly touched the ground; he had been away twice now since the night of the party. The day Horst called, he was due to fly out for the third time in ten days, but that morning further clients had to be seen. They conformed to the emerging type. One man had a face like an upended hard-boiled egg, huge-jowled; pasted below his bald top were little wings of hair, above his lip a small, close moustache. He wore sunglasses. Another man of about the same age. In a rather corny way he was very handsome indeed. He had all of his hair, which was quite long and thick, swept back over his head in a grey-white mane, and an imperial Roman profile, which he directed upwards.

In each of the other two cars was a young man. Both of these – and the driver of the Mercedes, who was about their age – looked very much of the regime: medium height, dark slick hair, olive complexions.

I overheard the egghead say, as they set off down the path. 'I hope you can do this real quick, John, because we haven't got time to mess around today.' His voice was testy.

While they were down in Marenkian's office the phone rang.

'Johnny, hall-o-o-!' Horst shouted. 'How are *you*?'

'Horst, I'm very well. How are you?'

'Oh, I'm fine. Very busy you know, but fine. Now, Johnny, I'm down here for a day or two, and of course one of my *duties* while I am here is to have lunch with my skipper, as we said.'

'I'd be delighted. Whereabouts would you like to go?'

'Ah, you are in Valbonne. Do you know the Colombe d'Or in Saint-Paul?'

'No, I don't.'

He told me how to get there.

'Next Tuesday?'

'No problem.'

'Oh, Johnny, a word to the wise. I would not say to Marenkian that you are having lunch with me. I am in his bad books at the moment.' He laughed.

'Not a word, Horst.'

I took Marenkian to the airport, and something strange, almost absurd happened.

A few minutes after check-in time he asked me to wait while he looked through his briefcase, and after a moment he began to swear to himself, something that was unusual enough in the normally unruffled lawyer. He was panicking – an extraordinary sight in a man who was usually so rigidly disciplined. Sitting on a bench in the bustle of the shiny new building, he stopped completely for a moment and closed his eyes.

'Do you have a phone card?'

I had one, and I gave it to him.

'Keep an eye on the bags, please.'

He hurried off to make the call. A few minutes later he was back.

'OK,' he said. 'I need a folder of documents I thought I had with me, I don't know why, and what I want you to do is to go to an address in Vence and get it for me. You will meet a woman called Madame Sospine, and she will show you where to find it. The folder is labelled *Factures 1979*. The address is

17 rue Pilatte, Vence. Bring the whole folder. Have you got that?'

'17 rue Pilatte, Vence. Madame Sospine. *Factures 1979.* OK.'

'I'll check in now and make arrangements for you to hand them across the barrier if necessary.'

'Right, I'll be as quick as I can.'

'You have an hour before the flight. It should be enough time.'

'OK.'

And so I met Madame Sospine, who surprised me.

I found the street without difficulty, which was a piece of good luck. With the ritual emptying for lunch, the road up to Vence was quite busy, and I had very little time.

Rue Pilatte was a cul-de-sac. The houses on either side were tall and most of the windows shuttered, their walls, already quite close at street level, seeming to lean in closer as they got higher, as though generations of suspended washing had pulled them together. That day the lines were empty.

I was surprised at the location, and wondered whether I had made a mistake. I had imagined that this place of safe-keeping would be an office service, the sort of establishment that would send and receive faxes and offer secretarial facilities. It would be bright and clean and modern, as such places try to be. But number seventeen was the dingiest house in this dingy street.

I rang the bell. Then, after a short pause, I rang again. Finally I heard some movement. A long time after this the door opened. I was hopping from one foot to the other in frustration.

A very old woman stood in the doorway. She had a pronounced stoop and a hunch, and very fine, thinning red hair – obviously dyed – that looked as if it would blow away in the wind. She wore a very old-fashioned pair of sunglasses. Evidently an eccentric.

'Madame Sospine?'

'Yes.'

'Monsieur Denner. I come from Monsieur Marenkian.'

'Yes, yes,' she said quickly, as if I was being indiscreet. 'Come in.'

I stepped inside, and she waved me past her with short, impatient motions of her arm, then bolted the door. Then she turned in the narrow hallway, cluttered with boxes and packing cases, and shouldered her way through. Two feet shorter – I stared at the top of her head – she was saying something I couldn't understand. She had a very strong regional accent.

'I'm in a hurry, madame,' I shouted. 'Monsieur Marenkian is about to catch a plane to New York.'

'Yes, yes, yes,' she muttered.

At the top of some steep, narrow stairs we turned to the right and into the room in which she obviously lived. It had the air of an obscure antiques shop. Against one wall was a vast wardrobe, against another an intricately carved sideboard made from wood so dark as to be almost black. Behind these hung heavy curtains, so that not an inch of bare wall was to be seen. In the centre of the room was a sloping table, and behind a velvet curtain at the back I glimpsed a chaise longue made up as a bed. I could see motionless, somnolent cats.

In the clutter, and in the company of this tiny old woman, I felt like a giant, and I stood there awkwardly while she sat down at the table, lifted its cloth, opened a drawer, removed from it a wooden box, and from that a bunch of keys. It was as she was going through these motions that I realized, from something in her way of moving, that she was blind.

'*Bon*,' she said when she had the keys in her hand, holding on to them tightly as old people sometimes will – as if they might suddenly take flight.

She was blind. It was a fairly remarkable place to keep documents, a place nobody would think of looking. And its owner was unable to read, anyway, in the very unlikely event she became curious – and bilingual. This was discretion on the grand scale.

She led me up another flight of stairs, steep and with worn grey wooden treads. A turn into a short, dark corridor, then I waited while she unlocked the door. She opened it and moved aside, motioning in her usual birdlike way. Inside the cupboard were piles of blankets, sheets, and other linen. She said:

'Move the pile on the left.'

I did so, and saw that behind it lay a small collection of pale-green cardboard wallets of the type Marenkian habitually used. One of them carried, on a small white label, the title *Factures 1979*. I picked it up and told the old woman I had found what I needed.

When we were downstairs she turned to me and said:

'Have you seen Jean-Robert?'

'I don't know him.'

She pursed her lips, the expression giving her an even more curious look beneath her sunglasses.

'You haven't met Jean-Robert?' she said with a tone bordering on disgust: I must be a real nobody if I hadn't met Jean-Robert. 'Huh.'

'Who is he?'

'Eh, he's my grandson. How long have you worked for Monsieur Marenkian?'

'Almost two months.'

She laughed.

'He's a good man, Monsieur Marenkian. I'm going to have my operation soon.' She pointed to her sunglasses. 'It's all arranged. A very famous doctor who travels all over the world. Have you brought any money?' she added, abruptly changing her tone. I was surprised.

'No.'

'Never mind, never mind. Forget that I asked. Of course that *salopard* Jean-Robert could have done something, but he was always too busy. Just like his father.'

She sighed at the recollection, then after a moment advanced towards me, waving both arms.

'Goodbye, goodbye now, monsieur, *voilà* . . .' she sang – an intonation she kept up until I found myself out in the dark, narrow street.

I got back to the airport about five minutes later than I should have done, slewed the Range Rover onto the taxi rank, and ran inside. Marenkian was standing on the terminal side of the customs barrier, remarkably cool now for a man about to miss his flight and doubtless a chain of meetings at the other end.

I handed him the folder.

'Close,' he said. 'But good work. I only have time to say this. Nobody save myself knows about the rue Pilatte; it's where my most confidential papers are kept. Not a word, OK? Not a word.'

'OK.'

'See you,' he said as he turned, and then he was away.

The thing was, I had been caught in a traffic jam for five minutes on the way down; and so, of course, I had looked in the folder. Inside it was a strange collection of share certificates: Tarquin Investment SA, Trajan Asset International, Trajan Fund SA. Severus International – and so on. With variations, they were like all paper money, laced with embroidered ink like prize-draw entries. They must be worth a bit, I thought.

When I got back, mid-afternoon, it was apparent that Bruno and Natalie weren't planning to waste any time. There was already a couple of cars in the drive, and two or three more arrived over the next hour, so that in the end there were about twenty people. I went through to the sitting room and spoke to her.

'Natalie,' I said graciously, because it gave me pleasure to be gracious with her, 'what can your devoted servant cook for you and your guests this evening?'

'My devoted servant can lie by the pool if he wants, or get stoned. Is there some bread and stuff?'

'Yes, and some cheese and cold meats. But, seriously, I have to go and do some shopping, and I was thinking I might cook a barbecue.'

Which is what I did: lamb cutlets by the armful that I marinaded in lime juice and chilli; green salad and burnt baked potatoes. Most of them seemed quite surprised that they were being offered food, and it made me realize what a bourgeois I was in that respect. These sybarites had drugs to take and love to make; they weren't going to waste time drooling over the pinkness of a piece of lamb.

This, at least, applied to Bruno's friends. Phil was there, also Nico and Sally; an English friend of Sally's who looked like a Burne-Jones nymph, with her long fair hair and dewy round eyes – straight from Winchester; a gorgeous black American girl and her French boyfriend; two rangy young men, handsome with high cheekbones, narrow dark eyes, and long ponytails. I could imagine all of them at a rock concert, an underground rave, perhaps even a degree show at the Slade. They sat on the grass and had slow conversations, or stared into space and smoked.

Natalie's friends you would have expected to find at expensive sporting events. Fit and brash, they had the air of the ski slope, and the DayGlo colours to match. They might snort cocaine to increase their vigour, but never anything hallucinogenic. As I cooked, I amused myself making comparisons between the two groups, who only seemed to converge in the person of Nico, who had a quiet authority in both camps. Natalie's, for example, would have no idea what Zen Buddhism was; Bruno's would subscribe. Bruno's would probably not enjoy water-skiing; Natalie's would see in it an art form. I recognized at least two of the Italians from Marenkian's evening party, and the other two or three Italian men looked similar. Boys, perhaps I should say; they looked as though they should be roaring round a village square on Vespas. The girls were small, shapely, mostly blonde, and mainly silent. They were what the subalterns used to call shagging pieces.

But the slick boys and their shagging pieces were absolutely in context here. They might think they were different to their parents, but in every important respect they seemed identical. Whereas Bruno's friends were only on the premises because Marenkian was away; and if he were to come back unexpectedly, he would be delighted to see Joey and Marco the Italians, but not Bruno's degenerate Americans.

Natalie appeared to become a little bored, perhaps even irritated, by the Italians, so she got up and left them, and they jeered and catcalled after her. She didn't turn as she sauntered away, but stuck a finger in the air.

Nico had been keeping an eye on her – detached, a free agent – and he sauntered in the same direction. Dusk had almost fallen; the evening was blue-grey and warm. The two of them fell into conversation like old friends as they walked down into the garden. They would go barefoot onto the soft carpet of pine needles, and perhaps he would take her there, and everyone would know, but no one would interfere. A picture of her flashed into my mind, soft and compliant, her legs apart, blindness in her eyes. I wanted her.

I started to clear things away and tried to swallow my sudden bitterness. I never had a problem pulling when I was a cavalry officer. It seemed to me as I circled around, picking up dirty plates, that I had fallen very far. It may be old-fashioned to grieve over a lost social position, but I was on heat. I imagined meeting her in London and taking her to Annabel's, or for a weekend's shooting on a Yorkshire estate, or to a dinner at the mess. There are some things that money can't buy, and she would have been intrigued by me and my world. Instead, her father had hired me, and I was just a part of the furniture, waiting on this foreign scum.

I noticed, though, and it cheered me up, that Sally was not really paying attention to whatever Phil was saying to her, and was giving anxious glances towards the shade under the trees where it might be supposed were Nico and Natalie. Nor did she confine herself to anxious glances; she got up and went down there to see for herself what was going on. For a moment, while I watched this, I was standing unoccupied. So that when Phil found himself deserted by Sally he came over and held out a joint they had been sharing.

'Those fucking Italians are an outrage, man,' he said. 'That was good food, though.'

'Thanks.' The joint contained excellent grass. 'Not as good as this grass.'

'Yeah, it's all right. Hey, that was a crack the other night. Sally told me you won fifty thousand.'

'Seventy, actually – about five minutes before we left. It was the only time I've ever won and not wanted to. The only time I've ever won that much. Probably the only time I will, knowing my luck.'

'Yeah. I got into the shit. Kept a few chips by mistake. Bruno caught me out.'

I handed the joint back to him and sat down in a nearby chair.

'Whoa, that's strong stuff.'

He sat down beside me.

'So how d'you find it, then, working for the Marenkians?'

I suddenly decided to like Phil. I hadn't gossiped with an Englishman, or anyone else for that matter, for months.

'It's fine. They're reasonable, and generous with money, and they seem like a nice bunch of people.'

'What do you think about Bruno?'

I laughed. 'I'm talking to a good friend of Bruno, am I right?'

He handed back the joint.

'Maybe.'

'I like Bruno. He can be a bit touchy, but . . . I wonder how happy he is.'

'He's *not* happy, man.'

I looked around, wondering where he was – and couldn't see him.

'See, one of Bruno's problems is that everyone's got an interest in him. His main function should have been to do what his old man is doing, and then take over the reins. But he can't cut it. So he's got his old man on his back, going, *Come on, Bruno, be a man. Keep it in the family.* Marenkian's saying, *I didn't build this up with my blood and sweat just to watch you piss it away.*'

'So Bruno should qualify as a lawyer and take over his father's practice.'

Phil wrinkled his nose. 'His father's practice?' He laughed. 'If you could call it a practice.'

'Well, it's tax and investment practice, isn't it? I assume that's why—'

'He's a fucking gangster, man. He launders money for some of the big gangsters here. Yeah, you know something, man. He ain't been in court for years. The next time he's in court he'll be in the fucking dock.'

Was he sailing quite that close to the wind? Was Phil a reliable source?

'He launders money? And what does that mean, exactly?'

Phil gave me a very puzzled look. 'How did you get this job?'

'It was a business associate of Marenkian's who knew that he needed somebody.'

'Who?'

'A guy called Horst Stacker.'

'Oh, right. And did you work for him before?'

'I skippered his yacht.'

'And that was it?' I understood his question. How could you be working for this family with that kind of background? For a moment I took the idea seriously, but then imagined my interview with Marenkian, and his asking: *Tell me a little about your criminal record, Johnny. Serious crimes only, please.* I laughed. Phil looked a little disgusted. He had probably wanted to know where I fitted in; perhaps his kind of sponger was only one rung up the ladder from the staff.

'So that's why they're so rich?'

'Yeah.'

'Marenkian doesn't take suitcases of cash to the Caribbean, though, does he?'

'What do you think that was, the other night? At the casino? I mean, that's a sideline, know what I mean.'

'But if they're trying to evade tax, why inflate the casino's profits?'

'Reynard's can stand it, and they've got the cash to get rid of. That's what laundering is. You take dirty money, like what Bruno gave us. It passes over the tables at Reynard's. In the morning the manager takes the cash to the bank. Where does it come from, they ask? Last night's takings. Then it's in Reynard's account. When they take it out, it's clean. You always get laundering where there's a casino.' He was looking even more irritated now.

'So how much would you say they're worth, then?'

He shrugged.

'Twenty million dollars, maybe. It's hard to say, man.'

I looked down the garden and saw Natalie, Sally, and Nico strolling up slowly, shadows emerging into the light. Nico was between the two, and they all seemed happy. Phil stared at them with a slightly sour, inscrutable expression.

'Don't try and get anything out of these people. You'd be wasting your time.'

'I wouldn't think of it.'

'No, I mean it, man.'

Strange: this fool was trying to warn me off his territory.

He continued, 'This shithole – Nice, Antibes, and all that – it's full of scroungers and conmen and people with some deal to sell.' Suddenly he smiled.

'And what does *your* father do?'

His smile disappeared. 'He's a yacht broker. One of the biggest on the coast.'

'Ah.'

Natalie, Nico and Sally arrived. Phil went and stood the other side of the main group, hoping perhaps that the three would move on. I sensed that he was slightly embarrassed to have been discovered talking to me.

'Hi, Johnny.' Natalie smiled. She really did have the most beautiful smile. It was very sudden, and her whole character shone out of it in a flash, like a window opened on the sunlight.

'Your devoted servant, madame, ready to do your bidding.'

'No bidding. Where do you get this stuff from? You should be in the theatre. Huh, Sally? My devoted servant – what'll we make him do?'

Phil was put out, poor guy – neither of them had taken the slightest notice of him. Nico didn't seem to mind; he was solid, and the girls could do what they liked. Nothing would faze Nico.

They couldn't decide what to make me do, and so they passed on to swimming, and they asked first Nico, then Phil, whether they would. *Not Nico; hard men don't swim*, I thought to myself as I sat half a mile away. Phil wouldn't either, for unclear reasons; he was probably following Nico's lead. Suddenly her eyes turned on me, shining, amused.

'Johnny, come on.'

'No, really. I couldn't.' My stomach tightened in nervous anticipation.

'Come on.'

'Natalie, I – I really don't think you should go swimming with the staff.'

'Johnny-y-y.' She fixed me with her eyes, grinning.

'Yeah,' said Sally, 'because we're not going down there on our own, right?'

'Johnny, I'm giving you an order,' she snapped.

I sighed. 'OK, I'll go and get my swimsuit.'

'No, no, come on,' they both said together.

'What?'

'Come on!' they shouted and, laughing, each took a hand and dragged me away. Phil and Nico looked at me blankly.

We ran down into the shade of the trees and got to the narrow steps that led to the pool. It was too narrow for three, so Sally let go of my hand and went on ahead.

In the dark leafy tunnel under the trees I could still feel Natalie's warm little hand in mine. I was wild with excitement and nervousness, and I kept saying to myself: *Calm down, don't get over-excited. It's only a game.*

She tugged at my arm and, when I turned, said, 'Did you do an E?'

'No, I just smoked some grass. Did you?'

She laughed. 'Sure.'

She slipped her hand out of mine and ran out onto the poolside. I ran after her. I was dizzy.

'Do you want the lights on?' I shouted. There were lights just under the surface.

'No,' she shouted back.

Sally was at the other end of the pool and she had almost undressed. Naked, there was some contrast between her and Natalie. She was paler and fuller, with quite large breasts that swayed as she bent to slip her knickers over her hips.

I stayed at the near, deep end.

Natalie joined Sally, who stood and greeted her, unabashed. She turned her back and shouted over her shoulder, 'Don't look,' and they giggled.

My desire was almost painful, and I had to turn round to hide it. *Jesus*, I said to myself, *I can't stand this.* Then I was naked, but so hard now that I didn't know how I could get myself in the pool without them seeing. I'd have to make a dash for it. One splash: who was it? I bent down to pick up my clothes. *Down, for God's sake; go down.* I couldn't let them see the state I was in. I hadn't had a woman for four months, and I couldn't let them see.

'Come o-o-n,' she drawled, amused; she could probably guess. I turned my head and there she was, halfway down the side of the pool, facing me. And the shock of that made me turn, and for a moment I was presentable.

She had a slender frame, quite sharply drawn; her thighs stretched up to her pelvis. Her breasts were broad and flat with big dark nipples and her public hair was thick and dark. She was no little girl naked. In the moment that I turned, a moment that lasted as long as Sally's five yards underwater after her dive, I saw all this, and our eyes met, and she glanced down at my cock, which still hung low, thank God, although it was twice its normal size. And I felt good about that, and ran down the pool and dived flat and sharp, thinking as I did: *You just had a good look, and you weren't embarrassed. Did you like what you saw, missy? Do you want some?* She dived too, and we all came up laughing.

The water was cool and incredibly sensual on my naked stoned body; it caressed my hips and buttocks like silk, like the wind lulling you to sleep. You come up for air and it flows off you, over your lips and down the back of your neck. I was aroused again, and I kept to the deep end, plunging into the underwater silence and up again to steal glances at Sally and Natalie splashing each other at the other end of the pool. Much of the time her breasts were just awash.

Eventually I couldn't resist it. *What kind of man are you? They haven't even objected to your presence – go and play.* I took a long underwater dive and came up near them, and growled. They jumped on me and ducked me. I came up, and they tried again, but I stood firm, and their hands slipped and slid on my wet shoulders. Then Sally tripped me and I went under.

I came up again and got a hand on each of their heads, and they both took deep breaths and let me duck them.

And then Natalie and I were left alone, almost as if by design. Sally suddenly crouched over slightly and put a hand to her face.

'I've got a bit of grit in my eye.'

'Anything I can do?'

'No . . . I'd better find some light.' And with her arm in the same position she stepped out at the shallow end and into the pool-house. A moment later a harsh, thin light came through the open door.

Natalie and I started to play a different game. We stood – the water at her collarbone and my solar plexus – two, maybe three feet apart. She stared into my eyes, a slight grin on her sharp, full lips. She knew the rules.

I reached slowly out to her head, singing softly 'Natalie',

put my hands on her wet hair, and ducked her! She came up spluttering. 'Asshole!' she said, and started to push me on the chest, once, twice, but I was ready for that and stood firm. Then a third and a fourth time, and I pushed my chest forward a little.

Then her hands stopped and she left them there, spread on my chest. Those slender fingers sent a shiver through my flesh, and slowly I moved towards her; we were only inches apart. Then there was a sudden burst of warmth as she felt me on her belly, and I felt her soft, rubbery belly the length of my cock.

She jumped back and, in something between a shriek and a laugh, she went, 'Johnny! Whoa!' She looked at me sidelong. 'Who-o-o-a.' But I knew from the grin on her wet mouth, her sharp white teeth, her eyes like black wine, knew as I had never known before in my life, that she wanted it as much as I wanted her. She flipped over and swam to the other end of the pool, fast. I followed. It was the last few yards of the race. At the end of the pool, at last, I would quench my thirst.

When I was halfway there the underwater lights went on. For a second I thought: *Come on, Sally. Come on!* But it wasn't Sally.

'Co-o-or, what a bloody peepshow, man.'

'Hey, fuck off, Phil,' Natalie said, and swam to the ladder. 'Fucking asshole.'

I went straight for the other end. Everything had disappeared, and I was only left with a feeling that I had overstepped the mark and almost been caught – that I could still be in trouble. Not one of the men here would take it well if they thought I had really been fooling with her. Sally came out of the pool-house and watched.

'Just as well Bruno's crashed, baby,' he said. 'Or you'd be in the shit.'

She had a towel round her by now, and after a second she went right up to him.

'I said fuck off,' she said in his face. Then she pushed him in the middle of the chest, and he fell backwards into the pool, and came up spluttering, his green shirt floating around him. Sally whooped and laughed, unconvincingly. There was something sour in the air.

Natalie smiled at me drily, turned and walked away up the steps. Sally ran after her. Neither of them turned back. Phil stood up and walked down to the end of the pool.

'Can I get you a towel?' I said, feeling a little foolish as I did so.

'Just leave me alone,' he said quietly. 'Stupid cow!'

So I left him alone. He was right, I suppose; I had been gloating.

The others regrouped but I slipped up to bed. Nothing I had experienced or heard that evening had made any impression on me; she had driven it all out and I was drunk on her image and my memory of her touch.

I fell into a deep sleep.

Chapter Eight

THERE IS A special pair of handcuffs for the courtroom. It is polished to a shine, and attached to the middle of its chain is a short length of fine blue rope. It is this that the gendarme picks up when the door opens and the word comes through to bring me in. The clerk of the court bustles and the other gendarme follows, and I am led in by the blue rope on my manacles, my stomach heaving.

Into an expectant silence, punctuated with the odd creak and cough and the echo of my footfalls on the wood, I am led. As the accused, I am last in of course; everyone can watch me. On my right the public, or rather an assortment of interested parties: the Marenkians, Sandrine, the little man with the goatee, the police. On my left the edifice of the court: a structure of boxes in which lawyers, jurymen, and judges sit. Mounted in all the boxes save that of the jury, which is now empty, are microphones. I am led to the dock, where my gendarme undoes the handcuffs. I sit, and they sit, one on each side.

For the first time I look at the judges – Dabremigne, my lawyer, has told me what to expect. They seem very young, and almost identical with their short dark hair cropped into fringes, their heavy-rimmed glasses, their thin mouths. They sit like three friars. I notice little things: under his dark robes the clerk of the court wears a pink lumberjack shirt; the prosecutor, with his florid face and cropped grey hair, brushes the underside of his nose with the ermine of his robe; another lawyer in the public gallery talks quite loudly with a frail elderly woman. Dabremigne points his hooked nose at me and smiles in reassurance. If only he knew, the clown. Next to him sits the interpreter.

Suddenly the judge, who sits in the middle of the three, pulls the microphone on its stalk towards him and speaks into it, almost whispers, it's so close. He has the casual, automatic tone of a man reciting something.

'Will the accused standup, please.' I stand, and the two gendarmes stand with me; also the interpreter, a woman with long red hair, ready for the start of her lengthy task.

'What is your name?'

'John Denner.'

'What is your age?'

'Twenty-eight years.'

'What is your profession?'

'Domestic servant.'

'What is your domicile?'

'I have no domicile, monsieur.'

A pause, and then: 'You may sit.'

As the lawyers whisper to one another, the lines are laid out. Another official hands the president of the court – this chief of the judges – a battered metal helmet from which he pulls numbered balls. The names of the jury are read out. I am told I have the right to object, but I don't exercise it. Now I only want one thing: for the charade to start. These leisurely ceremonials while you writhe are the most refined form of cruelty.

Then the names of the witnesses are called: Marenkian, John; Marenkian, Bruno; Marenkian, Natalie, Bonnaire, Claudine; Goodwin, Philip; Mammalio, Niccoló; Berthelot, Sylvain; Schenck, Beata. Other names I don't recognize straight off: policemen, forensic scientists, pathologists, the shrink to whom I have been obliged to talk.

Finally, after they have all been linked, and all manner of other formality has been completed, I am told to stand up, and my interrogation at the hands of that whispering president of the court begins.

'Monsieur Denner, stand up, please.'

I stand up and wait while he sorts through the bulging file in front of him.

'Do you have any chronic illness?'

'No.'

'What is your consumption of alcohol?'

'Moderate.'

'What do you mean by moderate? How many glasses of wine a day, for example?'

'Two.'

'And spirits?'

'I included that.'

'What about drugs?'

'No, I don't take drugs.'

'But have you in the past?'

'No.'

'And yet you attempted to smuggle six hundred grammes of marijuana out of Spain.'

'I was innocent of that charge.'

'I will state to the court that, on 27 August 1991, John Denner was convicted by a court in Barcelona, Spain, of attempting to smuggle marijuana, and sentenced to four years' imprisonment.'

This president will do a thorough job in laying the foundations for my conviction. Yet I'm not really frightened. It is as though being the accused in a murder trial is a nice new job I've landed, that the sentence and its aftermath will be nothing to do with me. I have a strange sense of camaraderie with the judges and the lawyers, as if they are my colleagues and we are all playing the same game.

But everything depends on the way I handle myself – years of my life. Because I can't rely on an acquittal, and if it all goes badly wrong I can only hope that this jury will think I was a good guy who made an awful mistake, that the murder was by accident not design. A slender hope. They look at me when they know they won't catch my eye, trying to size me up, trying to come to some conclusion about me. Do I look like someone who'd bludgeon a man to death? I wear a sort of hangdog, mournful expression, an extreme sincerity, like a funeral director.

'So for you the army was a little like a family? You said to the *juge d'instruction*: '"My best friends were there, and I didn't have a father or mother. And I suppose I got some of the guidance I would otherwise have got from my father from one or two of the more senior officers in the regiment." That's true?'

'Yes.'

'How did you feel when you knew your army career was over?'

'I was very disappointed.'

'How did your career in the army come to an end?'

Back to the drugs, eh? Little shit! It wouldn't be allowed in a British court.

'I was in the south of Spain, staying with friends. There was a woman there who asked me to take a parcel back to her sister in London. She had hidden marijuana in the parcel, and I knew nothing about it. The marijuana was found and I was sentenced to four years' imprisonment.'

'Was the woman your lover?'

'Yes. She was.'

He pauses. I don't dare look at the jury.

'Were you involved with any other woman at this time?'

I clear my throat. I feel dry, hot.

'Yes, Monsieur le Président.'

'What was your relation to this other woman?'
'I was engaged to her.'
'This was Elizabeth Whitley-Urban?'
'Yes.'

Something terrible has happened to my memory of Lizzie. I can only picture a photograph that appeared in *Tatler*, showing her striding along an improvised catwalk in a marquee with a determined look on her face. I can't remember her smile or hear her voice.

'Elizabeth Whitley-Urban was your fiancée in England at the time of your arrest?'
'Yes.'

Another pause, as if comment were needed.

'Did your engagement end as a result of the trial?'
'Yes, it did.'
'Was this because she discovered you had had an affair with the woman you say gave you the marijuana?'
'Yes.'
'Did her father, Viscount Storrington, not pay you to break off the engagement?'
'No, he did not.'
'Did he not go to Spain at the time of your trial and give you money?'
'He helped me with my legal bills, quite willingly. I didn't want to accept his help, but he paid the lawyers directly and gave them instructions not to accept any money from me.'
'He paid your legal costs, in fact.'
'Yes, he did.'
'In his interview with the *juge d'instruction*, he said: "I have to admit that I wanted him out of the family. I went to Spain and did what I could to help him, and I paid all his legal costs and put a bit of money in the bank for him besides. I suppose you could say I paid him off." Is that true?'
'He didn't pay me off. Perhaps he says that now, because

he's bitter. It's inevitable that – that he's not going to think very highly of me.'

'Is it true? Did he give you this money?'

'He wasn't paying me off, and there was no agreement between us.'

'Is it true that he gave you this money?' he insists.

'Yes, it is true.'

Another pause, while this impartial judge decides on the next step in the prosecution case. Of course I'm the perfect accused for a murder in France: a friendless Englishman with a few minor contemporary vices. Vices that this little monk can conjure into crimes, sear into the imaginations of these trembling bourgeois jurors.

'Did you take drugs in prison?'

'No.'

He questions me about prison, about Cap d'Agde.

'Did you know that Monsieur Marenkian had a daughter before you applied for the job?'

I stop; for a moment I can't answer. Of course I knew; Horst told me. Why should he ask such a question? 'Yes, I did.'

Another pause.

He's laying on this thin innuendo like gold leaf, and when he's finished it will look solid.

'When did you first meet Max Schenck?'

'At his house, late September, when I drove Bruno there for a consultation.'

'Did you have much contact with him? Did you speak to him? How did he treat you?'

'I took Bruno to his house. We hardly spoke to each other at all.'

'When did you next meet him?'

'He came to the house one night to consult with Mr Marenkian about the future course of Bruno's treatment.'

'And on other occasions?'

I pause for a second, genuinely trying to remember.

'He played tennis at the house one day.'

'And how did you get on with him on that occasion?'

'Not particularly well. He blamed me for the fact that we lost the game to Mr Marenkian and Natalie.'

'What sort of a man would you say he was?'

'I think he was very intelligent. He was probably very good at his job. I don't deny that he was quite an arrogant man. I think anyone would admit that.'

If I don't say it others will.

'What about his job? Was he doing a good job?'

'I don't know. Bruno seemed to value his help.'

'But you must have an opinion.'

'I think that if Bruno found him helpful, then he must have been doing some good for him.'

The sun suddenly shone through one of the high windows, and I looked at the clock. It was a quarter to twelve. And it seemed to me that years of my life were passing on this one day, draining away like the sand in an hourglass.

Claudine must have arrived at her usual time. I got down about ten thirty, suffering, and she had done most of the clearing up, and was a bit sour about it. She was sweeping the floor in a pointed sort of way.

But I was not in the mood to worry about her sourness or her pointed ways. I had let the previous night give me ideas, and I wasn't on her footing any more. I felt flat, though, and disappointed, and aware that whatever footing I might be on I still had to clean and do the shopping and cook lunch. If I had been a guest, Claudine would have dropped everything to make me some strong black coffee. Instead she told me grumpily that I looked ill.

I didn't have to court Natalie; I would be wrong to court her. I was independent precisely because I was the hired help. I thought of myself as her dog, which shows I was still stoned. I wandered about the house, which seemed full of dazzling sunlight. I had heard that American girls were all sexed up; that they gave blow-jobs on the first date.

I finally went out and, as I picked my way around the supermarket, I took the idea of Marenkian being a gangster and tried it on for size, like an unfamiliar garment, and to my surprise it fitted quite well. Phil was only corroborating, after all, what Natalie had already said. He might be unreliable and indiscreet, but he wasn't completely wide of the mark.

If it was plausible that Marenkian was a kind of gangster – and it was; I thought back to the sleazy antics of his party and the madness of the casino – how did I feel about working for him? It made me laugh, and it made me a little excited, and it intrigued me. It gave me a slight sense of power, a sense that I would have an invisible privilege, that I would be invulnerable. It amused me, too, to think that if Marenkian was the gangster's attorney, Horst, his client, must himself be some kind of crook. Film production, commodity dealings, and the sponsorship of powerboat racing and motor sport: nefarious stuff, cover stories. Most of all, though, it made me covet Natalie even more, fresh and corrupt as she might be, and the apple of her daddy's eye, ripe for me to pick and eat.

It was like that from then on. She wasn't at the front of my mind all the time, but she was *present*, and sometimes she sent me into a rage, and then I would literally go weak at the knees and in my stomach, and practically fall over. As I walked around the supermarket I pictured taking her very violently.

They were lying on the grass when I got back: the inner circle. I smiled at her briefly, so as to be discreet, but tried to put some intensity into it. She smiled back behind her sunglasses, sighed, and turned onto her back. Her black top left her stomach open, and I watched its supple flexing as she twisted.

By late afternoon, for no particular reason, I had come to the conclusion that I could never have her. The night before I had behaved like a virgin schoolboy, unable to control himself. I blushed for myself; it was hardly possible to make a cruder approach to a woman: *feel it – it wants you!* She had probably already laughed about it; maybe she had told Sally. I didn't have a hope; she was beautiful, intelligent, incredibly rich, the kind of girl every man in the Western world would want. She had the pick, and *I* hoped she might choose a drop-out her father employed to cook and drive the car. That beggared belief.

'Hello,' she said when she came into the kitchen at about six o'clock. 'I had to fight to get you.'

'Really?' I said, and was suddenly full of joy.

'They wanted you to drive them to Villefranche, but I insisted you had to stay here and cook dinner for me.'

'Mademoiselle, your devoted servant waits to do your bidding.'

'You know what I miss here sometimes? American TV. Oh, I know it's junk, but when you're out of it it just lulls you into a kind of stupor.'

'And satellite?'

'It's not the same. It's junk, too, but not the same junk. Like, when you want a McDonald's, fried chicken just won't do.'

'There's dinner exclusively for you. Name your menu.'

She sighed. 'I don't know. Whatever my servant recommends.'

'You don't want a McDonald's?'

'I don't think so.'

'Eggs Benedict – that's what you need.'

'Johnny, you'd have to make a hollandaise sauce.'

I was taken aback.

'You're right. But I can do that.'

'But I don't want you to do that. And don't look so surprised that I know there's hollandaise sauce in eggs Benedict. It's as American as apple pie.'

'Is it?'

'Just ham and eggs – and a croissant.'

'OK. What time?'

'Any time.'

'About eight?'

'Sure.'

Why hadn't I suggested a stew of mussels, artichokes, oysters, lobsters, powdered rhinoceros horn? Why didn't I drug her? Why did I have to be so normal? What did her restraint mean? Was she trying to put me back in my place?

She swam and left her hair wet, and came down in a white linen dress with no make-up and no jewellery, so that she looked very pure and calm, and very much like a Sicilian or a South American with her skin the colour of caramel, it seemed in the dusk, against the white of her dress. Such beauty as hers I felt I had never seen.

She sat on the terrace, I served her a drink and she said:

'Why did you only lay one place?' She seemed slightly annoyed.

'Well, I didn't really think about it,' I said, disingenuously, and she continued to look at me – and I forced myself to say something better than that. 'No, it's not that I didn't think about it. I just – didn't know whether you wanted my company.' I was conscious of what a weak figure I cut.

'If you want *mine* . . . I'm not going to order you.'

'I don't need to be ordered. And I don't need to be asked twice. Of course I'd love to join you.'

Then she stood up.

'Have a drink.'

'OK.' And I turned.

'No, no, I'll get it. What would you like?'

'I'll have a Scotch and soda. A highball, as you Americans would say.'

She turned and went to get my drink, and I sat and looked at the dusk. It was early November now, and still the Indian summer lasted. Everywhere else the landscape was burnt into pale yellows and greying browns, but in Marenkian's garden the grass was green, thanks to the sprinklers that soaked it every morning. Beyond the pines was that glow, a light peculiar to that part of the world: immense brightness, shaded and filtered. Near by somebody had set light to a bonfire, and there was a trace of blue smoke hanging in the air. She came back and we talked; I don't remember much of what we talked about before dinner, but I do remember the blue smoke in the shade of the pines, and a very great sense of contentment.

I had been thinking about what she had told me of her frustration and her ambitions, in the way you do when you're falling for someone, entering their lives in your imagination, developing that powerful sympathy with them; allying yourself to them and to their causes.

'So we were talking about the freemasonry – after we played tennis the other day.'

'Yeah.'

'England's like that, you know. Whatever anyone might tell you about the classless society and the way people are equal nowadays, you still have to be a member.'

'To go to the Royal Enclosure.'

I laughed. 'That. And a lot more besides. More important things, in fact, like jobs. It strikes me that in some respects I'm in a similar position to the one you're in.'

She looked at me. 'Being deprived of what's yours by right?'

'Yes.'

'Is your position that serious?'

'Well. I think I've got a claim to the kind of benefits that the English upper-crust can expect. But all those benefits are closed to me now.'

'Because of the drugs conviction.'

'That's right.'

'Surely in a year or two it'll all be forgotten.'

'Oh, no. It was splashed all over the papers, of course, but it's not just that. These people have got such long memories. Actually, it's not so much the individuals. It's the group. It's because they all know each other. It only takes one of them to remember the crime you've been accused of.'

'I know. In these groups there are one or two leaders, and the rest are sheep.'

'Can you get one of those leaders on your side?' I asked her. 'Isn't there someone in your father's close circle who could argue your case?'

She curled her lip.

'They all think the same way, Johnny. It's in the culture. They have a marital alliance planned for me. Oh, I'm not going to be forced into anything – don't get me wrong. But I'm constantly being given to understand by my father that if I could see my way to marrying Joe Catanio – who's one of the boys who was here the other night – or, at a pinch, Jean-Michel Marquand, son of one of his associates . . . all our problems would be solved. Because my husband could be involved in the business for me, and what would *I* want with the business if my *husband* was involved?'

'Perhaps he thinks you're more motivated by the money.'

'Yeah, maybe.'

'Whereas what you're after is – the fulfilment? Of ambitions?'

'Maybe. Maybe it's good that I have to make my own plans.'

'I must say it's extraordinary, in this day and age. And particularly when it seems so obvious a solution. Your brother is not – ready to take things on. So you step into his shoes. Anyway, tell me about these plans of yours.'

She smiled a curious, secretive smile.

'Oh, no,' she said. 'You'd be shocked.'

'And what makes you think I'm so easily shocked?' *Shocked! I could shock her right now. I wondered what she would do if I grabbed her.*

'You're an Englishman, Johnny. You're a gentleman.'

'And so you think I'm naïve.'

'I don't think this is your world.'

'Maybe it's not.' I held her eye. 'I intend to make it my world, though.'

'And how do you suppose you'll do that?' she said, smiling.

I don't know yet. You know, I think I can understand a little of your frustration.' I wanted her to share it with me, confide in me her shocking plan.

'The club doesn't admit new members, Johnny.'

'Some of your friends are children of your father's associates. Like the guys who were here the other night.'

'Some of them, yeah.'

'Whereas that's not true of Bruno, is it? Of Bruno's friends.'

'That's right. My father doesn't like a lot of Bruno's friends. He doesn't trust them.'

'Is that why he asked me to keep tabs on Bruno? Report to him who Bruno sees?'

'It may be. Particularly he doesn't like Nico and Sally.'

'And Phil?'

'Oh, no, he likes Phil. He dandled Phil on his knee. Phil's father is a yacht broker called Frank Goodwin, about the biggest on the coast, and he and my father have been friends for a long time. So he knows where Phil comes from – knows where to go if Phil gets out of line. People have taken advantage of Bruno . . .' She paused, and I had the impression that she was wondering whether she should continue with what she was about to tell me. 'You see, he went badly off the rails. He was studying at Princeton – law school – and he got into a very wild crowd that had nothing to do with Princeton. My father thought they had ulterior motives. He wanted Bruno to shake them off. There was a drug problem. But the thing is, right, I don't think they had any ulterior motive. My father couldn't accept that anyone would like Bruno for himself.'

'And were they so bad, these people?'

'Oh, yeah,' she said, and laughed. 'They were truly terrible. Really – grungy people. And they got Bruno into trouble. My father, who has got a lot of strings to pull, starts hearing from the faculty: "John, your son isn't doing any work; John, your son has been arrested; John, your son is in hospital." Bruno flunks out, and by this time my father had been over to see him several times. I think he tried really hard to get Bruno to break his links with these people. But he didn't succeed.'

'And what did he do then?'

'Bruno was arrested and charged.'

'With what?'

'With a serious offence.'

'What?'

'You're goddam curious, you know that?'

'I know it, I know it – I am. I don't even know why.'

'With possession of cocaine. Bruno was bailed, the case came up for trial, and he was freed. On one condition: that he should live here under my father's supervision, who vouched for him.'

'Convenient.'

'So he thought. There's a hypothesis that my father organized the whole thing.'

'You're joking. Could that be true?'

'It's possible.'

'Do you believe it?'

'No, I don't,' she said. 'But what happened was certainly convenient for my father. Bruno was working for him, stopping over in Anguilla and the Virgin Islands on his way to and from the States, doing the business. It was confidential stuff. He couldn't be allowed to just run wild.'

'Maybe something happened that led your father to believe that Bruno was messing things up. Maybe there was a breach of confidentiality.'

'Maybe.'

'Now this hypothesis that your father fixed a bust and a trial – is this what Bruno believes?'

'That's right. It has a kind of . . . Bruno flavour about it, doesn't it? In other words, no one in their right minds would believe it.'

You really don't like him, do you?

'But could your father really manage something like that?'

She paused for a moment.

'Well, it's not such a big deal. With his connections he could do it.'

Was Marenkian's arm that long? I was sceptical. But I wasn't really giving the subject my full attention. I didn't care what she told me, as long as she confided. It put us on another footing. My mind wandered to imaginings of her nipples brushing against the linen of her shift.

We moved on to other, less personal subjects. And I tried, with little success, to make her laugh. I opened a second bottle of wine: a bottle of Marenkian's Petrus '81. He would never notice its absence.

When it was down to the last inch she stood up. 'Whoa.' She swayed. 'Shit, that was too much wine.'

I looked at my watch. We had sat and talked for almost three hours, and it was near midnight.

'Here, I'll get you some coffee.'

'No, no, I've just gotta go to bed now.'

She started to turn, and I said: 'I know what you need. You need a swim.'

I immediately knew I had made a mistake.

'No, Johnny,' she said with an ironic little smile. 'I think a swim is about the last thing I need. I really do.' And with that smile on her face she turned and left me cold.

Chapter Nine

MARENKIAN RETURNED; as if avoiding him, she and Bruno went out. That night I lay back on my bed, naked with the heat, the silence of the room, the cicadas outside. She must be promiscuous; in my memory, sharp as a photograph, was what I had seen a few weeks before. The hand up her skirt, the veined forearm; she had shoved her pelvis forward, her legs had gripped. She probably took a few men a month, all those Italian boys she hung around with, they had probably all had her, and I imagined them in the sand, in the water, faceless, pumping her as she clung to them. They could take turns with her, she wanted so much.

I did try to put that image of violent porn out of my mind, and I thought instead of her face as she smiled, her tenderness. She liked me and she was willing to share some of her most serious concerns with me. I knew I wouldn't sleep until she came back. Who was she with now?

Just after two I heard her throaty little car pull up outside. The heavy front door opened and shut. I opened my door very quietly and stepped out into the corridor. I heard her go into the den to join her father. A low murmur of conversation began.

Now she was back, I told myself, I could sleep; although another voice urged me to creep downstairs and eavesdrop. I found it hard to resist the temptation, but I managed it – and ended up lying stiff as a board in bed, my ears pricked back and my hair, so it felt, standing on end.

Finally I did begin to drop off, and it was then, of course, that another car woke me. Bruno was back. I recognized the deep purr of the Mercedes, its weight crunching the gravel. He'd be in trouble . . .

The front door opened quietly and slammed shut. Again there was some muttered conversation. Then suddenly the noise of glass or china shattering on the terracotta floor.

I hesitated for a moment, wondering whether I should interfere, then put on a tracksuit and gym shoes and went downstairs. Bruno was standing in the hall. Next to him on the floor was a smashed bottle of whisky. On his other side, standing on tiptoes, was Natalie. She had hold of his arm, and she was whispering urgently into his ear. Marenkian was poised in the doorway of his study. I looked at him for some guidance, but he didn't glance at me.

He said to his daughter, 'Let him alone, Natalie.'

Bruno's eyes were fixed on him, and Marenkian's on Bruno.

Then Bruno turned to me for a moment, and our eyes met. At first I thought that the deadness in his eyes, the glazed, faraway look, was the look of a man who had gone over the edge, slipped into insanity. A second later I realized with absolute certainty that, whatever his mental state, he had taken a lot of drugs. There was no mistaking it. He blinked long blinks, often, turning his head from side to side, his mouth lolling open. He seemed barely to recognize me. He licked his lips.

Then, in an almost comical gesture, he bared his teeth languidly and growled, 'Hurrunguah,' and I almost laughed.

As if aware that his growl had been slightly comical, he staggered back to the sideboard behind him, picked up a wooden bowl full of walnuts and threw it on the floor. The nuts scattered across the hall, clattering on the tiles, bouncing at first, then rolling slowly into corners. Everyone stood absolutely still, incapable of responding – at a loss.

Finally Marenkian said, calmly, deeply, urgently none the less, 'Bruno, pull yourself together.'

Bruno turned back to him, stood swaying and staring for what seemed like five minutes. Then, with a sort of twisted smirk on his face, he spoke.

'You fuck. You fuck. You fuck.'

Then he turned, swayed towards Natalie, who with surprising self-possession walked over to me. She stood slightly behind my shoulder and grabbed one of my arms tightly with both hands.

Marenkian looked at her gravely and said, 'I'm going to call Max Schenck. Stay with Johnny.'

He turned into his office.

Bruno descended the steps into the living area. He paused and swayed again. Then he roared and clumsily swept his hand against a standard lamp. He roared again, up-turned one of the coffee tables and then, still shouting, pushed a sofa halfway across the room. It was a frightening sight: this big man, out of control. Natalie gripped my arm even tighter and pushed her face into my shoulder. I had to be ready to square up to him.

After he had pushed the sofa across the room, Bruno collapsed onto his knees in front of it and appeared to lose his ability to move.

Marenkian came out of his study. 'Schenck'll be here in ten minutes.'

He looked across at Bruno, and the expression on his face was very difficult to read. Then he looked at Natalie, who slowly let go of my arm but didn't make any move to go over to him. For a moment Marenkian looked very tired, his face long and deeply serious like an old Russian priest's, his shoulders hunched. Then he breathed deeply and pulled himself upright. He walked over and stood near Bruno, as if wanting to speak to him, touch him, but not daring to.

Everything was still and silent. Bruno stayed in the curious, prone position he had adopted by the skewed sofa, as if praying to the fallen standard lamp.

Then Natalie took my arm again, drew me back to the hall and whispered tearfully, 'Oh, Johnny, I'm – I'm scared. I don't know what he's gonna do. He's—'

'Don't worry. He's not going to touch you now. Look at him. He's – he's finished for tonight.'

'Oh, Christ, I tell you, that's not always the end.' And she looked up at me and said very slowly, 'He told me he was gonna kill me.'

It took me a moment to react to this.

'Hey, calm down. He's not going to kill you. That's the drugs talking. What is he on, anyway?'

'He's just drunk. Very, very drunk.'

'Do you think so? Didn't you see his eyes? You can't get that way with booze.'

'You're – maybe you're right. I don't know. I mean I don't know what – he's into.'

'Whatever it is, he should stop.'

'Oh, Johnny, can you just – can you just look after me? Just keep him away from me. I'm scared.' She pressed her face into my shoulder, and this time I drew her round and hugged her.

'Of course I will. You know where I am. Any time, just shout and I'll hear you. OK?'

She nodded, and stayed in my arms a moment longer. The circumstances seemed to permit it, seemed to turn things upside-down. Then she pulled away, gazed at me, laughed slightly in a tearful way.

She said, 'Hey, I'm sorry. This is weird, you know, your brother saying he's gonna kill you, you know. I can't believe it but it's true, you know, and I don't know what to do.'

Marenkian had been watching us, his gaze penetrating. He looked away, back to Bruno, and we all stood there, waiting for Schenck to arrive.

When the bell went, Marenkian motioned me to stay still, and he himself went to the door to let Schenck in. For a few moments they had a whispered conference in the hall. Then Schenck came down the steps into the living room, carrying a heavy brown-leather briefcase, and surveyed the scene, confident. His presence altered the atmosphere. There seemed to be a vigour in him, something you could almost feel, a physical authority. Even Bruno stirred at the sight of his mentor.

'Wait there a moment, please, then I will ask you to help me with Bruno,' Schenck said to me, politely, but with his usual slight contempt. He went down into the living room where Bruno was, walked round to the other side of him and put his hand on his shoulder. He said quietly, soothingly, 'Well, my friend, I hear this evening you are a bit wild. Ah, dear. This won't do, huh? We'll have to get you to bed, a great big fellow like you. It's not gonna be easy, you know. You're a big guy. A big guy out on the town. My God, look at you now, huh?'

He looked up, those sharp eyes ordering me to come down. When I came round to Bruno's near side I saw a pathetic sight: he was looking up at Schenck like a baby looks at its mother, his head lolling, grinning slightly, adoring.

Schenck said, quietly, 'Take his left arm,' and I did so. With some difficulty we hauled him upstairs.

When we had got him onto the bed Schenck said, 'Stay with him, please.'

He disappeared for a few moments, then came back with his briefcase, out of which he took a bottle and a hypodermic syringe. He went through the usual procedure, rolling up the sleeve, swabbing.

I had moved back a few paces but I hadn't left the room. So I said to Schenck, 'I think he might have been on drugs already this evening.'

Schenck looked at me sharply, paused for a moment. 'Really? What makes you think that?'

'His eyes, mainly. You don't get eyes like that from drinking.'

'Sadly, Johnny, some people do. This is part of Bruno's condition unfortunately.' Then he said, 'Thank you very much,' in a polite but unmistakable way.

Still, right in the doorway, I hung back. Schenck gave him the injection. At the moment the needle went in, Bruno raised his head in confusion and then, moments later, slid back down onto the pillow.

He murmured, 'Why can't they . . . why can't they . . . ?' and fell unconscious.

Then Schenck glanced up at me, and I left the room.

It was about half-past three in the morning when I got downstairs. Marenkian was standing in the hallway. Natalie was not to be seen.

'Well, Johnny,' he said. 'I'm extremely sorry that something like this has happened, and that you've become mixed up in it. And I thank you very much for your help tonight, which has been truly invaluable.'

Mr Marenkian, I'm very sorry, but I don't really feel I'm qualified to deal with this kind of situation. I think you need to have trained help.

That's what I should have said, there and then, but I didn't. There's a time and place for everything, and *that* was the time to jump ship. *That* was the tide in my affairs. Very shortly afterwards it became much more difficult for me to extricate myself.

So, missing the tide, I said, 'Not at all, Mr Marenkian. I'm sorry that you have – these things to worry about.'

He nodded, and there was a pause.

'I'm afraid these clients are still coming tomorrow, so we'll need to be in good shape. I'd like to have a longer talk with you then.'

'Certainly.'

Then Schenck came down, businesslike.

Marenkian said, 'Thank you, Johnny. That will be all for this evening.'

I set off upstairs and, as I went, heard the start of their conversation.

'He'll sleep well into the day now.'

'This is a terrible worry, Max.'

'Try not to be too concerned, John. It's not as bad as it seems.'

'Would you come in for a minute.'

'Of course.'

The door to the den closed and there was silence. I slowly climbed the stairs.

But the evening wasn't over.

As I turned the corner of the landing I saw Natalie. She was standing in the half-dark, biting her lip. She looked almost ill, sick with . . . it must be fear, I thought.

I said, 'Good night, Natalie,' and she didn't reply.

Then, as I continued up the stairs that led to my rooms, she called me, in an urgent whisper. 'Johnny.' She was breathing fast, almost hyperventilating. 'Johnny, I'm so scared.'

'Listen, Schenck has knocked him out with an injection. He won't wake up until well into tomorrow, I heard Schenck say. I'd be surprised if he makes it out of bed even then.'

'But he's woken up after those injections before. I swear. Oh, God.' And she looked up to the ceiling, biting her lip.

'He won't wake up. Believe me.'

She sighed heavily. 'I just wish I wasn't so scared. I guess I . . . I guess I know he wouldn't kill me but – he just looked so wild when he said it, he . . . And I know he's woken up before, and I'm just . . .' She went back to biting that full red lip of hers.

'Natalie,' I said, and put my hand on her arm, 'it's understandable. It's normal. Of course you're scared. Look, what I can do is this, I'll leave my door wide open all night. I'll hear anything that moves – and if there *is* anything, I'll be right out. OK?'

'Sure. Thanks, Johnny.' She looked up, her eyes moist. Her brown, rounded face seemed slightly flushed in the half-dark. 'Thanks.'

'It's a pleasure,' I whispered, and I put my hands on her shoulders, pulling her towards me with an imperceptible force. Her face looked up to mine, and then I kissed her lips, and for a second they opened and I felt her mouth. Then she twisted away, and she was gone. And I was standing in the dark corridor alone.

I heard faint voices: Schenck and Marenkian had emerged onto the terrace and were talking together. Then Schenck left, and I watched Marenkian walk down to his office. The lights went on inside, and I cursed the man for an insomniac and a workaholic – on the phone again through the night. Because I had decided that I was going to go to her, and while he was still up I didn't dare.

So I scrunched myself up and went to my room, where I was full of doubt, despite my resolution and all the favourable signs. I remembered the first time I had crept the corridors, in an old house in County Durham, after a dance. A really gorgeous girl I had danced with for hours, and who had taken a lift with me back to the house party. It was dawn when we returned. I remember the big, cool sky lighting up. And when it came to saying goodnight in the dim corridor, she said, 'See you later,' and winked! And she was ready for me, standing by the window in a towelling dressing gown, brushing her hair.

I was eighteen, and she was the first. But I've done the same thing since, telling them: *I couldn't sleep, and I needed to talk to you.* It works, but you always need guts to take the chance.

The outside door shut quietly, and I heard Marenkian come slowly up the stairs.

Then I heard the door of his bedroom close. I had no further excuse for delay. In my mind I went over her signals: our swimming-pool play, our intimate conversations, the momentary touch of her tongue. *What further invitations do you need?*

And yet I could be wrong, could be the desperate teenager unable to restrain himself; the naïve Englishman blundering into her bedroom uninvited, misunderstanding everything.

After what seemed an age of mental struggle, I stood up, put my dressing gown on and opened the door. I was going, whatever happened. In the pool she had licked her sharp white teeth in hunger. She wanted me.

In the silence, my bare feet made quiet slaps and squeaks against the terracotta, and I crept down and round the corner. There was no light under Marenkian's door. So I went on to hers, which was next to it. My fingers slowly gripped the handle, and I turned it, infinitesimally, and then a little more – and then, with a rush of my heart, I was in, the door shut behind me.

The unfamiliar room in which someone else is asleep – it's dark and warm, and you can sense them. They fill the room, and you can smell them sleeping. Her room was full of a drowsy, sweet scent, although it was a scent I couldn't describe. I sensed it but I didn't smell it. Under a crumpled sheet she slept silently on her side, an arm thrown out in front of her, her hair over her face.

For a moment – for five minutes, perhaps – I stood near the door wondering what to do. I was somehow unprepared for finding her asleep. I had held visions of her sitting at a dressing table or coming out of the bathroom and being casually ready for me, for she had to have realized, I thought, that I was coming.

I considered leaving, but put that thought aside. I had run

the risk of the corridor, and it would be cowardly to go back. So after those few cold minutes of indecision I went and sat on the side of her bed.

I could see the smooth curve of her shoulder, the honey brown of her back, and under her arm the lighter, softer flesh of her breast. Her hand lay on the sheet beyond her, and her face was pushed into the pillow, her mouth open in an expression of babyish pain. I was shaking.

Suddenly and violently she twisted in her sleep, and moaned something incomprehensible and I felt an overwhelming compassion for her and the sadness with which she seemed to be filled, and I reached out and with a trembling uncertainty of touch stroked her rich, dark hair.

She twisted again, and muttered, 'Please,' and I lifted my hand clear of her hair and then put it back.

I stroked her again, this time not so tentatively, whispering, 'Natalie, don't worry, it's me.'

She turned slightly, and sighed in her sleep and pushed her head against my hand, and I thought, *My God, I knew it, she's responding to my touch*, and I leaned down and softly kissed her.

She moaned once again, and again I chanted softly to her, and then her moan became an 'Uhnn—'. And then suddenly she twisted away again, and sat bolt upright, staring at me with her eyes wide open.

'Uh? What?' She shook her head as if to shake the sleep out of it, and screwed up her eyes. I was screwing up my eyes as well, and raising my hand to rub my nose, because sitting up suddenly had brought her skull into sharp contact with it, and it hurt.

'What?' she said again, and then she took another catlike jump to the other side of the bed, and reached behind her for the bedside lamp, and I realized that this time the gamble wasn't going to pay off.

She switched the light on, and of course I was looking – I couldn't help it – at her naked body. She saw where my eyes were moving, looked at me defiantly, and snatched the sheet up to cover herself.

'Hi,' I said weakly but with sincerity, and I took my hand away from my nose. I hadn't anticipated the reaction I was about to get. 'I just wanted to come and—'

'What the fuck are you doing?' She looked suddenly like Bruno, her lip curled.

'I couldn't sleep, I just wanted to talk to—'

'Fucking shit. Who the fuck do you think you are, coming in here? What gives you the right?' Christ – she was shouting.

'Natalie, I just came down here to talk to you. If I made a mistake I'm sorry, OK?'

'Some people just *take*,' she said with disgust, and the volume of her voice wasn't much lower.

'Sssh!'

'Don't tell me to be quiet!' she shouted, about fifty decibels louder than before. 'I give you an inch, I show a little friendliness, and you think you can come here in the night – to my room, goddamit.'

Suddenly I was angry, and I stood up. Who did she think *she* was, Mother Teresa? But I wasn't going to argue the toss, and I started to speak—

'Good—'

—when the door flew open, and Marenkian appeared.

He looked from her to me, obviously enraged, then back again, and said, 'Are you OK, honey?'

'Yes, Daddy, I'm fine, I'm—'

But he cut across her and addressed himself to me. 'What are you doing in here?' he snarled, slowly and deliberately.

And suddenly I was terrified. I really thought he was going to kill me, and I've never encountered someone who seemed to me suddenly so dangerous.

'Mr Marenkian, I thought that I heard intruders,' I said, 'and I came along here, and there definitely did seem to be noises coming from this room. I had searched the downstairs already, and I – obviously I surprised Miss Marenkian.'

'Don't lie to me,' he said quietly.

'I can assure you, Mr Marenkian, I'm not lying.'

He took a step towards me and I knew that he was about to attack.

Then Natalie said, 'That's why he was here, Daddy. I just got a shock and I was scared, right.'

'Is this true? Did he say anything to you about intruders?'

'Sure, of course he did.'

He looked at her for a long moment, then at me, and the silence was heavy. Then he said to me coldly, 'Go to your room.'

'I'm really sorry I caused this disturbance,' I said quietly, and left the room. I didn't think he believed me, but my skin was saved.

The hypocritical bitch, making that kind of show. Perhaps she had lost me my job – and perhaps I didn't want the job any more. Who was she anyway to make such a fuss? The silly, dirty, spoilt American tart.

Back in my room, I got into bed but I couldn't sleep. She had practically *asked* me up there and, although it seemed to me fair to turn me away if she had just been prick-teasing earlier, to come out with this pretence of outraged honour and offended virtue, to shout like that when she must have known damn well it would bring her father in – that was intolerable. I was livid. How dare she do that to me? I was worth a hundred shallow little whores like her.

Then I was struck suddenly, and as I had never been before, by just how low I had sunk: servant to this American trash, prostituting my background and my honour to these criminals. My life had once been so promising. I had once had everything – and now I was beneath respect, beneath contempt.

It was a bad night – there wasn't much of it left, anyway – and I wasn't about to do much sleeping. I crept down to the cellar and fetched a bottle of Black Label, which over the next two hours I half finished.

So in the morning I was in a bad way. My anger had curdled in my stomach – it was sour and watery, like what I vomited when I came back from buying the bread.

Marenkian was already up, and sitting out on the terrace. When he saw the Range Rover pull up, with me inside it, he stalked down the terrace steps.

I got out and he said, 'Come see me in my office.'

He walked down the path and I followed. He sat down behind his desk, while I stood.

'You were in my daughter's room last night. It seems you had a reason for being there, and you're goddam lucky she's confirmed that to me, because believe me, mister, I don't make threats. Maybe she's being kind and giving you an out. Anyhow, I'm gonna overlook it this time. But don't even *look* at her,' he said savagely, staring me in the eye. 'Don't even put your eyes on her, understand? Because there are oceans between you, and low life like you could never have her. Do you understand?'

'Yes.'

'*Never.*'

'Yes, sir.'

Then he sat back again in his chair and sighed. 'OK. We're not gonna say any more about this.'

'Right,' I said very quietly.

'You can go now. I'm not having any breakfast.'

'OK, Mr Marenkian.'

I turned and went, feeling too exhausted, as I walked back to the house, to feel the rage I knew would come later. I was aware of my humiliation without yet being able to feel it. *Low life!* I could not believe that he had called me low life. I was stunned by that. As far as I was concerned my career in the place ended as of that moment; nothing would persuade me to wait on any of them ever again. So I went to the kitchen and asked Claudine to deal with their lunch, then up to my room where I set the alarm for midday.

Today was the day, I had suddenly realized, of my lunch with Horst – and Horst might be able to help. He was a friend and associate of Marenkian's, but he might none the less be able to find me another job.

As I fell asleep, I felt a small corner of satisfaction that when I left this place I would regain, at least, a little pride in myself.

Chapter Ten

I WAS STILL enraged as I drove up to Saint-Paul, and suffering from a nasty, liverish hangover. Reckless with the car, I practically forced a few big Citroëns off the road as I gunned round the steep hairpins. The panorama down to the coast, the memories of the gallery in the trees I had once visited with my mother, the charm of the old hilltop village and the desecration of it with an underground car park, all left me unmoved. The only thing that interested me was the prospect of getting very drunk with very good, expensive wine – at Horst's expense. He owed me; after all it was he that got me the Marenkian job, foisted me onto the mad bastards. She was dirt, a dirty little tart. How could I ever have fallen for her?

Horst was already installed at one of the best tables, on the edge of the old stone terrace. He hailed me, a fellow well met. I decided at that moment, I don't know why, that I would be a little cautious about what I revealed to him, and how. After all, he was Marenkian's client and friend, and he had found me the job. He might not be sympathetic.

'Ah, I've been flying from here to there, a lot of *indescribably* dull meetings about finance, you know. I have spent quite a lot of time in Switzerland.'

'You've been raising money?'

'Oh, yes. Raising it, investing it, eating it, drinking it, you know? Retail, a small high-tech concern we are interested in, a film.'

'We?'

'My partner and I,' he said solemnly. 'My partner Yaroslav, who is the eastern half of the enterprise.'

'An equal partner?'

'Very unequal,' he said, and laughed at his joke. 'No, no, I heard what you said. Never, Johnny, never have an equal partnership with anybody. If you have a partner who is your equal, how can you control him? What if he goes mad and wants to – wants to do something *honest?*' He laughed again. 'How could you stop him? God, it's terrible, you know – I've been there.'

I was smiling by now. The man was good company; his jokes and a glass and a half of excellent white burgundy swiftly despatched had already half restored me.

'That's very interesting advice. I would never have thought of that.'

'But of course you don't, until it has happened to you. It's rather like a marriage failing – which is not usually anticipated on the wedding day.'

He clearly knew the place well. When he came to take our order, the maître d'hôtel addressed Horst by name, and our table was clearly one of the best. From our places we could gaze out over the steep dry slopes beneath the hilltop on which we perched so luxuriously, our starched linen and rows of wine-glasses in the dappled shade of fig trees.

He ordered a bottle of Vosnes-Romanée – we had made light work of the Montagny – and turned back to me.

'So-o-o, what about this weird family, huh?' His face was serious now, concerned. 'Honestly, you know, Johnny, I'm god-dam sorry if I got you involved with some *mad* people.'

'No, no, Horst, don't worry about it.'

'I *do* worry about it though, you see, because I feel *responsible.* I mean, like this idea of Marenkian's that you should follow Bruno around and spy on him?'

'I thought it was a bit sneaky. I had accepted the job, and all the terms had been agreed, and it all seemed nice and simple. And then Marenkian calls me in and says, "Oh, by the way, Bruno can't drive because of his medication." God, this wine is delicious. So, "Can you drive him?" he says. "I'll give you a bonus." "Well, that's no problem." And then he gets a little bit coy, and says: "Oh, and, I actually want you to go into the bars with Bruno, and stay with him – make sure he stays out of trouble."'

'Really? It *is* bizarre.'

'All of that would be fine. But what I found really irritating was what he *then* wanted. He wanted me to report back to him on everyone Bruno met, which put me at loggerheads with Bruno, obviously.'

'Bruno is temperamental. I know that about him.'

'Oh, yes, there's no doubt about that. I'll tell you something else, I can't work out whether Bruno is *really* dangerous, but he's already threatened me with violence.'

Horst laughed. 'So you're living dangerously, huh?'

'No. Horst, I mean it. He has seriously threatened me with violence. I went into his room in a completely routine way to change an insecticide plug, and he followed me in and started a *What are you doing in here?* routine.'

'Hmm. And is this part of his mental illness?'

'I should think it probably is, yes. But I've got to tell you that I don't want the hospitalization of John Denner to be part of his mental illness. "I'm sorry, your honour, but I had to beat the butler up as part of my course of treatment."'

'"And I have a certificate from my doctor."'

'"And anyway he was only our employee."' We laughed, then started to eat one of the most delicious lunches I have ever had, and dwelt on all kinds of subjects other then the Marenkians and their milieu. Much later on – two bottles later, I think – we came back to them.

'So you don't want to be Bruno's wet-nurse. Have you talked to Marenkian about it?'

'No . . . I find him quite unapproachable. Old-fashioned, I suppose.'

'Ye-e-es. He is old-fashioned, you know, in business. One of the *old school*.' This time there was irritation in his word emphasis. 'Marenkian, in common with a lot of the people in this part of the world, these people from the south of France and Italy – they don't understand what's going on in the wider world today. They've built this beautiful life for themselves in the sun. They've turned their profits into sun-dried tomatoes.'

'What on earth do you mean?'

'Ah. I'm sorry, Johnny. I get in the habit, you know, because the people I talk to about this are the people who are doing it. They're people who have recycled the money they made under the counter into building and agriculture and transport – for example in southern Italy, where they have been able to boost their profits with money from the EC: to build these wonderful high-tech farms with the most modern equipment. And this is a wonderful, comfortable life.'

'Horst, do you mind my asking this? You talk about under-the-counter money. What do you mean?'

He laughed again. He laughed more than anyone I knew.

'Johnny . . . Ah, well, we're good friends now, so I can tell you about it. Most of their cash is coming out of narcotics. It's obviously the most important market now. And, you know, if you're a certain kind of entrepreneur it's difficult not to get involved in it. But that market moves fast, and the opportunities now are in the East – and the East is what I know. Just think about it, Johnny; there is a world there – I mean East Europe and the former Soviet Union – which for fifty years was in the deep freeze! And now it thaws out, and of course there are all sorts of things coming out of the ice. People like John Marenkian can make money like they never dreamed. Why?

Because they have capital, and most of the people with capital won't invest it where it is not safe. You ask ICI, or Barclays Bank, and they say: "We will wait until the structures are in place, the safeguards." But we don't have to wait for that. We have our own structures, our own safeguards.'

'Right.'

'You ask what kind? OK, I'll be honest with you here, and it's not the most desirable thing always. But all of these states had enormous security apparatuses, and they employed thousands of people. All these guys knew was state security work, and in many cases their organizations were completely disbanded, so overnight they had nothing to do. Sad thing for them. But that is still the field they are going to gravitate to. When you've been the boss of a state security organization, you are hardly going to become a *window-cleaner*, huh?'

We talked around this subject for some time, and Horst kept coming back to his theme: the service he could offer to Marenkian and his clients; the numerous ways in which he could redirect their investments to give them returns greater than they could otherwise have dreamed of.

'Because that is my world, Johnny. That is where I come from. I know how to deal with these people. And I say to Marenkian: "Come into partnership with me. Let me make money for you. You don't have to lift a finger." But he won't do it. He is stuck in his old ways, he's too old, he's complacent. He actually – he actually believes in his own image now. That is his problem.'

'What, you mean his appearance of wealth?'

'No, no, he is very wealthy. His cultivated image of an establishment man of the East Coast, of Harvard and the Ivy League.'

'Which is not what he really is?'

'No, of course it's not. He has the training – don't get me wrong – but he's from the gutter. That's the way to make him angry: to remind him of what he is. Although I wouldn't advise it, Johnny, unless you've got a very big stick in your hand. You don't like working with him, I know that. Not just because of Bruno, huh?'

'Well . . .' We were on to the armagnac, and I told him. 'There was a misunderstanding between us yesterday. I was – I thought that I heard intruders in the place, and one of the places I went was Natalie's room.'

'So what's wrong with that?'

'Well, it was the middle of the night.'

I thought I was going to have to get up and pummel his back, he laughed so much.

'Oh, I love that. Fortune favours the bold, you say. But not this time.'

'That's right. Marenkian came in, and he wasn't too happy.'

'Still, she's tasty, isn't she – worth the risk. Well done.'

'I was given a very hard time about it, in a humiliating sort of way. Marenkian saying: "Keep your hands off my daughter. She's not for scum like you." He actually called me "low life", which pissed me off. OK, fair enough, I can understand that he doesn't want the hired help interfering with his one and only, but I'm not low life. If I hadn't had the Spanish misfortune, I'd be quite a catch for them.'

'There's no doubt. It's outrageous that you should be treated like that.'

'Fucking American crook. Excuse me, but who the hell is he to push me around?'

'There are limits, for sure. You have to treat people decently. And now you feel pretty goddammed embarrassed about working there, waiting on these people who treat you like shit.'

'I do.' I was drunk, by then.

'I tell you something. I feel bad about this, you know.'

'No, no, you mustn't.'

'No, really I do, because I should have seen this coming.

You're an intelligent guy with a strong sense of your own self-respect. And I've steered you towards a domestic position which gives you these problems. These Americans don't know how to deal with servants, anyway.'

'Huh!'

'Bloody interlopers.'

'You speak superior English, Horst, do you know that? You speak a superior English.'

'In my conversations with superior people,' he said. We were finishing our armagnacs. 'Another armagnac, I think. Fuck the Marenkians, Johnny. You don't want to stay with those assholes. It's outrageous the way they've treated you. Seriously now,' he suddenly said – and he meant it; he managed suddenly to seem quite sober.

'I could use you, Johnny. You've got charm, front, quick wits – God, I don't know what I was doing putting you into the Marenkians in the first place. I could use you to front my investment operations here, maybe in the UK too. I think you'd know how to deal with my clients very well.'

This sounded better. This sounded more like it. Something I could get my teeth into, something substantial, something that could make me a lot of money. Horst was a rich man, and working close to him couldn't fail to bring its rewards. We'd always got on well, and it seemed to me that we were close to becoming good friends. I could go a long way hitched to his coat-tails.

'And we could work together really well, Johnny. We could *make* work.'

'This sounds wonderful. Really interesting.'

'God, and now I'm drunk. Which is no time to discuss business, huh? But I mean this: this is a serious offer, and we'll get you out of there and into something where you can stretch yourself. And become *rich*, Johnny,' he said, his voice suddenly quiet. 'You want your own yacht? Eighteen metres, say? In my business they pay in yachts, Johnny.'

'It gets better.'

'Oh, yeah. But listen, we can't talk about it now. I'm not sober. Come and see me ... Can you make it tomorrow morning first thing? At the Meridien.'

'The Meridien? I thought you stayed in the Negresco.'

'No, I like to be a bit more anonymous, you know. Nobody *recognizes* you in the Meridien, even if they know you. Staying there kind of makes them go blind. I don't promise you that it will be immediate, Johnny, because I have partners – and even though they are not equal partners, they need to be consulted. But it will happen.'

'Here's to payment in yachts, Horst,' I said, and we raised our glasses. 'Here's to payment in yachts, goddam it!'

I went to bed again when I got back. There was no sign of anybody there and I wasn't much interested in looking after them, wherever they were. When I got up later, with another hangover, none of them had returned. 'Not much longer,' I said to the walls, holding tightly to a Bloody Mary. *Not much longer will I be a bloody servant. From now on people will wait on me; people will listen to my orders again. Payment in yachts.* I laughed. He was such a bloody salesman: the kind of man who could not resist the sales pitch, even when no one was buying.

The next day my head was reasonably clear. I served Marenkian his breakfast as usual, and took some pleasure in being slightly uncooperative.

'I'd like to see you this morning, Johnny.'

'Certainly, Mr Marenkian. Later this morning would be fine. I'm afraid I have to go out early on.'

'OK, that's fine. Come see me when you get in.'

So I went to the Meridien for my appointment with Horst, full of grim pleasure – triumph almost. This was snatching victory from the jaws of defeat. Natalie's noisy rebuff had been a blessing in disguise. Without it, in her arms, I would still have been a miserable servant, a lackey, I told myself. But with that stinging me into action, I would be one of Horst's right-hand men paid, if not in yachts, in one hell of a lot of dollars. Perhaps I *would* be sailing close to the wind. Perhaps I *would* be breaking the law. So what? I was already beyond the pale. That's what it all added up to. I had tried to claw my way back, and it hadn't worked. I had tried and failed, lost my good name, and nothing I did now would ever grant me admission to the Members' Enclosure. And I wasn't going to live in mediocrity for the rest of my life. Here was a once-only opportunity to team up with a real player, to take the shortcut. I could do it. I owed nothing to the Marenkians.

It was dim in the corridor of the Meridien's fifth floor, and the ceiling was low, and the place hummed with a cascade of white noise: a muffled waterfall of ventiliation and plumbing. My heart beat hard. Now, at last, I had a real chance.

'I'm sorry, I must have the wrong room.' Because the door hadn't been opened by Horst but by a short, thick man in his forties with angry, pockmarked skin. He stared into my eyes – his own were rimmed with red – and his lip curled.

'Or perhaps I do have the right room?' I said in English.

'For Horst?'

Another German?

'Yes.'

This must be the Russian whatever-his-name-was: the KGB man. He must be a real bastard, I thought. Without a word he pulled back the door and I walked down the corridor of the suite into bright smoky light. I could glimpse the opalescent sea through a gap in the muslin curtains. Horst himself stood among them as the breeze billowed them, looking for all the world like a music-hall sorcerer.

'Ah, Johnny, come in. Allow me to introduce my associate, Yaroslav, known to his friends as Yari.'

Yari put out his hand. He was a peculiar-looking fellow, in his dress as much as his face. He wore a black-leather jacket, black jeans tucked into black cowboy boots, and a black T-shirt, so that he looked like a guitarist in a heavy-metal band.

We were going to be colleagues, Yari and I, but I doubted we would ever be friends.

'So, welcome, Johnny. Come in. Have a seat. I've been telling Yari all about you, and he's impressed – wanted to meet you. I can't think,' Horst said, as he motioned me to a seat, 'how it is that we didn't consider having some better *presentation* a long time ago. I can't do everything myself, obviously. I can't be everywhere at the same time. And Yari's responsibilities lie at the other end of our operation in Moscow. But I have to tell you, Johnny,' he continued, settling now into his seat and down to business, 'not everything is straightforward. If I offer you a job with me, I will be handing you the opportunity to become a very rich man. That is a simple fact of the matter. But the kind of work that is involved is high-risk – very high-risk – and to do it you need to be incredibly resourceful, and you need to be tough. So I've been asking myself' – here he stood up and began to pace slowly up and down – 'and Yari has asked me too: *How can Johnny prove himself?*'

My heart sank a little; I had supposed our agreement as good as sealed. But I told myself not to be feeble. There is no such thing as a free lunch, they say.

'How can Johnny prove himself? Do you *want* to prove yourself?'

'Of course I do, Horst.'

'I'm not gonna hide something from you, Johnny, you know. My line of business sometimes involves dealing with violent people, lying and deceit. So I thought about this, and there is a very obvious way you start with me – to earn your spurs. You must stay with the Marenkians.'

'Right,' I said, cautiously.

'You stay with them, but you work for me. I'm going to put you straight on my payroll, Johnny, at an annual salary of one hundred and fifty thousand dollars, cash. If you like, see the period you stay with the Marenkians as a trial period. It's when you earn the right to work on the mainstream of my business. And now I'm going to talk to you about this trial period. I'm not going to talk about what happens afterwards – for many reasons but mainly confidentiality. Nobody gets to know about my business who doesn't work for me, you know? Just by coming here, Johnny, you're putting yourself under an obligation never to speak about anything we discuss. You understand that?'

'I *do* understand it.'

'So I'll say to you now: you can get up and walk out of here. You don't want that kind of commitment, that's fine.' He stared at me – and Yari, who sat at the other wall, also stared – and there was that moment of silence they say you can cut with a knife. As he had been speaking there had been a tension growing inside me. I hadn't been prepared for this, but I jumped. One hundred and fifty thousand dollars a year.

'I don't want to walk out, Horst. This is a big chance for me, and I'm going to take it.'

'Good,' he said, beaming. 'Now, let's talk about the Marenkians. Over the next few weeks I want to know *everything*. I want to know where they go, who they talk to, who they do business with, who they sleep with. Particularly I want to know about clients – anything about his investments. I want you to get into his office, I want you to read his documents, his mail, his diary, everything.'

'Right.'

'Now tell me about this Bruno business.'

I went through what we had discussed the day before. As I delved further into it, he seemed to become more interested. He wanted particularly to hear about Bruno's dealings with Schenck, and I gave him an account of what I knew.

'But this treatment could be perfectly normal,' he said.

'It could – I don't deny it. But if you put it together with the rest of what I've found out about Bruno it does begin to seem remarkably strange. Maybe – just maybe – history is repeating itself. Marenkian believes Bruno is being manipulated, and thinks the manipulators are people from his past, or his contemporaries in Nice, like this American, Nico. Whereas it's his psychotherapist. And who could be better placed to do it?'

'Who indeed?'

'I could find out more.'

'Go ahead, Johnny. The more the better.'

Then he resumed his minutely detailed questioning, almost two hours of it, in all.

Finally he sighed, 'Well, I guess that's about it. Oh, except for one thing. John Marenkian has certain – how shall I put it? Financial deeds of title, let's say. Some of them belong to me. Have you ever actually seen a share certificate?'

'I'm not sure if I have.'

'The ornate borders, formal language, the nomination of whoever it may be as a shareholder in whichever company – that is very everyday. Marenkian and myself – among others – work with a slightly different mechanism, which I will call a bearer share. What does that mean?' he asked himself. 'A bearer share is very simple. Instead of the share certificate being specifically nominated or made out to you or to me or to the steelworkers' pension, it is simply marked "Bearer". Now this is impossible in the mainstream markets, but not in many of the offshore tax havens. Tell me now, Johnny, what does Marenkian *do*, huh?'

'He invests money for other people. Money that they want kept hidden from the tax man or the authorities in general.'

'Right. And how does he do that?'

'I've actually overheard him briefing a potential client. He sets up a chain of companies, most of them based in tax havens. I'm not sure quite how they're linked.'

'One owns the next – really for putting investigators off the track. Let's say I'm Mr Tax Man and I want to find out who owns Lion Ltd. I go to the Cayman Islands, and at the companies registry there I discover that it's owned by Tiger Ltd in the British Virgin Islands. And Tiger Ltd, I find when I go to BVI, is owned by . . . Donkey Plc – you see? – in Anguilla or some such place. Still, if I am determined enough, I have now found Donkey Plc, so if I am the guy hiding his money, what happens if the investigator reaches my last company? What do I do, Johnny?'

'You keep your name out of the records.'

'OK, fine. But what about when I want to *get* my money? How do I *prove* I own Donkey Plc?'

'You have a share certificate with your name written on it.'

'But even that might be found – when the tax man breaks into my safe. "Ah, we always wondered who owned Donkey Plc." So the share certificate just says Bearer. No one can *prove* that it is linked to me. But if I have the share certificate, I own the company. Do you see? It's bearer shares. Bearer shares are at the end of Marenkian's chains. They are the key to his little operation. They are tens of millions in a safe. And he won't let them go. Oh, I'm not going to tell you *I* have any more right to them than the right of anyone else who can make use of them. But I could make that money work: I could multiply it by ten times in a year. And I wouldn't feel bad, because the people who got that money got it from cheating the *municipalité*, skimming contracts, selling drugs, taking bribes, I don't know what. They live in my world, so they take the fucking risk, man. I'll take that risk. I'll say to them: "Yes, I took your fucking money. What are you gonna do about it?"' Suddenly he was shouting. Just as suddenly, he stopped and looked at me. 'You gonna take that risk, Johnny? You up to that?'

I was taken aback, and didn't answer straight away. So he carried on, quietly this time. Yari sat still and expressionless, watching me.

'I want you to *find* these. I want to know where they are. Maybe you'll be able to take them, and you must know that if you do I'll pay you a bonus of one year's salary.'

I should have known, of course, that there would be a sting in the tail. Horst would hardly offer me a place in his 'organization', whatever that might be, on the strength of my table manners.

'You presumably agree with me,' I said, 'that this could be very difficult. If these documents are so vital to Marenkian, it stands to reason that he must look after them very carefully.'

'I don't *expect* it to be easy for you. The risk is quite high, but so is the reward. Effectively, three hundred thousand dollars if you succeed – and a place with me.'

'Horst, I don't need persuading. What do *I* care about these people? They don't mean anything to me. I just want to make sure that we're looking at something realistic. I mean, why don't you just break into his safe? Surely that's where he'd keep them.'

'No, Johnny, that's not where they are. Don't you worry about getting your *hands* on them. Just find out where they are, and I'll take care of the rest. Or, rather, Yari will. He is used to security work, you see.'

'But are you saying I won't get a bonus if I only *tell* you where they are?'

'Fifty thousand.'

Then, for a moment, I vacillated, and suddenly asked myself what the hell I was doing, consenting to go back into Marenkian's household as a kind of spy – or a thief. The thought that I might get caught sent a fear into my stomach. But I got a grip and said to myself: *This is your chance, and you have to take it, if you don't want to spend the rest of your life a grovelling servant and a failure. This is the road to riches!*

'A hundred.' Those bastards would find out about me. They'd find out who they could then mess up and humiliate.

Horst considered for a split second, then said, 'You drive a hard bargain. OK.'

'And what about something on account, eh?'

'Sure, Johnny. You learn fast.' He turned to Yari and said, quietly, 'Ten.'

And Yari produced from his pocket a green bundle which he handed to Horst, and Horst handed to me.

Ten thousand US dollars. *Ten thousand.*

I stood up. 'Horst, you've got a deal.'

He laughed. 'Hey-hey, money-money, it's so good. You know, I love the thought that you will have your own yacht very soon if you get this right. Would you hire a skipper?'

'No way. I'd only hire crew.'

'That's the way, Johnny. That's the way. Welcome aboard!'

Chapter Eleven

TEN THOUSAND dollars – that was something serious. When I got back to the car I took the cash out of my pocket and felt it. One hundred one-hundred-dollar bills. About seven thousand pounds sterling. About sixty thousand francs. When I squeezed the notes together hard – they were used, and some of them quite crumpled – the bundle was as thick as my finger. It so happens that I have never held so much cash in my hand in my life. So, while ten thousand dollars might not seem much in the land of the thriller or the movies, for me it was a lot. It was a paper bundle of freedom, and it had a big heart. I smelled it, then kissed it as if I were in a Western.

Talk about snatching victory from the jaws of defeat. Two days ago those people were spitting on me – that prick-teasing tart and her bent-brief father, not to mention their bloody nutcase of a son. Now I'll spit on them, I'll show them just exactly who can be treated like dirt. I'll show them that I hold good cards, too. I'll show them that in the game we're all playing I know who the winner will be, and I will be on *his* side, and I will reap the rewards.

But I had to deliver first. I knew that I had to prove myself, and that proving myself might be difficult. Could it be *dangerous*? Marenkian was a lawyer with some underworld clients, but he surely couldn't put me at the bottom of the Baie des Anges for messing about in his files, could he?

On the way up the steps to the house I ran into Natalie, and she said, 'Oh-ho, someone had a good lunch yesterday, Johnny Denner.'

'Really?'

'So that's good. When we play tennis today I might be able to beat you.'

'I haven't got time to play tennis today. I've got other things to do.'

'Oh, I see,' she said gaily. 'OK.' And she bounced off upstairs.

It cost me something just to be a *little* off with her.

I went to the kitchen, and after a moment the phone rang: Marenkian.

'Johnny, I hate to disturb you, but could you just come down to the office for a moment.'

'Sure.'

When I got there he sat me down in front of his desk. *What does he want now?* I wondered. *More apologies?*

'Johnny, I'll come straight to the point. Then I won't have to keep you any longer than necessary. I have to say that I overreacted yesterday. I spoke to Natalie this morning and she confirmed that there was no dishonourable intention in your action. And frankly I feel that the way I expressed myself was unpleasant. So I apologize.'

I was embarrassed.

'Please think nothing of it.'

'Well, it's generous of you to take it in that spirit. I would just like to explain to you my feelings. Natalie's my only daughter, and of course I'm protective of her – particularly in this part of the world. There are people who exist in order to use emotional relationships to make money, and a girl who's as beautiful as she is and also comes from a wealthy background is vulnerable for that. So I'm sorry I mistook your motives.'

It may have been generous of him to apologize, but we had

crossed a line, and there was no going back for me. So I suppressed my sympathy, smiled, and said, 'Thank you for saying that, Mr Marenkian. I understand your position and your feelings. And there are no hard feelings on my part.'

Horst, however, is going to find out all about you, and your family, and what your games are.

'I'll let you get away, then.'

'OK, thanks.'

Of course he had made me feel disloyal. But I hardly knew him.

I went to the kitchen and Natalie followed me in. She jumped on to the side and sat on her hands, swinging her legs and thrusting her pelvis forward.

'Found a new tennis partner?' she asked in a light, casual tone.

'No.'

'Given up the game, huh?'

Why don't you just go away.

'Certainly not.'

'How about that game tomorrow?'

'I don't think I've got time.'

'You're angry, aren't you?'

'Not at all. Just a little bit wiser about where I stand.'

'Oh, come on. If I hadn't made excuses for you – big excuses – my father would have torn you apart.'

'Uh-huh, I'd like to have watched him.'

'So would I,' she said, irritated – which pleased me. 'Anyway, if you're gonna sulk, that's fine. I'm not known for having to ask favours more than once. And from someone who owes me.'

'Natalie, I'm not sulking and I'm not angry,' I lied. 'But I *am* busy tomorrow. Now I might be able to fit you in on Thursday? How about that?'

She tilted her head to one side.

'Hmmn ...' she murmured, looking at me ambivalently, then left.

'Psychoanalysts, psychiatrists, psycho-I-don't-know-what, they are *salopards*, you know. But, I tell you, a thousand an hour, you realize? A *thousand*. They're not poor, it's certain.'

Jean served another customer, then came back, leaned over the bar and said confidentially:

'You're thinking of using one, you?'

'Certainly not. I have a friend who is considering it.'

'Ah, always a friend, huh?'

'No, really, it's true.'

'A woman?'

'No, a man.'

He shook his head, as if this was a very sad piece of news.

'That's bad. Psychiatrists are for women, you know.'

I laughed.

'No, no, I tell you, it's true. My sister was treated by a psychiatrist.'

'Was it good for her?'

He paused and sucked his lips, then blew.

'I don't know. She is better now, but it is possible that she would have got better without that.'

'Do they have to be state-registered in France?'

'Oh yes, of course they do. Your brain in their hands, you realize? It's a good thing to know their address.'

'Where are they registered?'

'I don't know. The *sécurité sociale*, I think. Wait.' He went to pull a beer. 'I'll get you the number.'

I later went to Schenck's, picked up a somnambulant Bruno, and took him back to the house. I had to help him up the stairs, he was that drugged up. Then I made the call.

'*Bonjour*, madame. I am thinking of consulting a psychotherapist in Nice, and I would like to check if he is registered.'

'Don't hang up, monsieur. I will connect you to that office.'

I waited, listening to Mozart.

A new voice explained, in answer to my question, 'We do not have a register of psychotherapists here, monsieur. It is not regulated by law. You should use a psychotherapist who is recommended by your doctor.'

'I see. Will this psychotherapist be able to prescribe – medication?'

'It is the doctor who gives medication, monsieur. It is not allowed for a psychotherapist. We have a register of psychiatrists, who are also doctors.'

'Right. Is there a Dr Schenck registered?'

'A Dr—?'

'S-C-H-E-N-C-K?'

'Wait, please.'

There was a pause.

'Here, in Nice?'

'Yes.'

'Yes, monsieur.' After a pause: '137 rue Jean Jaures.'

'I see. Thank you very much.'

'You should ask the advice of your doctor, monsieur.'

'I will. Thank you very much.'

I had other ideas, but I couldn't follow them up there and then. I had to vacuum the swimming pool, then try and charm Claudine a little. I'd be wanting her to do more of my work in future.

In the afternoon I went down to Nice. I was Horst's private eye, so I had to start somewhere.

I was looking for a *notaire* – or local solicitor – because I wanted to have a substance analysed, and I thought they might know who could perform the task.

I found one, left her office with a card in my hand: Gaston BERVILLIER, *Laboratoires SOPIC*. I called the number and made an appointment. Horst was going to get his money's worth.

For dinner that night *boeuf en daube* with morels. When I had finished serving it and they were occupied eating, I unobtrusively skirted the table and went upstairs to Bruno's room.

Very quietly I went into the bathroom. I was conscious that my movements might be heard below – unlikely, given the solidity of the house, but possible. I was mindful of our last encounter and his warning to me, so I crept round like a burglar. My presence in his room would put him in the mood for violence: I would be convincing a paranoiac of the truth of his delusions.

On the shelf sat the two small, archaically labelled bottles: THE TABLETS. Why should Schenck give his medicines so mysterious a rubric?

One of them contained a good number of luscious yellow and green capsules, and I felt no qualms about taking one and wrapping it in a square of tissue paper. The other worried me a little more. Five dark red capsules nestling in a slip of cotton wool. Bruno would surely notice the absence of one. Indeed, he was probably given a week's supply each time he went to Schenck, so this would leave him short for a day.

But I just sang under my breath, 'Sorry, Bruno,' wrapped one up and pocketed it. He would hardly suspect anything, hardly suspect me. He wasn't organized enough to know whether he had lost a capsule, or miscalculated, or taken two by mistake.

We played tennis, and I beat her comfortably. She seemed a little off form, and I was feeling fine and angry; and I hit the ball straight at her as hard as I could, if she dared to come to the net.

On the way back up she said, almost meekly, 'You're still angry with me, aren't you?'

I didn't say anything.

'Johnny,' she said, and stood still. 'I *know* you're angry, and I'm sorry. I really am. You know why I was like that? I sleep real bad, I have nightmares, I hear voices, you know? I get so scared because of Bruno, because sometimes I believe what he says, and I believe he's gonna go nuts, and that one night he's gonna come in and kill me. And you know what I thought?' She lowered her voice to something near a whisper. 'I thought you were *him!*' Then miserably she turned her face away. 'By the time I knew it was you I had started bawling my head off, and then it was too late. I'm sorry.'

My heart was full. 'Oh, Natalie, that's – I don't know what it is. It's mad, and terribly sad that you should think of your brother like that.'

'Yeah, but I really soured things for you – and I didn't mean it.'

She looked up at me, and this time there was no mistaking the message in her eyes: *Kiss me now.* I reached over and touched her cheek with my fingertips, dropped my tennis racket and put my mouth to hers, and her lips melted. I stroked my other hand round her back, but she pulled away unsteadily.

'Hey, let's go for a swim,' she said, smiling to recover herself.

'Natalie, I can't.'

'Come on. There's no one here.'

She took my hand and pulled me up to the house.

'Swimsuits this time, maybe,' she said with a little smile.

We collected them, ran down, and swam.

Afterwards she dried off, pulled a cushion off one of the
chairs, and sat cross-legged on it as we talked of nothing in
particular. Without seeming to make much of it, she slipped
the straps of her one-piece off her shoulders and then rolled it
down carefully over her breasts and her stomach, so that it
rested on her pelvis. Then, as if I wasn't there, she rubbed
herself with oil, and I watched her dark nipples slipping against
her fingers. Then she lay back and sighed.

I was enraged; she was flaunting herself at me, and I was
paralysed. I couldn't sweet-talk her, or kiss her, or stroke her.
So I stood up and turned away.

'See you later,' I said quietly, and walked to the steps.

'Johnny,' she said after a moment – and then again.

But I didn't turn back, and that cost me something, too.

While Bruno was at Schenck's, I went to Laboratoires SOPIC.
It was housed in a red-brick building in gothic style, to which
the good scientists had shown no mercy. There was a pair of
plate-glass doors in the portal at the front, and the interior was
all neon strip lighting and pearl-grey partition walls. I
announced myself to a white-coated receptionist and took a
seat. On the table were fairly recent copies of *Paris Match*, the
New England Journal of Medicine, the *International Journal of
Clinical Chemistry* and other scientific publications. I scanned
one or two impenetrable articles as I waited.

Gaston Bervillier advanced to meet me with hand outstretched. He had a head of thick auburn hair, a long, fine nose
that meandered its way through a series of curves from
forehead almost to chin, and a spectacular moustache teased to
points east and west of his face. His eyes were small and dark.

'*Bonjour*, monsieur . . . ?'

'Halliday.'

'Monsieur Halliday, what can I do for you?'

I hoped that he would be helpful.

'Could we speak for a moment in private, monsieur?'

'Certainly. Come this way.'

There was space for conversations with clients in a small room off the reception area, and we sat down.

'I explained my position to Madame Brudenell, and she suggested that I speak to you, monsieur.' This was not entirely true. I had only told the *notaire* that I needed a substance analysed. I had not told her that it might be a *controlled* substance. But I felt that her name gave me some credibility.

'I have a younger brother, monsieur. I have been looking after him since he was twelve years old, which is when both of our parents were killed. Well . . . he's been in trouble with drugs before now, and he promised me that it was over, that he had stopped. I believed him. Then recently I found some pills in his room. He says that they're from the doctor, but I don't believe him. Monsieur, I want to find out what these pills *are* before I decide what to do. I believe you can analyse them.'

'Certainly, with any chemical product it is quite easy to make an analysis. But don't you think this is a matter for the police, Monsieur Halliday?'

'I . . .' I had thought about this. 'He has already been in trouble with the police. That's one reason I don't want to go to them straightaway. But the other reason is that if I'm wrong, if these are perfectly normal medicines, then he would never trust me again.'

'Hmm.' He reflected for a moment, then said, 'Let me see.'

I got the capsules out and handed them to him. He opened each one gingerly and looked at its contents.

Then he said, abruptly, '*Bon*. We can make an analysis for you. For each of these it will cost 350 francs, plus tax. But I must tell you, monsieur, that if these are controlled substances, we are obliged by law to report them. You understand?'

'Monsieur, if they are controlled substances, *I* will report them, you can be sure. I will take my brother to the police. You can probably understand the difference.'

'OK. I hope that they are not.'

'So do I.'

He stood up. 'If you give your details to Mademoiselle Derelle at the reception, we will send you the results in two or three days.'

'I would much prefer it if I could come in here and hear the results from you direct. I really don't want my brother to find out, and he just might if things are posted to our house. It's very difficult to help people when they become involved in drugs.'

He looked at me very sharply, tutted, sighed and shook his head. 'Well, it's not normal procedure . . .' He paused, gripping his jaw with one hand. 'But come back next Tuesday. Goodbye, monsieur.'

We were back in the reception area by now, and shook hands.

'Goodbye, monsieur. Thank you very much.'

Then I gave my details to Mademoiselle Derelle:

Nom: Halliday, John
Adresse: 8 Residence Belair,
               496 rue Monceau,
               06000 Nice

Mademoiselle Derelle looked at me with great suspicion, and I suddenly had the idea that she was going to challenge my false name.

She said, 'Like the singer?'

'Pardon?'

'You have the same name as our singer, Johnny Halliday?'

'Oh yes,' I said and laughed weakly. So that's where I had got my neat alias. How simple can you get?

I left, hoping that they wouldn't try to contact me before Tuesday.

She knew she had overstepped the mark. But I was determined not to let her ingratiate herself with me. Natalie had flaunted her body at me, but I didn't have to be a slave to that. In mastering my desire for her, I knew I would be halfway to mastering her. She would yield up to me everything she knew, and if anyone helped me to attain Horst's ends, *she* would. Natalie would get my hundred and fifty grand for me.

Marenkian took Bruno to Antibes that night – and she asked me to have dinner with her.

'How about a date, Johnny? A date tonight by candlelight – like the one we had a week ago?' She smirked.

The night you led me up the garden path, you cow? The night you got me ready?

'I haven't got time, Natalie.'

'Oh, come on. I want us to be friends.'

'I haven't got time.'

She leaned back on the counter and then, to my utter amazement, began to cry. She shut her eyes and a big tear rolled down her cheek.

'Oh, Natalie, don't,' I said. She put her hand up to her face. *'Don't.'*

I started to move towards her, to comfort her somehow, but she waved me away, so I stood there helplessly. Then she wiped her eyes, recovering, and looked at me for a moment, intently.

'Will you have dinner with *me*?' I said.

'You haven't given me much respect,' she said quietly, then turned.

'Natalie, please have dinner with me.'

She was silent for a moment, then said, 'OK,' and left the room.

I had done my best to be indifferent to her tears, but it was wasted effort. I wished I had a heart of ice; now, I was even beginning to feel guilty. I started to wonder whether she hadn't been within her rights to throw me out of her room – summon her father, even. Perhaps she had only ever wanted to be friends; perhaps she was lonely here, frustrated with her father's obstructiveness and bored with her shallow young friends.

The truth, though, was that she simply couldn't do without my infatuation. Every woman wants the men in her life on their knees, particularly every young, beautiful, spoilt woman like Natalie. She sensed my indifference, and she didn't like it. Now she would drag me down again, to satisfy her petty vanity and lust for adulation. I could only fight her with indifference, and so continue a conflict which might just end in my screwing her.

One hundred and fifty thousand dollars. I had a job to do now, and she was going to help me. I would be her big brother now, and everything I did would be for her. I wouldn't lay a finger on her; I would listen and nod and smile while she confided, and when she had confided enough for me to give Horst what he wanted, I would screw her up and throw her away. Indifferent? I was one hundred and fifty thousand dollars indifferent.

We ate some delicious king prawns that I had glazed with honey and vinegar, accompanied by slices of aubergine, sweet peppers, and halloumi cheese, all charcoal-grilled. I sat and listened to the crap she talked: her father and the business first, then back to bloody Bruno.

After a while she came out with something new: 'You know he beat up the guy who used to do your job?'

Her gaze was tranquil and level. *Had you? Did he? My predecessor?*

'The guy was an asshole – he deserved it.' She laughed. 'Yeah, the way out of this job's in an ambulance.'

You're a hard-faced bitch.

'But he did worse to himself. He stabbed himself in the stomach one bad morning. You know those little toenail clippers that've got nail files inside them?'

'Yeah.'

'He stabbed himself with one of those. Listen, this was when I took him seriously. Anyone who does that is majorly fucked up.'

'But he's obviously totally unfit to take on the business, and therefore it's natural that *you* should take it on. I don't quite see what alternative your father has.'

'My father thinks that Bruno is going to get better.'

'That the good Dr Schenck is going to cure him?'

'That's right.'

'And do you think he'll manage it?'

'Yeah, I think there's a good chance he will. He's one of the best in the business.'

'Ever thought of going to him yourself?'

'Wondering if it runs in the family, I suppose. Mental illness? It doesn't. Or at least it may do, but it wouldn't matter because Bruno and I are both adopted.'

'Really?'

She suddenly looked surly.

'My real parents are Colombian.'

'Right.' *What? What are you talking about?* 'Do you know them? Have you met them, you know, again? When you were older?'

'No, but I know them. I found a photograph of their house. It's a beautiful, beautiful place: a white house high up in the

mountains above Bogota, surrounded by this lush forest. Full
of wild animals and birds, you know – the colours of those
birds.'

'Did you find the photograph here?'

'Well, no. It's strange, and I know it sounds strange, but I
remember it from before I was taken away, and I saw the
photograph in the *National Geographic*.'

You weird cow.

'I can see you don't believe me and that you think I'm
talking bullshit, but sometimes you can remember. And I
wasn't taken away until I was two, and I *can* remember. It was
incidental that the house was in there; it was a photograph of
an electrical storm, but I knew it was my house.'

'When you were *two*? That's quite late. So Bruno was four?'

'He's not my brother. They picked him up out of the trash.'

I stared at her.

'I'm not saying anything against him,' she said, 'but he's
not my real brother, right, and he doesn't come from my family.
Anyway, that's all part of his problem. He thinks Marenkian
took him away from his real mother, deprived him of – of his
family, of anything normal, and screwed him up, you know.'

'Do you feel that?'

She paused. 'A little.' Then she continued, 'I can remember
that house. It always comes back to me: this big, cool house in
the hills with stone floors and white walls. My mother was
always dressed in these big, loose white dresses, kind of – kind
of crisp and clean. And my father, white too. Linen suits, like
he had just been out at work.'

'What did he do?'

'How could I know? Marenkian won't tell us anything
about it. His story is that it's no good for us to know. I'm
gonna go back.'

I looked up at her.

'I'm gonna go back there and find them. I'm gonna go back

to my country, and I'm not going with a goddam pack on my back. Marenkian will buy my ticket, whether he likes it or not.'

Hispanic, honey-coloured skin, dark hair. I still wanted her.

She stood up and smiled a vague smile, then walked out of the room. I sat there for ten minutes, thinking she had just gone to the loo, but she didn't come back.

I wasn't sure what I could believe. Was she really a cuckoo in this nest? Or was she just another ageing adolescent with teenage grudges and fantasies? What did she think she would do in Colombia? Set herself up as the first-ever drug baroness? And what did she mean about Marenkian? The thought gave me a shiver of excitement – Natalie and I. She could cheat Marenkian, I could cheat Horst – ditch him. We would head off together. I saw her, lying on a bleached, bone-dry teak deck, under my eye, the sun burning, the wind cooling her golden skin.

Natalie and I, partners in crime: stories flew around my head as I lay in bed and began to doze off. In most of them she gave herself to me.

Then I felt a movement, and I woke up and saw her sitting beside me, and my stomach jumped a few feet.

'Hi,' she said very quietly. 'I – I couldn't sleep.'

'Hello,' I said. 'Come in. Make yourself at home.' I glanced at the door. It was closed.

She looked at me with hurt in her eyes.

'Are you scared again?'

She nodded.

Then she said, very quietly, 'Don't be mean to me.'

Now everything was different, completely silent, as if under water, the world above us fathoms away. She knelt on the bed above me. I sat up, and ran my slightly trembling hand along her haunch, slowly pushing her T-shirt up. Her crotch was thrust towards me, and I pulled her until it met my mouth, my hand for a moment on her buttocks, squeezing. She fell back on the bed and brought her knees up above my shoulders, and I went down. And she moaned, and I felt her thighs pressing against my ears and her calves and feet resting on my back, and my tongue slid against her, and then I forced myself free, because she was holding me there, and onto her, and my tongue went into her mouth as far and as hard as I could push it, and in a miracle – it had never happened to me before the first time – I rode into her as far as I could go, and I thrust and she scratched, I twisted myself round and kissed and bit and licked, and she bit my shoulders and got her fingers right in between my legs and she shook, and we came.

After everything she lay in my arms, saying nothing, and when I started to speak she put her finger over my mouth.

Nothing bad was left; she had swept it all away. I lay in that sweet exhaustion that is like nothing else. I had lost myself in her.

Chapter Twelve

'WHAT IS YOUR name?'

'John Marenkian.'

'What is your age?'

'Fifty-four years of age.'

'What is your profession?'

'Attorney-at-law.'

'What is your domicile?'

'4, impasse 8 Mai 1960.'

'Do you know the accused?'

'I do.'

'Can you affirm that you are neither parent nor ally, and that you are not in his service?'

'I can.'

'That nor are you in the service of the civil parties to the case?'

There is a short pause, the formalities over with. Then the judge settles slightly in his chair and continues:

'What is your deposition?'

Marenkian hardly pauses before launching on a fluid and reasonable exposition of the case. I admire, I must say, the efficiency with which he hammers the nails into my coffin. I can see the jury warm to him, regretful, as he seems, that a young man with such promise should have turned out so flawed, that someone he had tried to help had come to such a bad end.

'I took Denner on in September 1991 on the recommendation of a business associate I trusted. I was looking for someone who could cook well, oversee the running of my house, and do some occasional driving work. He seemed completely right for the job, and indeed he started very well. He was a hard worker, his cooking was good, and he approached the running of the house intelligently.

'There was a problem, however, which emerged slowly. He didn't seem able to draw the line between his place as a servant and the way things would have been if he had met my children socially. They're two or three years younger than he is. It's true that his job led him to spend some leisure time with them, particularly as he had to drive my son in and out of Nice on occasion. But I would find that sometimes the dinner wouldn't be on the table because he was fooling around with Bruno and Natalie by the pool – having a swim, playing tennis.

'This would have been OK – I had a word with him about it and he mended his ways, and I thought the problem was over. Then I started to notice something that made me more worried.

'It seemed to me that he was attempting to form an intimate relationship with my daughter, Natalie. She can be a little naïve, and she's young – she was only twenty-two at the time, and obviously I was a little concerned. Particularly when I found him in her bedroom late at night.'

Marenkian pauses a moment and coughs. He affects a slight stoop, and a faintly regretful, melancholy expression, and I suddenly see, knowing the way he's lying, what a superb actor and a superb liar he is. A pathetic figure, this sad, ageing father trying to fend off the sharks circling his gorgeous daughter. A heavy burden for his old shoulders. The jury lap it up, of course, particularly the older ones who are gazing rosily at him as he starts to lay it on really thick.

'You see, I've never wanted to restrict my daughter unnecessarily. And certainly not because of the social standing of any of her suitors. But I was worried about the real motives of this servant. Did he really want to make her happy? Or was he just interested in money? Because all I care about is her happiness.

'After a couple of weeks it became clear that she wasn't interested in him, and I was pretty relieved about that. He went on with his duties as normal and I thought the whole thing was over. The only difference, and I can say this with hindsight, was that he began to seem angry and brooding, but at the time I didn't take much notice. I was very busy; I had a lot of work.

'Then one day he took the car he usually drove, which is a Range Rover, and he drove it down the drive so fast that he actually crashed into the metal gate at the end.'

'We will return to this,' the president interrupted drily. He spent thirty long seconds looking at his notes while the court waited. Then he moved his microphone very slightly and continued.

'Going back to when you first employed Monsieur Denner. What did you know of his background?'

'I knew about his army experience, his background in England, and the fact that he had been skippering a yacht belonging to my business associate for the summer.'

'Did you know that he had been in prison in Spain?'

'No.'

'Did you see any evidence that he took drugs still?'

'Ah – no, not really.'

'But you thought that he had a certain problem with alcohol? You stated to the *juge d'instruction*' – here he read – '"I noticed that he was often drunk. There were occasions that he was ill in the morning and could not serve breakfast, and these followed drinking sessions."'

'He was sometimes drunk, but *often* would be an exaggeration, and it didn't interfere with his work very much. This was also towards the end rather than at the beginning.'

'Did his drunkenness affect his mood?'

'I wouldn't say particularly, although I'd have to say that often I wasn't there, due either to work pending in my office or trips abroad.'

'What made you think that he was developing an intimacy with your daughter?'

'They started to spend time together. At first it was just the occasional game of tennis, then I saw him paying attention to her in the garden. But it was this bedroom incident that got me seriously worried.'

'What did you hear?'

'Her voice. She was asking him to leave.'

'So your daughter was objecting to the fact that he had come to her bedroom at night.'

'Yes, very much so.'

'Did he have any reason for being there?'

'The reason he gave was that he had heard intruders.'

'Did you believe him?'

'Not really.'

'Was he drunk at the time?'

'I believe he had been drinking, yes.'

'Later did you have any reason to believe that he might have succeeded in forming an intimate relationship with your daughter?'

'No. In fact, I'm quite sure that he did not succeed.'

'Why are you sure?'

'Because of his anger, later. Because she threw him out of her room. At this time she stopped playing tennis with him. She also promised me that nothing was happening between them.'

'What did you think were his motives regarding your daughter?'

'I was a little concerned that they might have to do with money. I felt that he was taking an unhealthy interest in my financial affairs. I discovered that he had been asking various friends of my son what kind of money there was in the family. And I knew that someone had gotten into my office and had been disturbing confidential papers, although I have no way of proving who it was. But I'm always very cautious where my daughter is concerned.'

The judge pauses, and there is silence for a moment.

'Monsieur Denner, please stand up.'

I stand.

'You have heard what Monsieur Marenkian has said about your conduct of the job and your bearing towards his daughter. Is what he has said true and accurate?'

'Some of it is true, but it is not accurate. It didn't happen the way he describes it.'

'Is it true that you attempted to form an intimate relationship with Natalie Marenkian?'

'No. We were quite friendly towards each other, and we played tennis quite regularly, but there was nothing intimate about our relationship.'

'Did you make enquiries about Monsieur Marenkian's finances or business affairs?'

'No, not at all.'

He shuffles through his papers.

'I have a deposition here from Philip Goodwin, in which he says' – the president bows his head to read – '"Denner was certainly very interested in Marenkian's financial affairs. He always seemed to want to know how much Marenkian had, and where it came from. He asked me about it on several occasions." Is this true?'

'No, it's not true.'

'Philip Goodwin's statement, then, is false.'

'No, it's not false. It's—'

'It's either true or false.'

'It's an exaggeration. I gossiped with him on one occasion out of curiosity, but no more than anyone else would have done.'

The president stares at me dispassionately for my impertinence, then states drily, almost ironically, 'An exaggeration,' and makes a little note.

How dare he say that? It's either true or false! Court cases would be pretty easy if it were that black and white. He knows the shades of half-truth and qualification that it all rests on.

'Were you frequently drunk?'

'No, I was not.'

'Monsieur Marenkian's statement that you were often drunk is false, then?'

'Yes, it is.'

'He is lying.'

'He is mistaken.'

'Is it true that you had an intimate relationship with Natalie Marenkian?'

'No. As I say, we were just on friendly terms. We enjoyed playing tennis together. There was nothing intimate about it.'

'Did you attempt to have an intimate relationship with her?'

'No.'

'Not even when you went to her room at night?'

'No. I had heard noises and I thought there might be an intruder in the house.'

I don't look at the jury, and I don't need to look. I know what they believe.

'Thank you, Monsieur Denner. You may sit.'

*

At breakfast I smiled at her from behind her father and bared my teeth to make her smile. She smiled, and I had to wipe my face clean when he turned to look at me. You'd like that, wouldn't you, Marenkian, after what you said to me? All right, I haven't tried to take her away; I've just had her, here, and I'll have her again right under your nose, and we'll cheat you at the end of it.

I couldn't betray her. I had been certain about that from my first sight of her after the meeting with Horst and my stupid agreement with him. How could I have made that agreement? How could I have been so shortsighted? So I did something really very naïve: I removed the finger-thick bundle of hundred-dollar bills from the stoneware jar of dried beans in which I had kept it, pocketed it, and went to keep an appointment I had made only that morning. I was going to go and see Horst and extricate myself from my commitment.

In that dark corridor I experienced a small crisis of nerve, and I had to force myself to raise my hand to the plain hardwood door and knock on it weakly. Yari opened the door to me, and stood aside to let me walk down the corridor to the main part of the room, his eye meeting mine for a moment, the lids no less livid, the pupils glazed and indifferent.

Horst was bouncing around the room.

'So, Johnny, this is quick. We have something to say already? That's very good.'

'Ha-ha.' A nervous laugh that sounded stupid.

'Sit down, tell me about it.'

I sat, and waited while he followed suit. Yari stood by the window.

'Well, Horst, I have to be honest with you. I'm very sorry about this, but I've come here to tell you that I didn't really mean what I said at our last meeting. You're not going to like this, I know, but . . .' I reached into my pocket during the lame pause that followed, pulled out the ten thousand and put it on the table. 'The thing is, he mistrusts me already. The first thing he said when I got back to the house—'

'What are you talking about?'

'Marenkian. The first thing he said was—'

'I don't want to hear about fucking Marenkian. What the fuck are you talking about?'

Yari half-turned from the window and spoke into his clenched fist, which he held up to his face like a microphone.

'I didn't come here to hear this *shit*!' he said.

'OK, Yari.'

'I didn't come here to hear this shit to this goddam town.'

'Shut up, Yari. You're doing just fine. You're having a nice time.' Yari turned back to the window, and Horst turned to me.

'What are you doing? *What* are you doing? Are you trying to back out of our agreement?'

'Well, Horst, I just don't think it's going to—'

'One hundred and fifty thousand dollars a year, and the chance to double it.' Suddenly he grimaced as if at a twinge of pain. 'Yari, if you want to do something useful you could get me some Pepto-bismol. Listen to me. This is the opportunity of your life. OK, you're getting some cold feet. You're wondering about the honesty of what I'm asking, you're wondering about whether it's safe to get involved. The profit in this is immense. It's not strictly honest, but you see Marenkian has stolen from me, from his other clients.' I raised my eyebrows. 'Oh, God, *yes* – you don't think I haven't got a right to this, do you? You don't think he hasn't got it coming to him? I don't understand you,' he said, quietly. 'Are you timid, is that what it is?'

'No, not at all. I just don't think it's—'

'I'm not asking you to betray anything you believe in. To betray anything important. I'm being cheated by a criminal, and I'm asking you to help, and to pay you far more than the job is worth. And I'm offering you a place in my organization. God, I'm disappointed in you.'

Yari had come back, and stood looking at me with that troubled expression people wear when they're about to hit you.

'Horst, it's just a question of the practicality of the thing. What I was trying to tell you was that when I come back from my meeting with you he pulled me in again and more or less accused me of having ulterior motives; it's back to this Natalie thing. I mean, I tell you, Horst, he suspects me. I'm not even allowed into his office. And I feel that in those circumstances I can't take your money.'

'You leave me to worry about that. Johnny, that ten thousand is your first pay cheque. You don't have to produce something in exchange for it. OK, so maybe things will take a bit longer, maybe they're a bit more difficult. That's fine.'

'I just don't think it'll work.'

'Or maybe you're just bullshitting me, huh?' He cocked his head. 'Coming up with all these practical objections where there are other reasons?' My stomach chilled a little. 'Maybe you thought you could do this independently of me, huh? Do the job for yourself. Don't try it, because you would end up dead. I'm not saying *I* would kill you. But you would end up dead.' He paused again. 'No. No, it's not that, is it? It's because really you are an English gentleman, and you just haven't got the stomach for it.'

'No, no, that's *not* it.'

'It's just because you don't think you can do it?'

'That's right.'

'Well, Johnny, you let me worry about that, OK? You do what you can. You try. And if it doesn't work out, and you don't get everything I need, that's too bad. I'm not gonna mind.'

'I can't. I'm so sorry. I can't.'

'You're telling me you're not even going to try?'

'I'd be wasting your money.'

'I already told you about that,' he said, and his anger was slipping through.

'I know, I just . . .' I tailed off. I could see that I had taken the wrong line.

'I treated you like a king. I gave you a chance when you had come out of prison, and you had nothing. I gave you my lovely *Margherita*. Huh? I gave you a break. And these people have treated you like shit. But you won't even keep an agreement you've made with me. It's really out of line.'

Yari walked over and sat down on the sofa next to me, leaning forward, his face a few inches from mine.

'You listen to me now,' Yari said. 'We've got an agreement to get what is coming to us, and you are not *fucking getting out of it*. You understand me? So shut up with this. You've got two weeks.'

Then he returned to his place by the window, and there was silence.

Horst looked at me reproachfully for a while, then said, 'You see, that's business. You can't just change your mind and let people down, you know?'

I could see the way the land lay. It had indeed been naïve of me to believe I could extricate myself that easily.

'Of course I understand. I was being pretty foolish. But I thought you wouldn't want to invest this kind of money in a project that seems to me to have such a slim chance of success. You see what I mean? Whereas if you're prepared to take that risk, then of course I'm still very happy to help you.'

'Of course,' he said, and made a cold smile at me. Why had I been so stupid?

He picked up the bundle of notes and handed them to me. I stood up and he said, 'We will hear from you in five days.'

Yari, a very slight smirk on his face, preceded me down the

narrow corridor and placed his hand on the doorknob. But as I drew level with him he whipped it away, and with remarkable speed and accuracy grabbed my balls. Then he put his face up to mine and squeezed slightly, and I practically swallowed my tongue, more with shock than pain, although a freezing ache spread up my torso. I stood on tiptoe, my legs rigid.

'Got a fucking agreement, so get our fucking property.' His breath smelled of mint. 'Don't mess me up, or I'll come looking for you, and I'll put these' – and he squeezed them and it hurt, and I yelped – 'down your fucking throat.'

He let go of me, looked at his thick hand, then put it gently on my face, pressed my mouth for a second with his thumb, and turned away. I was very frightened, and disgusted.

As I waited for the lift my legs began to shake so badly I thought I would fall. I steadied myself by feeling the money in my pocket, but it didn't help much. Ten thousand? For the trouble I was getting myself into?

I was still shaking when I got to Laboratoires SOPIC. I sat in the reception area wondering what I thought I was doing, and just how this was supposed to help me extricate myself from the clutches of Horst and his psychopathic friend. That makes me laugh, I lied to myself: Horst claiming that Marenkian is a gangster. His little enforcer is like something out of a TV movie – grabbing me by the balls. I was still shaken.

Bervillier looked grave, and fearlessly honest.

'Monsieur Halliday, this is a serious problem that you have with your brother. The first substance that you have asked us to analyse is simply a tranquillizer, and so it is possible that it came from a doctor. It is a prescription drug. But the other, well, it is a little bizarre. Special. It is a mixture of an amphetamine and lysergic acid diethylamide, LSD.'

'I see.'

'This is very strange to me, I must say, and it is very serious for your brother, because this is a dangerous combination. Potentially very bad for him and, of course, against the law. It will have to be reported to the police.'

'Yes, I suppose it will,' I said slowly. Then I paused, and tried to make my tone appealing.

'Monsieur, I would like my brother to go to the police himself. I think that then he would be treated better.'

He raised an eyebrow.

'Well, I don't know whether this will be possible.'

'The thing is, I want him to give up the drug habit, and I feel he's much more likely to do that if *he* can go to the police. And perhaps they will be more lenient. And if I turn him over to them, he'll never forgive me.'

I was worried that Bervillier would call the police there and then, and I probably played my part quite well. As the man who had not foreseen the laboratory's legal obligation to notify a controlled substance.

'I must admit, I didn't quite foresee this.'

'I warned you, monsieur,' he said. 'You see that here on the Côte d'Azur there are people who are involved in drugs, and it is important for any laboratory not to be involved with them. Do you realize that in Nice we have a drug problem more serious per head than does Paris?'

'You said that you found this drug strange?' *I* certainly did. What kind of a treatment was speed and acid combined?

'I do find it bizarre. I also do some work for the investigating magistrates here, and this sometimes involves illegal drugs. And you have probably heard of designer drugs, which are a mixture of different substances. But there is only a little LSD in this pill. I cannot see that it would be a good experience for the person who took it.'

'Why?'

'Because LSD is a hallucinogenic drug and, for it to work,

a certain quantity is needed. With less than that quantity there is a – simply a sensation of disorientation. And the amphetamine acts as an excipient. That means that it enhances the effect of what accompanies it.'

'Is it at all possible that a psychotherapist could have given him these pills? He does go to a psychotherapist.'

'A psychotherapist?' Bervillier repeated, astonished at the suggestion. 'Certainly not. There are no circumstances in which a psychotherapist would give him these.'

'I see.'

'Do you know where he might have got them?'

'I don't, I'm afraid.'

'Well, I will make my report to the police at the end of the day, so you will be able to contact them now, if you wish. I am sorry that it only gives you two hours, but that is as much as I can do.'

'Thank you, Monsieur Bervillier.' Then he wrote something on a piece of paper and handed it to me.

'You should call Madame Cochourd. She is the investigating magistrate who deals with many drugs cases. I think that would be better than calling the police.'

'Thank you very much.'

I stood, shook hands, paid Mademoiselle Derelle, and left. Much to my surprise, I had discovered something.

I foresaw trouble, it was true, although the trouble I foresaw was not the trouble I eventually landed up in. If I took the bearer certificates – always assuming that was possible – Marenkian would know about it and he'd come after me. How much did I have to worry about him? So he was a gangster's lawyer; how dangerous did that make him? If I gave the certificates to Horst, would he bother to protect me? Would he really have any more use for me? I didn't entirely believe his pitch about a classy frontman for his investment activities. Would he even bother to pay me? But if I gave him nothing, Yari might take a course of action that involved my balls.

Natalie and I could take the certificates, go to Colombia together to find her family and their coca fields in the mountains, if that was what she had in mind, or any other mad scheme. I didn't care. I adored her with an unquestioning, complete adoration that I revelled in, a great, soft feather bed of lust and love into which I had thrown myself after one of my longest days. I couldn't leave. I couldn't go back to England.

I would confide in her; that was the first step. Carefully. I might have to edit the truth a little, but I could tell her something of Horst and his ambitions, and his desire for the information that would give him leverage over Marenkian. Information that she and I could cook up together – that was how my plan went; that in league with each other, we would palm off Horst with promises, take his money, and go. Take Marenkian's shares too. Take everything – why not? There was everything to lose.

I arrived at the little restaurant near the port, bursting with excitement. I had it all worked out.

There's nothing in the world like rushing to meet the girl you're in love with; nothing can make you feel so fresh, so completely alive, full to overflowing with joy. She smiled when she saw me, smiled from the shadows of the little table at the back. I sat down and she took my hand, and we enquired after each other's health, and she told me about the shopping she had been doing that morning, and showed me a little sequinned dress she had bought. It wasn't until later that I steered the conversation towards business.

'I think I can help you with your father. We know he thinks Bruno represents a threat to his business. He's worried about that. Now, just say you identified what the threat was: you found out who was trying to influence Bruno, and why. Maybe you even put a stop to it.'

She wrinkled her nose.

'This is a bit far-fetched, isn't it?'

'No, no, not at all. Hey, would you like some more wine?'

'No – well, maybe a glass.'

I called the waiter and ordered another bottle.

'Listen. I think I know something about this. Max Schenck – just what the hell is he doing with Bruno? Bruno comes back from his appointments with that guy practically unable to walk. And he's getting worse, not better.'

'So?'

'Well, who's the most likely person to be manipulating Bruno?'

'You're suggesting Max Schenck? Don't be stupid. The guy's a psychotherapist, and Bruno confides everything in him anyway – and so do his other clients. That's what happens when you go into analysis.'

'Yeah, but in your father's business information is money, isn't it? Just like in stockbroking or banking.'

'Sure. But forget any theories about Bruno and Schenck. He's devoted to Bruno, and to Bruno's recovery. There's no way he'd do anything to mess it up.'

'So why is Bruno getting worse?'

'Other factors. So he *has* got a little worse. Then again, without Max he'd probably be ten times worse still. You can't measure that. Anyway,' she said, 'none of that helps me. I don't want to win my father's trust.'

'No?'

'I'm interested in getting what I want, and getting out of here. Getting what *belongs* to me, my fucking inheritance, my reward for being stuck in this cage. I'm gonna take what I need and get out. Not too much – just what I need to get started. I can do it. I can get away with it. If I don't take too much, he won't come after me.'

Yes! I could have jumped up and hugged her. She was talking about cheating him.

'Wow.' I leaned back in my chair. 'You're serious, aren't you?'

'Very serious, Johnny. Completely serious.'

'How are you going to do it?'

'There are ways, technical ways. It's really a question of having the right information and certain documentation.'

'Well, well. And do you have both?'

'I have most of what I need.'

'Most but not all, eh?'

'Listen, Johnny-come-lately, why don't you just put away your insatiable curiosity?'

'Because you and me can be partners, babe.'

'I doubt it. What have you got to offer me?'

'You might just use me for sexual favours.'

'I don't need favours.'

'I do, though.'

'Johnny, you're a gentleman. You're an English gentleman. You know about as much about my world as I do about yours, i.e. fuck all.'

'You'd be amazed.'

'I would be amazed.'

I was a little stung by all this.

'The pills Bruno's been taking,' I said. 'You know he has two different kinds.'

She sighed.

'This again? Why don't you leave it?'

'No, I have some real hard evidence that something strange is going on. Those pills – I took one of each from his room.'

'You did *what*?'

'I took one of each from his room, and I took them to a

commercial laboratory to get them analysed. Look, one set of pills is a perfectly normal tranquillizer that you might expect to find in the circumstances. But the other is a mixture of speed and acid.'

'What . . . what are you talking about? This is ridiculous.'

'Oh, there's no doubt about it. Look.'

I pulled the green form from my pocket and handed it to her. She looked for a minute with a furrowed brow, then handed it back.

'OK,' she said. 'So it's a mixture of speed and acid, not that you could tell from what's on here. So?'

'So? Well, it seems potentially pretty counterproductive to me to give somebody *that* combination of drugs. It's illegal. And the guy who did the tests told me it couldn't be normal psychiatric practice.'

'Maybe it's some kind of new treatment. Some kind of innovation.'

'I find that very hard to believe. Have you ever done acid?'

'No.'

'I did in Spain. I don't know how to describe this in scientific terms. The hallucinogenic properties of the drug are one thing. But with a lot of people it also seems to be affected by their current mood, so that if you're in a bad mood, or feeling vulnerable, don't take it – because it'll make you much worse. In fact you'll have a bad trip. I mean, I can't imagine a worse thing to give to someone who's unstable emotionally.'

'Maybe with the speed it would be OK.'

I laughed. 'Really? Do you really believe that?'

'I don't know,' she said, with some irritation. My God, she took some convincing.

'Speed is a – what do you call it? – the labman used the word – an excipient,' I went on. 'I think it would accentuate the effect of the acid. But then Schenck is throwing in a few tranquillizers as well, so who knows? I also heard that LSD was originally developed for use in battle – to disorientate the enemy. But listen, this is serious, and *not* above-board, and no one's going to tell me it is.'

She gazed ahead, distracted.

'Could the chemist have got it wrong?'

'You don't want to accept this, do you?'

'What do *you* think?'

'Why not?'

'Well, isn't it obvious?'

I didn't answer.

'I mean you know how I feel about my father, anyway,' she eventually continued, 'so I should be the last to care, but if this is what he's doing then it's just sick. That he could do this to Bruno. Who the fuck does he think he is? Bruno would be better off with nothing, with no money, but with his sense intact. I don't know what we can do. I just don't know what we can do.'

'You're saying that Marenkian is behind it?'

'Of course he is. It's just a kind of restraint. It'd be useless to say anything to him, because he's responsible.'

'Anyway, he'd want to know what I did to discover this, and why I did it.'

'Why?'

'What?'

'Why are you doing this?'

'Natalie, I did it for you, because I love you, and I want us to be in this together, and I want to help you get what you want.'

'Don't. You're interfering in things you know nothing about.'

'I know a lot more than you think.'

'Well, leave it at that.'

But I couldn't do that.

'Did you know we have a rival?' I said gaily.

'What are you talking about?'

'OK, forget about Bruno. We'll leave him out of this.' I had the ten thousand in my pocket, and I pulled it out and slapped it on the table.

She picked it up and said, 'Jesus, what have you been doing?'

'Oh, that's a payment in advance. A gift, you might call it, actually. Considering I haven't agreed to do anything for the guy.'

'Who?'

I raised my eyebrows.

'Come on,' she said, very aggressively, almost shouted.

'Horst.'

'So you've got what – ten thousand?' she said contemptuously, flicking through the notes – 'belonging to Horst Stacker. Why?'

'Intelligence on your father's household. And, more than anything else, the location of his bearer shares.'

'Why did you take it?'

'So we can give him false information and take the shares ourselves.'

She paused, fixed me with her eyes. 'How do you know about those?'

'You told me.'

'I did not.'

'Yes, you did. When we were by the pool, you explained to me the structure of his business, and the use he makes of various offshore systems.'

'But I never mentioned bearer shares.'

'Well, give me some credit, then.'

'I didn't say I was going to take his shares.'

'You said you were going to take something, and we can safely assume it's not going to be his cuff links.' I chuckled. The wine had got the better of me for a moment.

'You . . .' She narrowed her eyes. 'You're living in the

clouds, you know that? You're living some kind of fantasy. Do you really think you can just take Horst's money and not do anything for it? Jesus, you're stupid.'

'Hang on a minute.'

'No, you fucking hang on here, because I know what I'm talking about. Don't you understand that if you take some-body's money you're signing a contract?'

'A contract that I don't intend to honour.'

'You will *have* to honour it. He's a powerful man, and he'll come after you if you don't. That's what makes the world go round, honey. If Horst Stacker lets people see that an amateur Brit can rip him off, they'll be crawling over him in a day.'

'I'm not going to rip him off. He's asked me to do something, and I'm not going to do it for him. I thought you would be interested to know about it.'

'Listen, I tell you, Horst is a non-starter. He's a dog sniffing around for a scrap. He thinks Marenkian has lost his touch – and he's right – so he's moving in. Looking for an opening. But he won't find one, because no matter how much Marenkian has lost his touch, he's still more than a match for Horst.'

'And Schenck? You're telling me he's just the shrink.'

'Just stay out of it,' she said. 'Just stay right out of it. I have to go. You shouldn't get involved in any of this.' She stood up. There was no mistaking the coldness of her tone. 'Take my advice. Just leave it alone.'

'Let's go back.'

'No, I have to go somewhere.' There was a look on her face that shut me up. She looked disgusted.

'Listen, I'm only trying to help,' I said.

'Sure.'

She turned and left the empty restaurant, and I sat down and took a slug of wine. It seemed as though I had played things rather badly.

I got back to the house in time to take Marenkian to the

airport. There was the usual calm preparation, and he strolled down to his office for the last time as I brought his spotless black suitcases down the stairs. As he was on his way, the phone rang.

'Marenkian residence.'

'Denner, you know who this is. Go down to the Meridien, Wednesday, seven p.m.'

'I can't talk now, and I can't make seven.' That's only two days.

'Eight p.m.'

'That's only two days.'

'I'll call you.'

'Eight p.m., Wednesday, you fuck.'

Don't let him think you're nervous.

'I can't talk now. I'll call you later.'

I put the phone down. I was in trouble.

Chapter Thirteen

WHILE MARENKIAN was away, Natalie disappeared, and I looked after Bruno cautiously.

He was looking terrible. There were dark smudges under his eyes and a ragged three-day growth of stubble. He had withdrawn himself from proceedings; he wore a furious scowl that seemed to deepen every day, his lumpy forehead protruding further and further over his deep-set eyes. They didn't glow now; they were dull and glazed. Occasionally I saw them following me, and I wondered whether Natalie had spoken to him. Tonight I would find out. She would come back and talk to me; she had to talk to me.

Half an hour after his return Marenkian called me down to his office.

'Somebody's been in here,' he said, and from the way he said it I could tell that in his mind I was the likeliest candidate.

'I'm not aware of anyone—'

'I'm not aware,' he said sarcastically. 'Who's been coming to the house?'

'Nobody – apart from myself, Claudine, Monsieur Pierre, Bruno. It's really been very quiet.'

'So, Bruno's been out seeing people? And you've been driving him, because that's your job, right?'

'No, he's stayed here. He told me he didn't want to go out.'

'So, he's had people here? Friends?'

I shook my head. 'Nobody.'

'Come on, Johnny, you can tell me.'

'Really, I promise you, Mr Marenkian – nobody's been here.'

Natalie, you clever bitch, you've been in his office, haven't you?

'That doesn't make things look very good for you, does it?' he said menacingly.

'I haven't been in here, Mr Marenkian,' I said. 'I give you my word of honour.'

He was silent for several seconds, holding my eye.

'Someone has been in this office,' he growled. There was a deliberate, repressed violence in his tone that chilled me. 'I will find out who it is. If it isn't someone from outside the household, it must be someone from inside. If I change the code, the card won't work.'

What? Oh, I get it.

'Mr Marenkian, I have not been in this office, I promise you. I have no idea about codes and cards.'

There was a moment of silence, then the tension passed.

'OK, Johnny. As a matter of fact there isn't a code on the door. But I know about Horst Stacker's interest in my affairs.' My stomach turned over, and I devoted everything to keeping my face blank. Did he know? 'And he is out of his depth. If you see him, Johnny, you can tell him that. You can tell him that he is way out of his depth. He comes to you with any propositions, don't touch them. Understand?'

'Yes, I do,' I said.

'You can go.'

While I was down there, she had come back. She was in her room. I went up there and shut the door.

'He knows you've been in his office.'

'What?'

'He knows you've been in his office.'

She had a shirt in her hand which she dropped on the bed.

'I have *not* been in his office.'

'Somehow, I don't know how, he knows that someone has been in his office during his absence. He's just been interrogating me about it.'

'Well, I *haven't* been in his office.'

'Come on, Natalie.'

'How dare you?' she snarled. She literally snarled at me; her mouth was twisted and her eyes furious. 'How dare you imply that I'm some kind of sneak thief in my own house?'

'I'm not implying anything. You told me about your plans.'

'What plans?'

'To take your father's money.'

'That's bull. I didn't tell you anything.'

'And you didn't sleep with me either.'

'I told you about my frustrations here and the hopes I had of working with my father. And if you thought I meant anything else, I'm sorry that you misunderstood me.'

I watched her for about thirty seconds, weighing up what to say next.

Eventually I just said, 'OK,' and turned on my heel and left the room.

She left the house, came back a day later. I decided to pretend nothing was wrong when I encountered her in the corridor.

'Come up and see me tonight?'

She looked at me and narrowed her eyes. 'Yeah, sure. I have to go to Nice tonight, so it might be late.'

'Any time.'

'OK.'

I touched her arm. 'I want you now.'

'Hey, don't,' she said, and shook my hand off. 'Do you know what will happen if my father finds out about us? Or if Bruno finds out?'

'Yeah, I know.'

'Just leave it lay, OK?' Then she turned and went.

I knew from the movies what the sexual dealings between servant and mistress should be: he brutish, feral; the pampered girl his victim-plaything; his careless, calloused hands bruising her silky flesh. She the flower of her rich hothouse; he a dog from the gutter. He would be the villain of the piece, not her! She was the bitch, hot between the legs, picking me up when it pleased her, then dropping me, calling the shots. And now? She was bored with this weak-willed, passive Englishman. Perhaps someone was already taking my place in satisfying her demands.

That night she didn't come. And this wasn't just a matter of love, or even lust; I needed her help to deal with Horst. She was my partner now.

The next day she came down late, in a swimsuit tight as a second skin. She looked up at me mildly, and I stood staring at her.

'Some fresh coffee?'

'Sure.'

'OK.' I fetched the coffee and brought it back. Then I stood there again, awkward all of a sudden.

'Did you sleep well?' I asked.

'Uh-huh,' she said. We stared at each other a little longer, and then she turned to go. There seemed to be nothing to say.

'You said you'd come to me.'

'I felt strange.'

'Strange?' I tried to keep the irritation out of my voice, the pleading irritation, petulance. 'You should keep your appointments with the doctor.'

'Really? Is this a rule of the house?' She didn't smile.

'Sorry?'

'Oh, you're apologizing.'

'I took you seriously. Why didn't you come?'

'Listen, I don't have time for this bandying.' She walked

across the room towards the French windows, a pale blue towel thrown over her bronzed shoulders.

Then it became difficult even to speak to her; I couldn't seem to catch her alone. I knew she was avoiding me, and there was nothing I could do. It was very difficult.

A day later she said to Marenkian: 'I'm going to meet the Spanish crowd at La Napoule.'

'When will you be back?'

'Dunno. I might stay there if they've got a bed. Don't wanna drink and drive.'

'OK. You be good, now.'

'Am I ever anything else?' she said, and turned on her heel, swinging her bag.

She didn't come back that night. I heard the beat of her stereo in the drive at about seven the next evening. I was out on the terrace serving drinks to Bruno, Marenkian and a French couple. She was introduced to the Frenchman and his wife, and then threw herself into one of the seats.

'God, I'm exhausted.'

'Would you like a drink?' I asked.

'Oh sure, thanks. Can you give me a beer.'

'You should have called to let us know whether to expect you for dinner. At least to let Johnny know.'

'Oh, yeah,' she said, and then smiled sweetly at me. 'I'm sorry, Johnny.'

'Don't worry,' I said. 'There's plenty for everybody.'

'Oh, good.'

'How was La Napoule?' I heard Marenkian ask as I climbed the steps, but I could hardly hang about to hear her answer. She was ditching me. I couldn't believe it; a night in the sack and she was ditching me. It couldn't be true.

When I went in with the coffee I made a blunder. Marenkian had taken Bruno to the other side of the living room to look at some photographs, and I thought I could safely whisper to Natalie:

'I've got to talk to you.'

She pursed her lips. 'No.'

She turned away, and Marenkian and Bruno turned around, as if they sensed something untoward, and for a moment stared at us.

After I had cleared the dining table I sat in the kitchen thinking about something: in the army they used to call me Double-O, and I would pretend to be flattered, because at that time I was obsessed with Ian Fleming and James Bond. I had every one of the books; I had read them all several times. What they meant, though, was that I was a fantasist, a mediocrity who wanted to make an adventure of his dull life. And it was true that I used to spin a starting pistol round my finger, and genuflect for the kill. I wondered whether that wasn't what I was doing now.

So it was a dismal evening that I dragged out with the help of whisky, in the kitchen, until finally I felt numbed enough to sleep. I trudged up to my room, shut the door and reached up to undo my shirt. I suddenly knew that I was exhausted.

A dark shape flew into my field of vision, and at the same moment I felt the blow of a fist on my forehead. My head cracked back against the door. A very sharp pain that soon disappeared. And momentary darkness, probably because I closed my eyes. I almost fell over. In fact, I think the bastard practically knocked me out.

Naturally it was Bruno, but I had never expected him to lie in wait. There should have been a build-up, there should have been a scene; it should have happened in front of the family. But I had no time to brood about that. I had half fallen over, then recovered my balance somewhere to the left of the door.

Snarling, his little eyes dull, his face bright red, he lunged at me again slowly, and I just managed to get away from him. He grabbed my shirt around the shoulder, but as quickly lost hold of it and fell back on the bed.

'Bruno, what are you doing?' I said.

'You fuck,' he whispered. In one motion he pushed himself up off the bed and came at me, swinging a fist. I managed to push him off, and he almost fell.

'Bruno, stop doing this,' I said.

But he came at me again, and this time his fist hit me full on the side of the head, just above the ear. I was really shaken, and deafened.

Then he said, again, 'You fuck,' and shook me by the shoulders, before slamming me against the door.

I was in trouble: disorientated, my head numb. I thought: *Surely Marenkian will hear this and come along?* When I looked at Bruno again, he had his fist raised behind his shoulder, ready to smash into my face. I knew that if he hit me again I would be making a last-minute booking at the Nice casualty department.

I had a bit of luck. Just as his great ham fist came for me, I twisted away. It brushed the side of my temple and hit the solid wood of the door – an expensive, well constructed door – with a resounding crack. That fist had been travelling fast.

He gave an almost childish, high-pitched cry of pain and backed away a pace, holding his injured fist in the other. I breathed hard and my senses sharpened. There was something comical about the way he clutched his hand, his face contorted with pain. I felt a sudden rage at the thought of how hard he had been trying to hit me, and I kicked him in the balls and scored a direct hit. He doubled up, started making a strange coughing noise, like a cat with furballs, and collapsed on the floor.

And then, I'm afraid to say, I kicked him in the stomach, to obviate the risk of his making an early recovery.

I felt flushed with triumph for a moment, breathing hard,

my heart beating furiously. Then I started to feel dizzy and faint, and I had to sit – and then lie – on the bed. I could hear Bruno making groaning noises on the floor. I expected my head to start hurting, but it didn't.

After a few minutes I sat up and looked at him. He was still doubled up, his hands in his crutch. I must say I then felt a strange sensation: an affection for him, a desire to comfort him, show him that I had nothing against him.

'Bruno . . .' I said, and I had to catch my breath as if I had just completed a long run, 'Bruno, I don't know what you thought when you came in here, but you're wrong. I'm on *your* side, I promise you. I'm not trying to do anything that – anything to harm you.'

He ignored me. Perhaps he couldn't speak, perhaps he was winded.

'Are you all right?'

No response. Jesus, what had I done to him? If he was badly injured I would be in trouble.

'Are you seriously hurt?'

After a while he shook his head. Thank God for that.

'I've got no reason to harm you.'

Then I felt quite ill, and I had to lie down again, and we must have stayed in our respective positions for about twenty minutes this time, or even half an hour. I wondered what to do with him. He couldn't just lie on my bedroom floor all night. Not a proper employer–servant relationship. I got up.

'Bruno?' I said. There was no response. 'Look, you can't stay here. Bruno, you can't stay here.'

He groaned and used his favourite word a few times, then there was silence. Out in the street we would have been taken for a pair of drunks.

I pulled at his arm and said, 'Come on, get up. Go back to your room, for Christ's sake.'

Then, much to my surprise, he did get up, still groaning,

and turned towards the door. I followed at a safe distance – you can never tell – then he turned and surprised me again, not by getting violent, but by saying, 'You don't understand . . . You don't understand how terrible this is . . . Oh, shit.'

He turned and went. He was clearly on the verge of tears.

Pain woke me up earlier than my alarm would have, and I lay there with a stiff jaw, a painfully bruised back, a head that growled and threatened every time I moved it. I felt as though I had an indescribably bad hangover, much worse than even the previous night's whisky merited. I probably had a mild concussion: I felt slightly nauseous. It seemed to me that I was going to find it very difficult to get up.

But there were good reasons that I couldn't stay in bed. One was the uncertainty of my place in the house after a fight with Bruno. I supposed now that it was true that he had beaten up my predecessor. He had done a good job on me too; although I had won the battle he had probably inflicted more damage on me than I on him. Would he tell his father? Would it matter if he did? It seemed possible that he might also stay in bed sick, although the bastard usually slept until lunchtime anyway. It also occurred to me that lying in bed might not make me feel any better. Even during those few minutes after I had woken up I could feel the bruises on my back, and I didn't want to put my weight on them any longer. I dragged myself out of bed and looked in the mirror. It was the usual morning face, with one exception: the right side had a patch of bright red, as though burned.

The previous night's violence had left me feeling fearful and disgusted. But I also had a sense of power, strength, satiated lust – I don't really know what. It filled me with something, made me bunch up my muscles and grin at myself in the mirror. The memory of my violence strengthened me. I could see how people became devoted to it.

I washed, dressed, and went downstairs. There was nobody around, so I made a lot of strong coffee, drank some of it and left the rest in a thermos, laid the table, took some painkillers, then got the car out and went into Valbonne.

There is a stretch a mile or two before the town where the road sweeps down through woodlands used by the locals for weekend picnics. There are broad verges for them to park their cars, and little tracks under the trees. I was taking the drive slowly, trying to think, unconscious of the late autumn colours, when a broad grey saloon jumped into my rear-view mirror as if from nowhere, then gunned its engine furiously and started to pull past. *Bloody maniac*, I muttered to myself, and turned to stare at him as he went by.

Yari sat in the back seat, looking not at me but at the road ahead. Then he appeared to point and say something to the driver, who cut in front of me and then slammed on his brakes. It happened so suddenly that I hit the verge, skidded and bumped along it for thirty yards, then swerved to a halt at an angle to the road and stalled the engine. *Horst and Yari!* My stomach practically hit my tonsils as I sat behind the wheel, panting. Was it two days since he had called? Three? *Oh, my God.*

By the time I had got my hand to the ignition key and my foot on the clutch, Yari had hopped neatly out of the big Peugeot. He wore an expression of faint distaste.

'Out,' he said. I complied; he got in, turned the Range Rover round and parked it neatly.

While he did that I went over to Horst, who had stepped out of the other car.

'Horst, what the hell's going on?'

'Don't speak to me like that. Shut up, and speak when you're told.'

I did shut up. I was frightened.

Yari swept up behind me and grabbed my wrist.

'Come on, honey,' he said, and walked on, dragging me along behind. He was phenomenally strong; I didn't really try to break his grip, but it didn't falter. Horst walked behind us, and after him came the young local who had driven.

I could feel something digging into my wrist, and I looked down. Every one of his fingers had a ring on it: a gold coin, a band of interwoven silver, a signet ring, and one other I couldn't see but could feel cutting into my flesh. Suddenly we turned off the verge under the trees, down a steep bank and into a little hollow enclosed on three sides. It was a dim, grimy little place strewn with rocks and old soft-drink cans and beer bottles, their labels washed out to a pale blue.

I stumbled as we went down, and Yari let go of me. Horst and the young Frenchman followed. That fear in my stomach had got worse, and I was feeling sick. I wondered whether I would be able to control myself. But it seemed to me I had to brazen it out.

'Horst, what is going on?'

'Shut up.'

'I'm very close to getting valuable information for you, and you're about to beat the hell out of me? I've only had a week to work on this. What am I supposed to do?'

Yari planted his feet wide apart, then pulled the rings up his fingers and my throat constricted. One punch would rip my face apart. He raised his left hand and pointed at the Frenchman.

'*Jean-Robert, viens ici,*' he said in appalling French, and the boy swaggered forward. Then with incredible speed Yari hit him on the side of his face. The boy screamed and coughed at the same time, and swayed on his feet, one hand up to his cheek, then suddenly dropped into a run up the slope of the hollow. But he slipped, and scrabbled for a moment like a trapped, blinded animal. One punch could do that, as Yari well knew; he took a second to knead his knuckles before he took a couple of steps forward and picked the boy up by the scruff of the neck, pulling him backwards down the bank, his outstretched hands flapping about, his feet searching for a hold. Horst walked over.

'You stole what is mine,' he said to the youth in French. 'Now you are fired.'

Yari had been holding the boy up; he was cut in what looked like three places, and in one of them the skin had been scuffed back to reveal a glimpse of translucent pink flesh, wet like a passion fruit, and dark blood. Now Yari dropped him and very quickly, before the boy had a chance to move, stamped on his face with his heel. My face curled up as my eyes closed in disgust.

The boy wrapped himself into a ball and lay shaking, emitting only a thin moan. Jean-Robert? I remembered Madame Sospine.

'So,' said Horst. 'You are close to having some valuable information for me?'

I tried to answer him.

'Yes, Horst.'

Yari pulled something out of his pocket: a handkerchief. Laboriously he wiped the blood off his rings.

'What kind of information?'

'I – I think I know what Schenck has been doing.' There was a quaver in my voice. I couldn't help watching Yari still wiping the blood off his rings.

'Uh-huh.' Horst seemed completely uninspired. 'What about the bearer shares?'

'I don't know about that yet, but maybe the two are linked.'

'Keep looking. I want to know where my property is. I've wanted for a long time to get that property back. I've worked very hard for that. You get it for me, you do yourself a favour.'

'I'll try.'

Yari had knelt down by the boy on the ground and turned

him over, and the boy had put his hands weakly over his face, as if trying to keep the sun out of his eyes. Yari's hand wandered down and rested on the boy's belt.

'Leave him alone,' Horst said sharply.

Yari stood up and walked a yard or two out of the hollow, where he rested his head against a tree. He suddenly looked like a man in despair.

'Don't be late again for an appointment. Never fail to return a phone-call from either of us. Now you can go. Ring me on Sunday at the hotel.'

Without another word I climbed out of the hollow and headed back to the road. The Range Rover had left a skid mark on the verge that I gazed at for a second. In the last five minutes, it seemed to me, an age had passed.

Chapter Fourteen

NATALIE WAS standing outside the house when I got back. I don't know whether she had been waiting for me. As I caught sight of her I felt like crying. I was getting worn down. I was crowded with nerves suddenly, and I knew I was going to her like a stranger, and that I had lost her.

'We haven't talked for days, Nat,' I said to her. 'I *need* to talk to you.'

'I had to be away,' she said blankly, then, changing her tone, 'What's happened to your face?'

'It was Bruno. If I hadn't got the better of him he would have hospitalized me.'

There was the ghost of something in her eye, but she remained silent.

'I've just seen Horst.'

'Listen, I'm not going to talk to you about this.'

'I have got to talk to you. Come on, you owe me at least a conversation.'

She was impassive for a moment, then she said, in a very tired voice, 'OK, I'll talk to you. Where?'

'Ah – I suppose we'll have to talk on the tennis court.'

'I'll see you there in a minute.'

We turned towards the house. Marenkian was standing on the terrace, just outside the French windows. I wondered how long he had been watching us, how obvious to him our intimacy might be. I went up the steps.

'Morning, Mr Marenkian. I'm very sorry I wasn't here at breakfast. The car played me up in Valbonne and I think I flooded the engine, so I was stuck for a while. I was just telling Natalie about it.'

He looked at me coldly for a moment, then said, 'Sure, Johnny,' and turned away.

A few minutes later I had changed, and I went down to the tennis court.

She was already there, bouncing a ball on her racket. I felt ridiculous in my bright tennis gear.

'I've just seen Horst,' I repeated.

'Don't talk to me about that.'

'I *have* to talk to you about that. I have to do something about him.'

'Now you listen. I'm talking to you just once.'

'But what's gone wrong, Nat?'

'Don't talk to me about what's gone wrong.'

'I love you.'

'It's too late to tell me that now,' she said angrily.

'I built all my hopes around you. I wanted to help you. I wanted us to be partners.'

'You built this up in your own mind. *You* built this fantasy about us ripping my father off. Oh, I know, we talked about it, and I shouldn't have claimed we didn't – but it was just talk. It didn't mean anything. I'm not going to steal from him. It was just a joke.'

'But you let me think it was serious.'

'If I did that, I'm sorry.'

Silence.

'I have to explain to Horst. I don't really know what to do.'

'I told you not to get involved with Horst. He's a goddam animal, and his partner is five times worse. I tell you what I'd do: come clean with Marenkian. Tell him what Horst has been trying to do. Marenkian will deal with Horst. Believe me, he'll handle it, and there'll be no more Horst to worry about. Come on, Johnny, you'll be OK.'

Silence. She had softened a little.

'And what about us?' I said. 'I mean it, Natalie, I love you. Can't we give it another try?'

'It's kind of ruined it, all this. I just wanted to have some fun, and I like you – but you want something serious, and I don't. I can't do that. I'm not ready for a relationship right now.'

She bowed her head and closed her eyes; she had begun to cry. Her jaw was thrust out a little and her lips twisted, and the little white diamond of a tear glittered on her golden cheek, impaled for a moment by the sun. She stood with her arms by her side and allowed me to enfold her in mine. Then suddenly she dropped her racket and clutched on to me as hard as she could.

'I was never—' I whispered. 'I just thought I was going to be a bloody servant.'

She felt my lust, detached herself from me, and slowly, almost mournfully, picked up racket and ball. Then she turned to go. She wiped her eyes with her hand: her red eyes, wet, tired. For an instant I could see what she would look like when she was fifty.

'I can't talk to you any more,' she said, and she turned to walk off the court.

I was exhausted and injured by what had passed between us; it felt as bad as being in a fight.

'Natalie, don't go away. Please.'

She went on walking.

I was like a rabbit in the glare of the headlights; I was an Englishman with not enough brains and not really enough courage, and I had taken a battering. I got myself a bottle of Black Label and took a couple of inches out of it. The first made me feel worse, but the next produced an improvement. Then I made a decision, quite easily. It didn't matter to me any more what she did. Those plans had all been foolishness. I was going to take matters into my own hands, without her help. I didn't need her.

I sat in the kitchen, staring into space. After a few minutes Claudine came in and dropped another piece of the jigsaw into place; at any rate she confirmed something.

She asked, 'Anything for Madame Sospine?'

'Who?' I asked.

'Madame Sospine. The old woman in Vence. The linen. Are you all right?'

'Yeah, I'm fine, thanks. Tell me, Claudine, you taking any documents up there for Monsieur Marenkian today, are you?'

And although she immediately said, 'Documents? I don't know what you mean,' she was a poor liar. For an instant her eyes had slanted away.

It made me laugh, that: he sent his bearer shares up and down with the laundry. John Marenkian, you are charged with the laundering of money and linen tablecloths, simultaneously. A few minutes later he himself appeared.

'Has Natalie gone out?'

'Yes, she has.'

'Will she be back for lunch?'

'I'm afraid I don't know.'

'Where's Bruno?'

'He's in bed, I think.' What if I had done him serious damage? I supposed I didn't care very much.

'Goddam it,' he said.

He left the kitchen and I heard his heavy tread across the living room floor and up the stairs. If Bruno told him what I had done, I would be in trouble, and I wasn't ready yet to make my move. I decided it would be good to check. So I crossed the living room and hall, and took the stairs up to the half-landing between the ground and first floors.

'That's not it,' Bruno was saying plaintively. (Maybe I couldn't hear everything that was said, but this is what I did catch.) 'You shut me out . . .'

'I'm waiting for you to be ready to take on these responsibilities.'

'Huh.' There was a silence. 'Why did you get me busted out of Princeton?'

'Bruno,' Marenkian said patiently and emphatically, 'you've said this before and I can tell you that there's no truth in it.'

'That's what *you* say.'

'That's what anyone with sense would say.'

'Well, there are some people with sense who think otherwise.'

There was another silence.

'All right. This time you are going to *stop* seeing Schenck.'

'No way,' Bruno said. 'Max is something I've got. He's *for* me. He's on my side – unlike anyone else around here.'

I felt sorry for Marenkian. What could he say to this nonsense? It sounded as if he was at a loss too. There was another silence. Then Marenkian talking, too low for me to hear. Then Bruno, then Marenkian, all unintelligible.

Then Bruno said, 'You made me what I am, so don't complain.'

'What the hell do you mean by that? Do you think you can blame everything in this life on your upbringing? That's the kind of thing you talk about with Max Schenck, I suppose?'

'Yeah.' Then Bruno laughed. 'What else do you talk about with a shrink?'

'Let me tell you something. You can't go through your life blaming me, or a family you don't know, or some incident in your childhood for – for anything and everything that you do now.'

'Why not?' Bruno said with a sneer in his voice. 'It's kinda convenient.'

'OK.' Marenkian suddenly raised his voice, and the rhythm and timbre of his speech changed. His long vowels and measured tones became clipped and military.

'We won't talk about this, then, because there's nothing to say, but I just want to ask you one thing: why in hell are you still in bed at this time of day?' He was shouting by now. Then there was a pause. I stared at the bright afternoon sunlight streaming through the door at the top of the stairs, waiting for it. *Johnny kicked me in the balls and I'm sick.*

'I just don't feel good today, you know. I just don't feel good.'

'Today and every day. Get up now.'

So he was keeping quiet about our altercation.

'I have something else to talk to you about.' Marenkian reverted to his usual measured tones. 'So come see me in my study when you get down.'

I heard him move rapidly towards the door, so I started down the stairs as quickly as I could. My trainers made a squelching sound on the terracotta that I was sure he must hear. A moment of panic, and then I turned up the stairs again and almost collided with him as he came down round the corner.

'Oh, Mr Marenkian, there's – there's an American on the phone,' I said. I felt as if I were reddening slightly. 'I think it's an international call.'

He looked at me sharply. 'Who is it?'

'He wouldn't leave his name.'

'OK,' he said, and continued down the stairs. I followed, thinking: *You fool, why did you say, 'There's an American on the phone'? When would you ever say that?* The nuances of language can tell those who are aware of them when a person is lying. Lawyers must come to detect such nuances.

As I crossed the living room, of course, he called me, and I put my head round the door of the den.

'There's wasn't anybody,' he said.

'Oh? Perhaps he got cut off.'

'No idea who he was?'

'I'm afraid not.'

'You didn't take the call in here, evidently?'

'No, in the kitchen.'

'I'd like you to step in for a moment and shut the door, please.'

I did so, and we both sat down.

'Bruno won't be seeing Max Schenck any more.' Then Marenkian continued slowly, 'If by any chance he asks you to take him there, I would be grateful if you could simply refer Bruno to me. In other words, don't take him to Max Schenck, whatever he may say. You know, of course, that he can't drive as a result of the medication he's taking. Do you have the keys to both cars?'

'Yes.'

'Well, keep your eyes on them, please. OK?'

'Certainly will.'

He went on down to his office in the grounds, and about ten minutes later Bruno followed him, and stayed there for a time. Then suddenly – I hadn't noticed him walking back up – I heard his voice on the terrace.

He screamed inarticulately for about a minute, rounding off with, 'A prison! A fucking prison!'

I began to feel much worse. A dull ache appeared in my neck and made its presence more and more forcefully felt. I went and lay on my bed. A voice told me that I was deluding myself again: spinning myself a yarn about taking these seasoned pros to the cleaners. How could I have believed she was serious about conspiring with me to rip off her own adoptive father? She couldn't face it when I wanted to turn her dreams into reality. It had all been bullshit: all that rubbish about her weird ambitions. She had just wanted to fuck someone new.

But I was in love with her.

My eyes filled with tears.

Later I dozed off, and dreamed not of her but of another woman, with whom I lay in bed and whom I felt had known all my life, who was my greatest friend.

I was woken up by that sixth sense that tells you that another person is close to you, and which seems to work even when you are sleeping. Still barely awake I saw only a dark shape, and then I shot up suddenly. Bruno was standing above me, his arm raised. I half rolled, half jumped off the bed and onto the floor. Then I was up on my feet.

'Keep away from me, Bruno, all right? Just keep away from me.'

'No, no, listen—'

'Keep the fuck away. I mean it. Keep away.'

Bruno had been close to the edge, and now he was sliding off it. He could have brained me as I slept. Revenge for my having kicked him in the balls? Yes, it was possible for a madman like him, a psychopath. For a moment everything seemed clear. Of course Marenkian had to keep him under control, knowing what he was capable of: really insane things, much worse than bar-room brawls. In the circumstances it was not unreasonable that drugs were being used. Perhaps even Schenck was not up to the job any more.

Then Bruno did something odd. In a curiously feminine way, a look of supplication in his eyes, he raised his finger to his lips and went 'Ssh!'

I stared at him for a second, and rubbed my shoulder. I had jarred it as I fell off the bed. Then I said, 'Get out of here.'

'Please. Just a minute,' he whispered. 'Don't say anything loud or my father'll hear. Look, I'm – I'm sorry for yesterday, I

– I've got this terrible anger, you know. I just can't control it. And, after what Natalie said to me, I just flipped, right?'

After what Natalie said to me? What had Natalie said to him? I wanted to know but I hated to ask him. If I had to hear something about her, I didn't want to hear it from Bruno. Yet who else was I going to hear it from? And he didn't have the self-control to deceive. I got up and pulled on a pair of trousers.

'What did she say to you?'

'I knew that – I knew that . . . my father, he gets people in here, right' – he spoke very hesitantly – 'so he can control me, you know. He doesn't want me to – live my own life. Listen,' he suddenly came out in a rush, 'he won't let me see Schenck, right. He won't let me see Max Schenck. Will you take me there? I know he says *no*, I can't, but just take me for an hour. I won't tell him, you know. I won't tell him a thing—'

I interrupted him. 'Just tell me what she said to you.' I spoke even more coldly than before. It's always men who are down that get kicked.

'Listen,' he said, giggling with embarrassment and waving his hands about, 'she told me that you were spying, right – for my father – that you were coming into my place and looking through my things, and you had been stealing my medicine.'

'What?' I was suddenly furious.

'You know that was what made me flip, right, and I'm really sorry for that, because now I don't – well, I don't really believe her.'

'Do you really expect me to believe this shite?' I said to him, my head throbbing with anger.

'Listen, man, she lies. She lies a lot. That's the way she is. She lies just for the hell of it. She's that kind of person. She's a liar.'

He had obviously never heard of the messenger who brought bad news.

'And I don't think she likes you too much, you know,' he added.

Little do you know, you fool, I thought. And then, like the Englishman I am, I turned cold and formal, like my school-teacher father or my commanding officer.

'I'm afraid I can't take you anywhere, Bruno. Your father spoke to me earlier today. He expressly told me to refer you to him. That's all I can do.'

'Look, please – I've got to see him.'

'The answer is no.'

'Listen, I had an idea,' he said, growing more and more feverish. 'I knew maybe you wouldn't want to do it, so' – and he reached into his back pocket – 'I've got this letter. Please just take it to him. You don't know how much it means to me. Please.'

He held the letter out in front of him, an imploring look on his face. But I hardly remembered he was there. I could only think of what he had told me Natalie had said. How could she say those things about me? The man who loved her?

'Please take it,' he said.

'No, I can't. I'm sorry.'

He stared at me in disbelief, then sat down on the bed. He put his fist up and pressed it against his forehead. There was silence for a while, and then a great sniff. With his other arm he clutched himself and rocked forward slightly. With a mixture of compassion and disgust I realized that he had started to cry, and I thought back to the casino, a few weeks before. What *had* happened to him?

Then I felt ashamed that, whatever my own circumstances, I could be so indifferent to this suffering. Yet I still loathed him.

I said, 'You need more drugs from him, don't you? That's what it is, isn't it?'

He shook his head, and murmured, 'No, it isn't that. I swear to you.'

'Well, I've got something for you to look at. Something you should see,' I said, almost taunting him. I went to the chest, pulled one of the drawers open, and rummaged among my clothes until I found the copy of the poems of Walt Whitman in which I had hidden Bervillier's analysis of Bruno's pills. Who in that household would ever want to read the poems of Walt Whitman?

'I found two of your pills.' He looked up at me in surprise, his eyes red and wet and his great brown ham of a face puffy. 'Yes, I did take them, and I had them analysed. For *your* good. If a doctor is giving a patient pills that are making him worse, then that seems strange to me.'

'They don't make me worse. They help me see inside – you know – become aware of myself and who I am. Whatever kind of shit that is. Whatever kind of shit I am.'

'Read it,' I said, handing him the paper.

He held it in his hand for a little while, not looking at it; recovering, perhaps, from his tears. He glanced at it, then laid it on the bed.

'I dunno,' he said.

'But, Bruno, this is a mixture of acid and amphetamines. It can't be good for you. It's what has made you feel so strange. No ordinary doctor would prescribe it.'

'But Max *isn't* an ordinary doctor, right? He's got ways of helping me that no ordinary doctor would know about. I can't explain it. He's just the best thing for me. I trust him more than anyone. Johnny, please take the letter.'

I walked over to the window and looked out.

'I don't know, Bruno.'

'The whole thing about his treatment, right, is that Max finds out the deepest things that are – aren't right, you know.

And then you act them out, you get in touch with them, so you can understand them and deal with them. The pills help you do that. See, this combination releases you from your inhibitions.'

'I can't believe that's right, Bruno. These are hard drugs, illegal drugs. People damage themselves with these.'

'But it's controlled, it's low dose. It's an important part of my treatment. So much of the treatment's gonna be ruined if I stop now.'

'Why doesn't your father want you to visit Max any more?'

For a little while he didn't answer, then he said, 'He's jealous. And he's ashamed of himself because he knows that he's at the root of it. There's things that happened in my childhood, abuse, and Max is finding that out and helping me get over it. My father can't take that. Johnny, please take the letter. I've got to at least talk to Max. I can't just leave it there.'

I stood there for a moment, vacillating, and then made up my mind.

'OK, give me the letter.' Perhaps Bruno had a right to expect something from me after his openness. He stood up with the letter in his hand, beaming with gratitude.

'But let me tell you something: I'm not bringing you any drugs from Schenck. Those you'll have to find some other way of getting, or he'll have to get them to you. I won't be your courier.'

'Hey, that's OK, Johnny. That's OK. Thanks.' He backed his way to the door.

The trouble was, I didn't see how Bruno could be lying. He was too much of a fool. If I accepted what he said, I would have to convince myself that she had simply made a mistake. To tell him that I was spying on him for his father, had searched his belongings, stolen his drugs, a mere *mistake*? Those were tales calculated to incite him, to set him against me. I stared from my window at the tops of the pines and thought of the evening he had spent smashing things. She had been whispering in his ear then. What had she whispered? The thought filled me with rage.

But another voice said: You're in love with this girl. How can you accept the evidence of this violent, malicious, paranoiac nutcase? He has a need now of your services, so he has to find a way of excusing yesterday's ambush. That Natalie incited him is probably the only story he could think of. Have the strength to believe in her. Find the strength.

That night I had a dream in which I walked through a series of rooms, searching for something. The rooms were almost identical, save for the fact that each was darker than the last.

Chapter Fifteen

SHE BOWS HER head before the judges, pure, with the simplicity of enormous expense, a single lily in the surrounding grass, and it is certain that every juror can see what the fuss is about. The men take trouble to look impassive, but you can almost feel their fascination and desire; the women make little effort to hide their disapproval. She wears a white suit, and she looks almost like a bride.

The monkish president is well trained enough to hide any attraction he might feel; one of his assistants is impassive, and the other looks faintly amused, as if reflecting to himself how easily some people mistake cheap baubles for works of art. I could shake him by the hand.

'Can you affirm that you are neither relation nor ally, and that you are not in his service?'

'Yes,' she whispers.

'State what you know of this case.'

'I . . . I met John Denner when he came to work at my father's house in September 1991. He was . . . a kind of butler and a driver and cook.' Her voice is low and hesitant, and she has an air of regret, perhaps even shame. The women jurors begin to melt a little. And the court is very silent, because even with the microphone you have to listen very carefully to catch what she says. (Not that it matters, with the interpreter translating, but everybody wants to hear the sound of her voice.) 'We got on OK because . . . we played tennis together, and he seemed like a nice guy. We don't have, I mean my brother and I don't have many friends here, and so it was good to have someone around, and we kind of became friends.

'But then he seemed to ... he seemed to get ideas that we were more than friends, and he wanted ... to take things further. I suppose I was a little naïve about it, because I liked him, but not like that, and I never thought of him as a lover, just as a friend. He came to my room one night, in the middle of the night, and he obviously wanted to sleep with me, but I said no, and he wouldn't go away, he was really harassing me. Then I got a bit scared, because I thought this could turn into a situation where he might try and rape me or something, and so I shouted so my father would come.'

'And your father did come?'

'Yes.'

'Did Monsieur Denner come to your room to look for intruders or burglars in the house?'

'No. He said he needed to talk to me.'

'Monsieur Denner, stand up, please.'

I go through the ritual of denial, and convince nobody.

'How did he react after this incident?' the president continues.

'He was OK. He was a little angry at first, but I decided not to hold it against him that he had done that, and I thought of it as just a misunderstanding, and anyway he'd had a bad time from my father. So we were friends again. But then I realized I'd made a mistake. He just seemed to become totally obsessed. He was always trying to see me alone and arrange meetings, and he kept telling me he loved me. I kept telling him to leave me alone, but he wouldn't, and I kind of felt sorry for him. He even ... he even told me that he wanted to marry me, and that we could run away together, and that he was going to get hold of some money.' She bows her head.

'Did you encourage him in this?'

'No.'

'Did he ask you about your father's money?'

She paused before answering.

'Well, yes, he did. I thought it was just curiosity. But he asked more than once.'

'Did you have the impression that he was trying to get money from your father through you?'

'I didn't at the time. But I see now that that's what he *was* trying to do.'

The president pauses and pulls out another file.

'Were you at this time involved in an intimate relationship with Dr Max Schenck?'

'Yes, I was.'

'Did Monsieur Denner know of this relationship?'

'No, he did not – at the time.'

'Please describe to the court how he discovered the relationship.'

'I had gone to see Max – Dr Schenck – because I was worried about the way Johnny was becoming obsessed with me and . . . he had just asked me to marry him, but I had said no, he had to leave me alone . . . And maybe I would have seen Max anyway. And while I was there Johnny came and banged on the door. He had followed me there, because he was doing that too: he was following me around. And he banged on the door and he was shouting.'

'What was he shouting?'

'He was shouting things like "Bring her out here," and "I know you've got her in there." So Max went to the door, and Johnny started saying, "I'm going to kill you, you bastard."'

She pauses, lets it sink in.

The president also pauses.

'How did Dr Schenck react to this?'

'He didn't take it very seriously. He said that being a psychotherapist he was good at reading the signs, and he told me not to worry about it. He said that he could tell if someone was really capable of violence or if they were just making threats. And he said that Johnny was just making threats.'

'Do you remember what else Monsieur Denner said?'

'He called me some names.'

'What kind of names?'

Her voice is at its lowest whisper, delicate, and hearts are bleeding for her now.

'Bitch. Whore.'

'Anything else?'

'He said, "You're gonna regret this."'

Another pause.

'What happened after this?'

'He wouldn't speak to me after that. He seemed to have changed, and he was just really angry and bitter and brooding.'

Another pause.

'Do you have direct knowledge of the events of the day of Dr Schenck's death?'

'No, I haven't. I was . . . away from the house.' She sniffs, and somehow manages a small tear, a tiny stain on the silk of her cheek.

The others are asked whether they have any questions for her, and they say no, and she steps down.

She knows how to lie – I'll give her that.

It was six o'clock, and she still hadn't come back. It was time to go, so I went, Bruno's letter in my pocket, Schenck's name written on the envelope in elegant copperplate and, in the top left-hand corner, STRICTLY CONFIDENTIAL in capitals, double underlined.

I wondered whether Horst would be at all satisfied with my account of Bruno's leaks to Schenck, and Marenkian's response. It might hold him off for a week at any rate. I would need at least that time to find what I needed.

There was a car in Schenck's drive.

It was Natalie's car.

I couldn't believe it – I said to myself: *No it isn't. Her car has an orange sticker in the passenger window – this one hasn't. There are plenty of these cars about. It isn't hers. How could her car be here?* But the sticker *was* there, on the other side. KICK IT: that's what the sticker said. I moved back towards the Range Rover, as if her car were watching me. It seemed to me significant that it was parked in his narrow drive. If this was her first visit, if she had come to consult Schenck about his involvement with Bruno, confront him, perhaps, with what she knew from me, she would have parked in the street. But she had parked in his drive, where she doubtless always parked, where her car wouldn't be noticed by a passer-by: a passer-by like me. Her car was intimate with the place.

The bitch. The foul whore. Inside, she was giving herself to that fat German bastard.

I stood vacillating for several minutes. I tried to convince myself that there was no sexual betrayal involved, but I couldn't accept that; everything about her was sexual. I felt cold and impotent, enfeebled, robbed of my manhood. I had excited myself with fantasies about her sexual exploits with other men. Now one of them confronted me and nauseated me. Now I knew why she had ditched me. A new man. Probably *not* new, in fact; we had probably been sharing her.

I could have just walked away, but that would have been cowardice. I had to revive my strength, and the only way I could do that was to summon a violent anger against both of them. Then I could face them, feeling whole again, *and* face myself, and do my worst. So I worked myself into a fury, taking the sickness of my fear and turning it into a fever of rage.

Then I walked up the path and banged on Schenck's door with my fist.

There no response for a little while, so I banged again. Then I heard footsteps, and the door half opened. Schenck stood in the eighteen-inch gap. He was wearing a white shirt, the top three buttons open to reveal a barrel of a chest, carpeted with dark hair. There was a steady, calm weight about him confronting my twitching, nervous anger.

He looked at me casually, not in surprise, not really even in mockery, although there was undoubtedly something mocking in his refusal to make any acknowledgement of my presence. He looked at me like the servant I was. The sight of him disgusted me. What was she doing with this old man?

'You've got Natalie in there, haven't you?'

Still he watched me without replying, a faint smile on his face, and then he gave one of those short breaths through his nose that are like little bursts of laughter.

'Haven't you?' I repeated furiously.

'I don't see that it is your business,' he said precisely, then turned and began to shut the door.

But I didn't let him. I put my foot inside and shoulder up against it, and said, 'Bring her out, you fucker.'

He was very strong, and he had a lot of weight behind him, and I was dismayed that he was able to hold the pressure I put on the door with one arm. He didn't even need to use his shoulder.

Then he heard something inside, turned, and said, quite distinctly, 'Go back in the sitting room.'

I took advantage of his loss of attention to release pressure and then push hard. The door slid back, but only a few inches. In one movement he shook his head in irritation, his lips pursed, his expression indicating that I had become a tiresome nuisance to him, and reached into his pocket. There was a metallic snap, and to my enormous surprise he had a flick-knife in his hand. He held it up at the level of my chest, and I looked at it and backed off.

Then he said, 'Go away now. Otherwise I will cut you. You understand?'

I took one or two steps back, and growled, 'I know what you're doing. I know what you've been doing with Bruno.'

'Do you? Goodbye.'

'You're going to regret this, I can promise you that. You're going to fucking regret it.'

He gave me a cold smile, turned, and shut the door.

I shouted, 'You're going to fucking regret this. You too, Natalie, you whore. Fucking whore,' I screamed. I turned and walked back down the path to the street. There was a low wall, and I smashed my fist against it and opened up a knuckle, and that calmed me down a little. There was only silence.

Then I heard a rustle and turned, expecting to see Schenck. But, instead, in the garden of the next house I saw the small face of a middle-aged man with a hooked nose and half-moon spectacles, which disappeared as soon as I looked at him: a curious neighbour, who wanted to see but not touch.

I was shaking, and I felt very peculiar, as if I were about to shatter. I had been dismissed like the servant I was. I burned with hatred.

The curious thing was that this possibility had once suggested itself to me, and I had dismissed it as too predictable, too cheap and obvious. Now I knew why she had constantly steered me away from my suspicions of Schenck.

So I would do the obvious. I would go to Horst and tell him everything I could. Yari would see to them both; they could hold hands in hospital.

I pushed my way rudely through a large gathering of men in suits in the foyer of the Meridien: American cardiologists, as a placard by the desk announced. Of course I wanted someone to take exception to my jostling, but no one did. People steer clear when you're in that frame of mind.

Yari sat in a corner of the dimly lit room, and Horst and I remained for the most part in the middle. My anger made me decisive.

'OK, Horst, I have a story for you. I think it might interest you. But I don't want Yari anywhere near me.'

Horst laughed amiably. 'Sure,' he said. 'I'm sorry he doesn't like you, Yari.'

'Asshole,' Yari muttered.

We sat down.

'Marenkian's bearer shares – you're not the only one who's interested in them.'

'Do you know where they are yet?'

'No,' I said, completely without apology. 'And I don't know whether I ever will. I think you're right. I don't think they're in his safe. Anyway, as I say, you're not the only one who's interested in them, and Marenkian knows it. I think I told you a while ago' – God it seemed a long time – 'that Marenkian was worried that somebody was trying to influence his business, or perhaps find things out about it, or perhaps, indeed, do what *we're* trying to do. And his worry was that people were trying to do this through Bruno, Bruno being somebody who's easily influenced and who seems to have a problem with drugs and alcohol. He was worried enough about this, as you remember, to ask me to report back to him on everyone Bruno contacts. But Nico Mammalio, who could have been the only real culprit in any of this, went back to the States, yet Marenkian obviously had reason to believe that his problems were continuing.'

'What is all this crap?' Yari said, and I turned on him.

'Shut your fucking face, Yari,' I told him. 'You don't want to hear this, piss off.' Yari stood up, a very ugly look on his face, and Horst said:

'Sit down, Yari. What Johnny's saying is very interesting, and I don't want a lot of tiresome interruptions.'

Yari looked absolutely livid for a moment; then he turned and left the room, slamming the door behind him.

'Don't worry about him. He's a goddam peasant, I tell you, but he won't revolt.'

We laughed.

'This is the kind of thing I want, you see. This is good. I'm not looking for the holy grail – just stuff that will help me in my work. Anyway, continue.'

'One thing that was certain about Marenkian at this stage was that he knew that someone unauthorized had been inside his office while he was away on his most recent trip. It wasn't me. It probably wasn't a stranger. It probably wasn't one of the servants. For one thing, neither of them speak any English. So it was most probably Bruno or Natalie. A pair of cuckoos, they are – did you know that?'

'What do you mean?'

'Both of them were adopted in Colombia, apparently.'

'Well, well.'

'And now one of them is dipping his hand in the parental purse. And it would make sense that it's Bruno, as he apparently knows a lot about Marenkian's business. For a while he was co-opted as a sort of junior partner, so he has more information at his disposal than Natalie, who knows nothing about the business.'

'Could he be acting on his own account?'

'Why should he? He's going to inherit whatever there is, anyway. And actually how could he? He's in no fit state to plot anything. No, Marenkian thinks that Bruno is under the malign influence of somebody else who's out to profit. None of Bruno's friends fit the bill. So what about Max Schenck, Bruno's psychotherapist?'

'You have spoken about him already.'

'It so happens that at the same time I was doing a little – investigative work into Schenck. Schenck is a very trusted member of the entourage. Marenkian's known him for years, and it's his task to keep Bruno under control, and perhaps to cure him as well – you never know. Now, I drove Bruno to his appointments, and it was quite obvious that Schenck was using a heavy regime of drugs on him. Bruno was practically in a coma when he came out. And he seemed pretty strange at other times too.

'Anyway, I wondered whether the pills Schenck gave him might have something to do with his state of mind. So I purloined one of each – he has two kinds, and he *needs* them, can't do without them – and took them to be analysed at a laboratory.'

'Really?' Horst said, laughing. 'I am impressed by this. Perhaps you should join the police force.'

'Yeah. Anyway, one of them turned out to be a mixture of acid and speed. Not really the thing to give to someone who's clearly on the edge. A sort of guaranteed bad trip.'

'Well,' Horst said reflectively, but made no other comment.

'So why would Schenck do this? To keep Bruno under control? Or to get information from him about Marenkian's business? Marenkian no longer trusts Schenck. He's forbidden Bruno from seeing him. He's gone so far as to order me not to drive Bruno there. I even confronted Schenck.'

'Did you, indeed?'

'He didn't deny that he was up to something in relation to Bruno, but it's difficult to know precisely what. I might be able to find out.'

'And so might I,' Horst said. *That's right, Horst.*

'You see, I think Marenkian's probably on the right track. I think the man has shrewd instincts.'

'So do I, Johnny. I don't underestimate him at all.'

'I'd pay Schenck a visit, if I were you. That would be my next step. I'm sure you wouldn't be wasting your time.'

'Maybe so. This has been useful, anyway. What's *your* next move?'

'I'm going to try and get closer to Bruno. He trusts me a lot more than he used to. I think he could shed quite a lot more light on this. In fact I think that if anyone other than Marenkian knows where the bearer shares are and how to use them, it's Bruno. Unless he's already told Schenck, of course, in which case Schenck knows too.'

'Sure.'

'I thought I might collect a month's salary too. As you can see, I'm getting on with things.'

Horst smiled, paused for a second.

'Sure, Johnny,' he said. He went through to the bedroom and came back with another bundle of notes.

'I'll see you in about a week.'

'OK,' I said, took the bundle, shook his hand and left. *Like hell you will. I'll be on the other side of the world.*

I started drinking again once I got back to the Marenkian house. The skin was tight around my head, and my stomach felt like a lead plate. It must have taken me five or six glasses to get rid of the tension.

I'd show her. In a year I'd be rich, hard, and her filthy shrink would have been run out of town. She might think he was cool and tough. But he couldn't be a match for Yari. Yari'd smash his face for him.

The next morning I sat in the kitchen staring into space, sick again. Claudine bustled around quietly; she had very little to say to me. I suspected she had somehow found out about my affair with Natalie and disapproved; that she had principles on the relations between servants and the daughters of their masters. Or perhaps she was just jealous.

After breakfast I went quietly up to Natalie's room, and even more quietly opened the door. The sun streamed in. She hadn't been back the night before.

Claudine was standing behind me as I turned, scowling,

back to the corridor, a little smile on her sallow face. I walked past her and down the stairs, hating her as much as anyone else, hating her for seeing my pain.

The thought was indecent: his crude, ageing bulk covering that delicate young body. His desiccated old hide scratching against the silk of her skin. I did nothing for a while, just sat in the kitchen, swallowing bile.

At about midday Bruno came in, bleary-eyed, twitching and nervous. He looked around him and shut the door.

'Did you see him?' he whispered urgently.

I was tired of Bruno, tired in every way, and I just said: 'He wasn't there.'

'Oh shit. Goddam the guy. God!' And he started pacing around the kitchen. 'What did you do with the letter?'

I had forgotten the letter. I hadn't given it a thought since he had put it in my hand.

'I put it through the door,' I said.

'Shit,' he whispered, staring at me, then started pacing round the room.

'Why hasn't he called me? He knows I've got to talk to him.'

'I don't know, Bruno.'

'I've got to talk to him. I need to—'

Then his pacing brought him to the little rack above the counter where the keys hung. He stopped dead, looked at me, then defiantly, like a little boy, grabbed the keys to the Range Rover.

'Put them back, Bruno,' I said.

'You come near me, I'll kill you.'

'Just put them back,' I said, but I didn't move. I wasn't going to have another fight with Bruno. He turned, ran through the living room and out to the car. He had it started in a second, and he roared down the drive.

The electronic gates started to swing open, and it then occurred to me that I could use the button by the front door to shut them again. But should I? Really, did I care? As it was, I hesitated just long enough. I pushed the button and gazed down the drive. The gates began to swing shut. Bruno just drove for them, and I knew that he wouldn't stop. So I jabbed the button again. They juddered, and started to swing back open. The front of the car went through, but he somehow managed to catch the rear bumper. The car was impeded for a moment, there was the roar of its engine being revved to the limit, a sliding sound on the gravel, and then a crack of metal. It finally shot through, and the right-hand gate sprang back on its hinges.

After a moment I pushed the button again, but the gates wouldn't move.

This happened in a matter of seconds, of course. Marenkian came running up the garden.

'What in hell was that?' He was out of breath.

'It was Bruno, I'm afraid. He went into the kitchen and took the Range Rover keys – and he was away before I could stop him.'

'Why did you open the gates?'

'I didn't. He opened them with the remote in the car.'

'Why didn't you shut them?'

'I tried, but he was driving straight for them. In my judgement he wasn't going to stop.'

He was silent for a moment. I couldn't read his face. Then we had a brief, listless discussion about the gates. He was anxious that they should be repaired as soon as possible, preferably that afternoon. But in the event I never got hold of anybody to do the job. I couldn't have cared less.

Another bad mistake, as it turned out.

She came back at about three, wearing sunglasses even though the light was pale, and walked slowly up the steps to the French windows, looking cautiously around her – for me, perhaps.

I stayed in the kitchen, where I could see her. Looking at her made me feel weak, defeated – a cuckold.

She came into the kitchen, her glasses now off, and stood there waiting for me to speak. That was something I couldn't stand, so I walked around, absurdly looking into cupboards and drawers, as if searching for something.

'I have to talk to you,' she said.

I said nothing. I went and looked out of the window. I was so weak.

'Johnny, I have to talk to you.'

Still I said nothing. She sighed.

'Johnny, please. Don't just ignore me. I have to talk to you. I have to explain.'

'Oh, why bother?' I said, still not turning.

'Because I want to. Please don't make it too hard for me.'

'Too hard for you? Jesus.' There was silence again for a little while. Then I said, 'I just don't know what you can say that can possibly . . . mitigate this. You've been lying all along . . . so what's the point?'

'Listen, Johnny, we can't talk like this – here. Please just give me a little time. Please.'

This time we went no further than the little paved yard at the back, dim and forlorn, its surface scattered with pine needles, the trees beyond it filtering the weak, white light. Finally the weather had changed, and it was cool and overcast. The place was very quiet.

She leaned listlessly against the whitewashed wall at the rear. She was wearing a short black skirt I hadn't seen before, and I stared for a moment at her legs.

She said, 'Listen, you've gotta talk to Horst again at seven, right? I think I know what you can tell him.'

'It was yesterday I talked to him.'

She was silent.

'Had some tips from your boyfriend?'

'What?'

'About what I might tell Horst.'

She didn't reply. I paced some more.

'What happened to the gates?' she asked.

'That was Bruno's handiwork. He was so anxious to see his protector – your boyfriend – that he took the Range Rover keys and busted out of here. But why should you care? He's someone you've betrayed.'

'I haven't,' she said very quietly.

'Oh no?' I said, and paced again. 'Actually,' I said, 'one thing I do want to know is why you want to bother to justify yourself to me. I surely can't be of any use to you.'

'I like you,' she said even more quietly, almost inaudibly.

'Oh, don't be ridiculous. It was obviously just a bit of fun for you. But what I really don't understand is how you could stand by and watch what he's doing to Bruno.'

'He's helping Bruno.'

'Oh, bollocks, he's not doing anything of the sort.'

'He's a powerful man, I – I couldn't end it with him. I wanted to when I got to know you, but he wouldn't let me, and I couldn't do it.'

'What's wrong with you? He wouldn't let you? What's wrong with you to need some fat old man in the first place?'

'I don't know.' There was a desperation in her voice.

I started pacing again, muttering to myself. I wanted to know more, so I held my fury in check.

'How long has it been going on?' I asked quietly.

She didn't reply.

'Come on, how long has it been going on?'

I looked at her and thought: *God, I could kill you. I could beat the hell out of you and nobody could stop me.*

'About a year,' she said very quietly.

'What happened?'

'I could tell you he forced me, but it wasn't that. He used to

come round here a lot, used to have lunch and dinner with us –
when Marenkian would still have him in the house. I was sick of
young guys. The young guys down here are rich punks who don't
have anything to do, who don't have anything to say. I had just
about had it, anyway, with this place. It was things like the way
he talks, and what he says. He's wise and experienced. He has
horizons that are far wider than any of the people down
here. And he understood me.'

'Did he seduce you?'

'Don't, Johnny. Don't ask me.'

'Come on, just tell me. Did he seduce you?'

'No,' she suddenly said, defiantly. 'I seduced him, OK? You
wanna know that? You wanna know how I went down to his
office?'

Perhaps I was showing now that I was another of those
young punks.

'But how could you just – two-time me like that? Why didn't
you give him up? Why did you have to start with me in the first
place?'

I could hear the dogged, pleading tone in my voice.

'Listen, I wanted you. There's no plot, for Christ's sake.' She
almost smiled. 'You're a lot more sexy than you realize. That's
one of the things I like about you. But it's too late for that now,'
she said sadly, and turned away.

'Maybe . . .' I said, agonized, 'maybe – give him up, for
Christ's sake. Just give him up.'

'He knows about you.'

'What did he say?'

She paused, and then laughed slightly. 'The same. The same
thing.'

Suddenly I was bitter and furious again, more than before.

'OK, well, you fucking go to him. Just do that, you bloody
whore.'

And then she was angry too.

'Oh, yeah? Listen, who the hell do you think you are? What kind of standards have *you* got? You took Horst's money and you agreed to spy on my family. When you were supposed to be *in love* with me, *baby*.'

'I did not.'

'Yes, you did, Johnny – although you might be thinking of cheating Horst now. There was one point when you were going to give him what he wanted. Oh, yeah.'

'Yes, I would have cheated him, for you. Would you cheat Max Schenck for me?'

'*Would have* cheated him? So you've changed your mind? The thing about Max, Johnny, is he really knows how to deal with these guys. Horst and that piece of Russian shit that trails around after him.'

'Meaning I don't.'

'Johnny, you're an English gentleman. You have to be a totally different kind of animal to play in this game.'

'And that's why you're with *him*.'

'Because I'm playing that game.'

Well, she had laid her cards on the table now, and I was so tempted to do the same, but I said to myself: *No – don't tell her what your plans are. Don't tell Schenck what you intend to do; for that's what it would amount to.*

'Johnny, you should get out of here,' she said. I think she said it with a real compassion and concern. 'Horst, Max, and John Marenkian are going to slug it out, and Horst is gonna be the first to go. Max could eat him for breakfast. So could Marenkian. You'd just get fried.'

'Thanks for the advice,' I said. 'I might possibly take it. Now why don't you go back to your boyfriend.'

This time I turned and left her. And I thought to myself: I've given you a good break. I told Horst all about Schenck, and your name never came into it, and it very easily could have done. And I haven't even boasted to you about it; I haven't even taken the credit. But your money's on Schenck, your vision clouded by your perverse sexual preferences. The two real professionals in this game are Horst and Marenkian. The two amateurs are Schenck and myself. Now, I'm not really a player – rather, nobody knows that I'm a player – so I'm running a risk, but a limited one, I hope. Whereas you, Schenck, now everybody knows that you're a player, my friend, partly thanks to me. Bruno, Natalie, Horst know; Marenkian suspects. Not a good position to be in.

We'll see, my darling, just how your fat old horse turns out. We'll see whether you don't come running to me in the end. Me leave here now? No way. I've had enough of running away and taking it lying down, and having no money and no future. Deal me in.

Chapter Sixteen

HE PAUSES AGAIN, then turns back to Marenkian.

'When did you first meet Dr Max Schenck?'

'We met in Zurich in about 1967.'

'What were the circumstances of your meeting?'

'Purely social. We were introduced by a banking acquaintance.'

'What is your knowledge of Dr Schenck's career?'

'When we met he had quite recently qualified. I believe he was very highly thought of. At that time he held a junior post at the university. He also practised, of course, as a Jungian psychotherapist. Quite by chance, I then met him some years later in New York. It was probably 1981, '82. He was teaching at the University of New York and he also had a private practice. We had dinner, and he told me that he was disillusioned with the politics of his institution, and to some extent with teaching in general, and we got to talking about the opportunities down here, where I had been living for three or four years.

'He moved here about a year later and set up a successful private practice. He also had a professional interest in the psychology of aggression, and this led to some specialized work with criminals, and he appeared in the courts here and elsewhere as an expert witness, and I believe his services were highly valued. I certainly had a great deal of respect for the man, and . . . when my son' – the first and last time Marenkian stumbled – 'needed a little help in getting over a difficult period, I turned to Dr Schenck for his advice, and he was able to help.'

'Were you present when Monsieur Denner and Dr Schenck met for the first time?'

'I was, yes.'

'Was there any friction between them?'

'None that I was aware of.'

'Was there any friction on any other occasion?'

'I don't think so, although I'd have to say that Max Schenck was capable of being a little high-handed, and he certainly had a very traditional manner with servants.'

A long pause.

'Did you know that your daughter and Dr Schenck were having an intimate relationship?'

'No, I did not – until after his death.'

'Did you approve?'

'No, I did not. It saddened me. I felt that my daughter could find a better way to be happy.'

'Were you angry?'

'In the circumstances, given the tragedy of his death, no.'

Another long pause.

'Describe, please, what you know of the events of the sixteenth of November.'

'Denner took one of our cars, a Range Rover, and drove it down the drive so fast that he actually crashed into the metal gate at the end. He then drove straight on – he didn't stop. I came out of my office to see what had happened, and I was surprised naturally, and I didn't understand what was behind this behaviour, but my son Bruno told me that Denner seemed to have been in some kind of rage, but that he wouldn't talk to Bruno or tell him anything about it. I was angry with myself, because I hadn't done anything about Denner, which really I should have done. As I said, he had seemed to be developing a strange attitude and there was also his anger, and his heavy drinking.

'When he returned, he really seemed very upset. What was more alarming was that his shirt was heavily bloodstained and his knuckle damaged. We assumed he had been in a fight, but he wouldn't speak to us, and he went straight to his room. He didn't cook anything for us that evening. He did do something, though, that seemed very strange. When he thought nobody could see him – but in fact I did – he took the T-shirt he had been wearing, the one with the bloodstain, out into the yard, and burned it.'

The clerk of the court goes solemnly to the cardboard box of evidence that sits below the judges' bench and takes from it the T-shirt, in a plastic bag. He holds it up to Marenkian.

'Are these the remains of Denner's T-shirt?'

Marenkian studies the charred purple fabric.

'It looks like the same shirt.'

'Continue, please.'

'Later on Bruno discovered, by a coincidence, that he needed further supplies of his medication from Dr Schenck, and so I asked Denner to take him down there. Obviously I knew nothing of what had happened to Dr Schenck, and I felt that Denner should be made to do his job, and so I asked him to go down to Nice and collect what was needed. He refused point-blank. He seemed very upset by the idea of going to Dr Schenck's house at all. But he couldn't give any reason for not wanting to go, and I insisted, and there was an argument, but finally he went.

'He got back much later, and told me that Dr Schenck had been killed, and I called the police. And when the police arrived we had to account for our movements, of course, and I felt I should tell them what I knew of his involvement.'

*

At about six thirty Bruno came back.

The three of us gathered in the long sitting room to receive him, brought out of our respective hiding places by the distinctive sound of the Range Rover's engine. We stood there in the evening light: a tableau casting shadows on the terra-cotta. Marenkian was centre stage; Natalie behind, near the stairs, haughty, avoiding my eye. I stood near the door to the kitchen, unsure whether they'd allow me to stay. I still didn't know all that I needed to know to win this game.

Bruno strode through the French windows with the swinging gait of a circus clown.

Marenkian said, 'Bruno, where have you been?'

He replied in a sing-song voice, 'Hello, everybody. Here's the car. I'm just fine, you'll be glad to know.' Then he grinned, and stood there looking with an inane expression from one of us to the next.

'Give the car keys to Johnny,' Marenkian ordered.

So he still trusts me. Will Natalie give me away? Not to him.

'Hold your horses,' Bruno said, and laughed.

'Give them to him, Bruno.'

Then everyone noticed – at the same time it seemed – that Bruno had dried blood all over his neck and T-shirt, and a nasty-looking cut on his left ear. He seemed also to have broken the skin on his knuckles.

'What have you done to yourself?' Marenkian said.

'These Frogs, they're so rude, you know. They're just so rude.' He laughed, and then underwent an abrupt change. 'Oh,' he said, and his legs almost buckled under him. Marenkian walked over, put an arm round his back, and guided him to one of the sofas, where they both sat down.

'Why did you have to go and . . . take the car?'

'You wouldn't let me go anywhere. Oh,' Bruno moaned

again, and slumped on his side, and began slowly to curl up into a ball.

'Bruno, what's the matter?' Marenkian asked. 'You've been in a fight. Are you badly hurt?'

Bruno was shaking his head.

'Did somebody hit you in the belly?'

Bruno kept shaking his head, still curled up. Then he turned his face upwards. Again he seemed completely smashed.

I looked across at Natalie, still standing at a distance. The expression I saw on her face was not nice. There was a contempt there, one might have said; like frigid laughter. Then her father was gazing at her too, and his voice betrayed his anxiety.

'He went to see Schenck, didn't he?'

'I don't know,' she replied, with some attempt at instilling a little concern.

'Help him upright,' Marenkian said angrily.

She stood still for a moment.

'I – Daddy, I feel sick.'

Like hell you do, you bitch. 'Johnny, call Max Schenck, please. Johnny!' He almost shouted. I had missed him the first time. 'Tell him it's an emergency, and he must get here straight away.'

'Yes – yes, sure,' I said, and went over to the phone.

Natalie went upstairs.

I dialled Schenck's number and got his answering machine.

'Dr Schenck,' I said flatly, 'this is Johnny Denner calling you on behalf of Mr Marenkian at six o'clock on Thursday. Could you come to the house as soon as possible, please.'

I wondered what he'd make of that. He probably wouldn't believe me. If he did receive the message, I'd have to see the bastard again. Open the door to him and take his coat.

'OK,' Marenkian said, 'let's get these cuts clean.'

I went to the kitchen, and got the first-aid kit, then, on

Marenkian's instruction, sat down next to him on the sofa, handing him cotton wool, strips of gauze which I had cut with a pair of scissors, a bottle of proprietary antiseptic, and sticking plasters. The cuts on Bruno's ears were nothing to worry about, but his right hand was a bit of a mess, the skin folded back from two of his knuckles and a deep gouge across the back of his hand. I hated to think of the damage done to whoever had been on the receiving end. Perhaps Bruno had been unlucky, as it were, and scored a direct hit on some teeth.

With another dramatic mood swing he seemed to return to near-normal. He submitted to his father's nursing quietly. It was a touching scene, somehow, and Marenkian had a certain dignity, his sleeves rolled up, carefully administering first aid. He was calm and methodical, gently working out the dried blood and any dirt that might be in the wounds. It no longer seemed likely that Bruno had taken an overdose, which thought had crossed my mind, and doubtless Marenkian's – hence his willingness to have Schenck back in the house.

The shoulder and half the chest of Bruno's T-shirt were covered in blood. I had glanced at it queasily, and wondered how he might have attracted such a quantity of the stuff.

Marenkian looked at it uneasily, then said to Bruno, 'Take your shirt off.'

Bruno did so, slowly and a little painfully. Marenkian took it, handed it to me, and said: 'Burn this, will you, please. Right away.'

'Sure.'

I took it through to the kitchen, then outside to the barbecue. I stood with the shirt in one hand and the plastic bottle of kerosene in the other, thinking: *If I were working for Horst, I wouldn't burn this at all. I would burn something else, and keep it, because Marenkian must have a reason for wanting it burned.* But I didn't want to land Bruno in anything. He had enough troubles already. And I wasn't working for

Horst any more. So I soaked it in the liquid and put a match to it.

After refusing something to eat and being refused pastis Bruno went up to his room to rest.

At about seven o'clock the phone rang. I answered it, and I got a surprise.

'Marenkian residence.'

'Yes, Johnny,' Horst said quietly and deliberately. 'You won't have to stay there much longer. We have made some progress, you know, and we are quite near a solution now. Give me Marenkian.'

I told Marenkian it was Horst on the line, and he took the call in his office. I didn't dare eavesdrop.

At about ten the internal phone rang.

'Come down to my office, please, Johnny. I need you to go to Nice.'

Now, perhaps, I would know what they had said to each other. When I entered he asked me to sit down, and poured me a brandy. Was he about to make me a counter-offer?

'Well, Johnny, I feel as if you've been here a lot longer than you have, given the things you've seen. I want to thank you for your – forbearance.'

Horst can't have told him anything about me, then.

'It's really nothing at all,' I said.

'I don't think it's nothing. I think it's more than we could expect. But, of course, you know I'm going to ask you not to say anything to anybody about Bruno's . . . movements, and his situation.'

'Sure. OK.'

'I'm sure that this is another of his brawls, and that the Frenchman with no manners will be at home with a steak on his head. But I didn't want to question Bruno about it this evening.'

'No, I'm sure it wasn't very serious, although he had me a bit worried with the – with the fact that he doesn't usually drive.'

There was a pause.

'Yes.' He was closing the subject. 'Anyway, not a word. Bruno has been here all afternoon, right?'

'Right.'

'And Horst – surprising to hear from him. He was telling me that he's been in Moscow for the last month, and he's flying back there tomorrow. Going to come and see me with a business proposition – and he asked me to send regards to his skipper. Says he's going to give you lunch.'

'Right.'

'Although you're our butler now, I told him, and we wouldn't want him to wean you away from us with the kind of expensive lunch he likes so much.'

'No, no. No chance of that.'

'Well, watch out. You probably know there are no free lunches in town. Now, this little trip to Nice – it's for Bruno's medication. We have to get him some. I'll be honest with you. I've decided he should take a holiday from seeing Max Schenck, but he does still need the medication. I've just called Schenck and told him you'll be down to pick up a package some time before eleven. He told me he might be working in the basement, but you're to go right into the house – call out to him if he's not around.'

So Schenck wanted a confrontation. What purpose could that serve? Would he try his luck – have a go? Nervousness sprang into my stomach, and my mouth felt dry. I couldn't face up to this – I had had enough. 'I'm sorry, Mr Marenkian, but I've had rather a lot to drink tonight. Would you mind very much if I went tomorrow morning?'

He looked up at me with sharp disapproval.

'Yes, I *would* mind,' he said simply. 'I'd mind very much. Bruno is sick and he needs his medication. That must be the priority.'

'Oh. I see. I didn't realize he had run out.'

'He has. I don't think you need worry about a little drink-driving, Johnny. You're sober enough, and they don't enforce the law very seriously. I'd like you to set off now, please.'

So I walked back up the garden, fetched the car keys, and went. It was hard to know what else I could do.

Behind the wheel I talked aloud, inciting myself into a state of readiness, arming myself for the confrontation with my rival.

'I've had to come and see you, Schenck, you fucking arsehole. I've been *ordered* to see you. Haven't you got any bloody shame? Fucking both of them, you scummy old man. This is your speciality, is it? Your code of conduct?' Then I paused for a minute, reflecting that he would laugh in my face. What did he care about codes of conduct?

'What are you talking about?' said Bruno's voice in my ear, and I jumped a foot in the seat, and with a convulsive twist of the wheel practically drove off the road.

'Bruno, what the hell are you doing in here?'

'Going to see Max Schenck, who has something that belongs to me.'

He again had that unnatural sing-song lilt in his voice, a dangerous lilt.

'We're going home,' I said, and slowed the car.

He suddenly snarled, 'Fuck, we are,' and he poked a kitchen knife against my neck, just below the ear, and for the second time I practically drove off the road. 'You fucking drive the car.'

'OK, Bruno, OK. No need for this, there's no need for the knife, Bruno; I'll take you there, OK?'

'He has something that belongs to me, and I'm going to get it back.'

'OK. Please just take the knife away, OK?'

He paused for ten or twenty seconds, then pulled it away from my neck.

'OK, Bruno, we're going to go and see him, both of us.'

He slumped back in the seat and said nothing for some time. I was bolt upright, and the back of my neck tingled with its exposure to this nutcase with a knife. I thought of stopping and jumping out, but every light was green. So I resorted to talk. *Talk him down.*

'What do you want from him, eh?'

He ignored the question.

'What do you want from Schenck? More drugs?'

'Why do you wanna know, huh?' he slurred. 'What do you care about Max Schenck?'

'I don't like what he's doing to you.'

'He doesn't give a shit about me.'

There was a pause.

'Really? What makes you think that?'

'I found out.'

'What did you find out?'

'I found out.'

He liked that phrase. I left it there, because an extra edge had crept into his voice, and he still had the knife in his hand.

'So what has he got that belongs to you?'

'He has fucking sinned, man. He's fucked me over. He's taken everything I've got. I'm gonna get what I own. I'm gonna get it back, fuck.'

We drove through the crowded town centre to the familiar street on the edge of the hill, and stopped. The foreground of silent houses was black as ink against the glitter of lights in the valley below.

'What have you got to get back?'

'My property, Johnny.' Bruno was more alert now as he climbed out of the back and shook his shoulders, the knife still in his hand. It was an eight-inch Drieszack, and I winced at the thought that he had been holding the tip under my ear. One pothole and eight pints of Denner would have been on the floor.

'I have to collect some medication. That's why your father sent me down. Why don't you just wait for me?'

He looked at me strangely, sceptically. I could hear the distant breath of the traffic.

'I tell you what,' I said, without much hope. 'You want to see him, you want your medication, so I'll give him a message. I'll get back from him whatever he's taken.'

He thought. A car passed.

'No. I wanna talk to him.'

I sighed. 'OK.'

The house was dark save for a dim light coming from the study across the hall. I walked across to it, saying quietly, 'Dr Schenck? Hello.' It was very quiet in there.

Papers were scattered in the hall outside the study. I went through the door. The room was a mess; all the drawers had been emptied on the floor. Schenck was slumped in a wooden swivel chair by the desk, slumped at a peculiar angle, one leg out in front of him, the other jammed under the chair, his head twisted to one side. I think I realized at that moment that he was dead. His posture was so unnatural; he looked as if he had been shoved into the chair by somebody, his left arm forced between his leg and the arm-rest, his right laid across his stomach.

I became aware of Bruno beside me. He murmured in a high-pitched voice, 'Oh fuck. Oh shit. Oh, Max. Oh shit.'

I suddenly realized that I mustn't let him crack up, although I suddenly felt very strange myself.

'Bruno, get a grip,' I whispered. 'Stay there. Don't move. Don't move.'

I went over to Schenck. It was all right from the back –

just. But from the front it was disgusting. Somebody had beaten his face with incredible savagery. It was blown up, the skin stretched tight. The eyes were closed, the nose swollen to a great plug, the lips bloated, lumpy, and broken. The colours were – well, there was an overall waxy white-yellow, with patches of a purple and black. And the whole was drenched in shiny blood, blood which was also on his shirt and spattered on the chair, the desk, everything around him.

I stood motionless for a moment, bracing myself to do one thing I had to do, in humanity. I touched his arm, avoiding a splash of dried blood. He wasn't cold, but he wasn't warm either. He was dead.

Bruno stood with an extraordinary expression on his face. (But then, so did I. I had felt my face twisting into a grimace of disgust.) His shoulders were hunched over, and he was breathing very fast, and I thought: If he goes on like this, he's going to faint, and we won't get out of here. I looked at him, and for a second the thought crossed my mind: Could *he* have done it? Is that why he came back hysterical and bloodied this afternoon? But I dismissed that almost straight away. I didn't believe him capable of it. And he seemed genuinely surprised.

As if reading my mind, he started a continuous shaking of his head, still breathing fast, and repeated in a soft voice, staring at me with imploring eyes, 'I didn't do it. I didn't do it. I didn't do it.'

'I know you didn't do it, Bruno,' I whispered, and put my hands on his upper arms. 'Get a grip of yourself. We've got to get out of here, and we've got to look normal. Take some deep, slow breaths, now.' He looked very ill, and swayed slightly.

'Breathe slowly.' He started to ventilate more normally, and he steadied himself.

'Listen,' he said, 'I've still gotta get something. This notebook.'

'What notebook?'

'It's a notebook that belongs to my father. I have to find it.'

'Bruno, we've got to get out of here.'

He ignored me, pushing past me with the evident object of getting to the wooden filing cabinet in the corner at the far side of Schenck's desk. So, before I could stop him, he came face to face with the battered corpse, and he stopped for a second, and put his hand up to his mouth, and retched. It was a dry retch, thank God.

He stood by the filing cabinet, staring stupidly; its contents were on the floor. The same applied to the desk.

I said again, 'Bruno, we've got to get out of here,' and again he ignored me.

You *sent* me down here, Marenkian.

'Bruno, the police may come any minute. We can't be found here.'

'I know, I know. But I gotta get this notebook.' He squatted on the floor and started rifling through the papers.

'This is no time to get some notebook,' I said.

'The notebook is the reason for this. I've got to get it.'

'We haven't got time.'

'Shut up,' he said, surprisingly.

He crawled around on the floor among the papers for a little while, then stood up and sighed, looking around him for inspiration. Then he went to the bookcase above the desk. At about the level of his eyes was a row of tall, thick, green books: the collected works of Jung. My mind drifted away, despite the body in the chair. For the last twenty-four hours I had thought I wanted to see this happening to Schenck. But I knew now I hadn't been serious. I felt a certain regret for him, a real sympathy. I wondered who would mourn him. Natalie would mourn him, but I wasn't glad of that. *I* had done this to him. In a sense *I* was guilty of this. Bruno ran his eyes over the books, one hand raised. Then he pulled out the eighth volume, held it by the spine and shook it. Nothing fell out. He replaced it, took out the seventh and repeated the performance, with the same result.

'Christ! Come on, Bruno, are you going to shake every one of these fucking things?'

Why did you send me down here, Marenkian?

'Wait. Just wait a minute.'

He took out the ninth volume. Nothing. Then, more and more frenzied, he shook every one of the books, but there was nothing in any of them.

By that time we had been there for at least five minutes. It had occurred to me to leave without him, but I decided against it. I urged him over and over to drop it, but he wouldn't. He rummaged through the other books on the shelves and looked under the sofa, chairs, and rug.

'Goddam it,' he muttered.

He looked in the curtains, and turned the prints on the walls. Then he went over to the telephone, a heavy, old-fashioned one, studied it, then slowly picked it up. Nothing there either.

Did you know that Schenck was dead? Did you send me down here, knowing that?

'Bruno, I'm going now.'

To send the police in after me? Not with Bruno here, surely, I thought, then realized Marenkian couldn't know Bruno was with me.

'Bruno,' I said, 'I'm going now. You can come with me or not. But I'm going.' And I turned and walked.

Finally, when I reached the front door, he caught up with me and grabbed me by the arm.

Then he said, very intensely and deliberately, 'Did you see what he did with the letter I sent him?'

'No. I just put it through the letterbox.'

'I've got to get it.' He had frozen.

'No way, Bruno. We've taken enough time.'

'I've got to.'

'Bruno, I'm going now. Get in the car with me, or stay.'

'I threatened him in this letter. I threatened him.'

'Nobody's going to think you killed him. Come on.'

Still he stood there, so I got in the car, started the engine, and manoeuvred in the parking space, ignoring him. And just as I was pulling out he ran to the car and jumped in.

As we drove fast down the hill we were passed by three police cars in quick succession, sirens wailing. It was possible they were going to Schenck's, but we didn't hang around to find out.

Chapter Seventeen

MARENKIAN, YOU bastard. So charming, weren't you? Now I know why, you cunning bastard. The blood was dry, and the temperature of his body about the same as the room's. You wanted the police to find me there, didn't you? You spoke to Horst, and he told you what he had done. You and Horst are good friends really, aren't you? Were you looking for this book, too? Both of you? Is that why he was beaten so badly?

In the dim industrial outskirts I saw a bar open. I pulled in.

'Do you want a drink?' I said.

'Yeah.'

'OK.'

Feeling old and heavy-limbed I walked slowly into the bar behind him. There were a row of three booths at the back, and we occupied the furthest of them. The barman strolled round to us, took our order, and brought us a beer each.

We drank the first one in silence, then ordered another.

Bruno said, 'I don't understand how he could've let that happen.'

I looked at him but didn't reply.

I thought about Natalie, grimly, about the shock this would cause her, about the grief she would feel for him. Could I tell her? Something more: that green set of the collected works of C. G. Jung had made me imagine Schenck when he was young, at a time when he must have been a dedicated psychotherapist,

when he must still have had some principles. His life story had
had a sudden, appalling ending.

Bruno said again, 'I just don't understand it. I wish he had
listened to me. But it was always me listening to him.'

'Did Natalie ever see much of Max Schenck?' I asked.

'No,' he said. 'She used to see him occasionally when he
came to the house for lunch, which he did sometimes. That
was when he got on better with my dad, but for the last couple
months my dad wouldn't have him in the house.'

'Really? Why?'

Bruno twisted his lip and shrugged.

'He didn't trust him, I guess.'

He paused, then looked up.

'But who the hell did it?'

Oh, well, I thought.

'Horst Stacker. That's my guess. Or probably not Horst,
but this little Russian heavy he takes around with him, name of
Yari.'

'Why?'

'What do you mean, why?'

'But you must know something, I mean you – you work for
Horst, don't you?'

'I don't work for him. I work for your father. I don't know
why everyone seems to think I work for Horst.'

'It's what Natalie said.'

'Well, you said yourself that Natalie was a liar. You were
right about that.'

There was a silence, but I could feel him looking at me.

Then he said, 'Yeah, she's a liar.' There was another silence,
which he broke with, 'I just don't understand it. You see, Max
was so strong – not just mentally, but physically too. I don't
understand how he could've let that happen.'

I didn't know what to say to him.

'Do you *really* think it was Horst?'

'Bruno, I don't know who else it could have been, but then I don't know anyone else. Let's have a whisky.'

'OK.'

I shouted the order.

'Why do *you* think he was killed?' I said.

'I don't know.'

'So tell me about it.'

'What?'

'Your visit to Max this afternoon.'

'I didn't see him. He wasn't there.'

'Come on, Bruno. How many people do you think are going to believe that? You go out this afternoon; you come back bloodied. You've been in some kind of very violent encounter. Five hours later we find Max Schenck dead.'

He rose to the occasion. 'Hey. If I had killed Max, why would I come back here now?'

'To get the notebook you keep talking about. We took a hell of a risk there, staying and trying to find it. So how about you tell me what it is, this notebook?'

'It's nothing, man. It's a personal thing.'

'It's a *personal* thing. Did Schenck get killed for it?'

'No. I don't know why he could have got killed.'

He was starting to look angry.

'This notebook also happens to be something that belongs to you. You were talking about it in the car on the way here.'

'I didn't know he was dead when I said that.'

'And some time in the next few minutes you're going to ask me to forget that you hid in the Range Rover. Your father's going to be pleased. Another mistake.'

He was silent.

'Tell me something. Have you run out of medication?'

He looked puzzled. 'No. I still have some.'

So you did send me down on a pretext. I almost regret we weren't caught; that would have landed you in it, framing your own stupid son.

'What's the notebook?'

He was thinking hard, his eyes darting from me to the table, the glass, his cigarette.

Then he said, 'OK, I'll tell you what it was.' He seemed more lucid now than he had been for weeks. He breathed a deep sigh. 'You may know that my father's specialty is the movement of funds between companies, one owned by another, in a chain of—'

'Yeah, I know all about that,' I interrupted.

'Well, ultimately you have to keep a record of it all: a personal disposable record.'

'Right.'

'Which is why my father keeps this small notebook of hand-written lists. A is owned by B, owned by C. Augustus by Claudius, Claudius by Nero.'

'Companies, you mean?'

'Yeah. Nero Asset International, Claudius Investment SA, that kind of thing.'

I said something very slowly to him. 'Just finish explaining this concept to me. So all these companies are owned by *other* companies. They make a maze. It's hard to investigate them. OK, I understand that. But where does it end? If someone gets right to the end of a chain, what does he find?'

'Bearer shares. Certificates with no names on them, just "Bearer".'

'So whoever holds the shares owns all those companies?'

'Sure. But he has to know where to find the companies in order to use the shares.'

'And where to find them is in the notebook.'

'Right.'

My God!

'And are you telling me this is the notebook that Schenck had?'

He pursed his lips and nodded.

'How the hell did he get it?'

Bruno looked down for a while, reluctant even to speak. Then he slugged back the whisky and told me.

'I took it from my father. I – oh shit, this just sounds so fucking crazy but Max made me take it from my father.'

'He what?'

'He got me to take things from my father.' He paused, then said quietly but insistently, as if he were trying to convince himself that it had been reasonable: 'It was a part of my treatment.'

'Oh come on, Bruno. How could stealing your father's papers be part of any treatment?'

He looked stubborn and slightly petulant.

'You don't understand.'

'No, I don't.'

Bruno stared into the distance, miserable.

'He ripped me off completely. He deceived me into taking things that he wanted, and he told me that it was a part of my treatment.'

'What do you mean, it was part of your treatment?'

'You wouldn't understand.'

'Try me.'

He sighed, twisted his jaw and said, 'That it was therapy. I've had problems for a while, right? And so I went to Max, and he really helped. We talked a lot about my father. And he – Max, I mean – he said that if I wanted to be strong and well, I needed to get rid of the influence of my father – that my father was keeping me thinking like a kid. That I couldn't develop my own personality until I had freed myself from his dominance. And he knew that my father wouldn't let me become involved in his work, and he suggested that I should go and read the stuff that my father worked on, that then I was, like, taking some of his strength doing that. Maybe it helped me a little, I dunno, but then he said, "OK, if you take some of this stuff and bring it to me, documents and that kind of thing, then that will help," and there wouldn't be anything wrong with doing that because I was just kind of – borrowing it, like it would be like an exercise or a game, you know, and he was my doctor so it was all confidential. That's what he called it: an exercise. A therapeutic exercise. Role playing.'

'Didn't you think this was strange, what you were doing?'

'You see' – he said, and struggled for words – 'it was like – it was like a kind of game, and – and it *did* kind of feel good, and I *trusted* him. You see, it – it all took place over a long time, and it seemed to make sense. Ah, shit.'

He put his fist up to his face in a gesture I recognized.

'I've just screwed it up again, and now I'm in such bad trouble because they're gonna think it was me.' He seemed on the verge of tears.

After a moment I asked, 'How long did he have the notebook?'

He shook his head and sighed. 'Two months. Three maybe.'

'How did he justify that?'

'He didn't.' Here his voice hardened. 'Oh, sure. This is where even I stopped believing in it. It was totally by chance that I found the notebook in the first place. It's one of my father's most important documents – the key to his whole business. I just – I guess I just wanted to say to Max, "*Look at this*!" This is my father's *bible*. He takes it with him everywhere. He updates it once a week, every week, on Friday night. You can take any one of his companies and look it up in the notebook. And you can find out where it is, and which other company owns it, if any. It's the key that unlocks the whole thing.'

'And you gave it to Max.'

'I gave it to Max. Shit, I didn't even know what I was doing, and the drugs he was giving me were – I didn't know what time of day it was.'

'And this was about two months ago. So Marenkian's known all this time this valuable information was missing, and he hasn't done anything.'

'He *is* doing things. He's very confident, and doesn't panic, you know? I thought I was gonna take it back, like the other things. But Max wouldn't give it back to me. He started asking about the shares. He started saying to me: "Hey, Bruno, for the next part of your therapy you need to start taking things that have a real value. Like some of the share certificates relating to these companies." And I said: "Listen, I don't know where these certificates are or how I can get them." And I was thinking: What are you really interested in? Me or my father's money? I told him to give the notebook back and he wouldn't. Then I wrote the letter I gave you.'

My God. Bruno's letter. I still hadn't opened it, believing I knew what its contents would be: a tiresome plea for drugs. I had been wrong.

'That's why I needed to find it. The police are going to find that letter.'

'What did it say?'

'I threatened him,' he said quietly. 'I said if he didn't give the notebook back I'd kill him. Shit.' He shook his head slowly. 'Shit.'

After a while I said, 'I wouldn't worry too much. Your father'll protect you. But he'd better not know you were there tonight. That wasn't in his plans, I don't think. I'm going to drop you well away from the house. And you've got to get in without anyone knowing. OK?'

'OK. Hey, Johnny. Thanks, man.'

'It's all right.'

We had stopped.

'I don't think the notebook was there,' he said. 'I think that whoever killed him was looking for it, and that's why the drawers were emptied. Or maybe they were looking for anything belonging to my father. Horst would have been very thorough. He might even have seen my father by now.'

'What?'

'Well, he works for him.'

I struggled not to let him see my surprise. Bruno needed to respect me.

'But maybe they didn't find it,' I said.

'OK. But if Max didn't have it, who would?'

'Good question. Come on, Bruno. I'm going to circle. I'll see you in the morning.'

'Madame,' I said to myself as I sped along the Vence road, 'there is an emergency. I know it's the middle of the night, but I must collect the *Factures 79* file for Monsieur Marenkian. No, I can't explain. Yes, I know – the second time. But please, madame; I must hurry—'

If she didn't play ball I'd brain her.

The living room was lit by a single table lamp, and Natalie lay on the sofa, eyes closed, a Walkman beating its beat into her ears. She didn't hear me, and for a moment I stood there, wondering what the hell I was going to say, wondering how I could attract her attention without touching her, wondering how much she knew and, more than anything else, what her stake in his game had been. Max knows how to deal with him, she had said. Max had miscalculated, and now his game was over.

I was disgusted by her.

She seemed to sense my presence, and she opened her eyes and looked at me, switching the machine off.

'Hi. How was the party?'

She stretched, then swivelled to a kneeling position on the sofa, and said, 'So how's Max?'

Bitch!

I stood expressionless.

'Oh, come on,' she said.

I had no pleasure in saying it. 'He's dead. Somebody has killed him.'

She stared at me, an involuntary smile of shock flickering around her mouth. Then she turned away, faced the wall.

I stood in silence before finally saying, 'I'm sorry.'

Another silence, then she said, 'I'll have to tell my father.'

I agreed with her, and the nerves rose slightly in my stomach. She turned back and looked at me, and her face was as I had never seen it. I can't really describe the expression: wooden, narrow. But her eyes were full of black flame. She got up and slowly walked out.

I had to wait ten minutes before Marenkian came down. He was wearing a silk dressing gown and his grey hair was slicked down.

'Natalie tells me Max Schenck has been killed.'

'That's right. Bludgeoned to death.'

'Have you called the police?'

He was very calm, made no pretence of surprise.

'I didn't need to. They were on their way up Cimiez Hill as I left. I only just missed them. Their timing was very nearly perfect.'

'That would have been very unfortunate for you.'

'Very. And for you too, though you didn't know it.'

'What do you mean, Johnny?'

'Bruno was with me.'

He became quite still.

'He stowed away in the car.'

There was what seemed a long silence, and it was with some difficulty that I held it.

'He didn't go down for medication, of course. Because he hadn't run out.'

A pause.

'You're clearly implying that I was setting you up,' he said slowly, then shook his head. 'You're wrong. I was determined that Bruno should never go to that guy again. I had finally realized that Max Schenck was an unscrupulous and unprincipled individual who was using his profession as cover for other, unpleasant activities. I've been aware of this for some time. But very recently I was approached by a business contact who provided me with the details of an actual extortion. It involved the brother of a property developer who had confessed to Max Schenck certain unpleasant paedophile crimes. Schenck had blackmailed him.

'With regard to Bruno his approach was different, of course. He was using Bruno to obtain confidential information relating to my clients. I had to stop Bruno from seeing him, but one thing that stood in the way was that Bruno required a continuing supply of these drugs. So I asked Schenck for a supply to tide him over until he could enter a new treatment. That's why I asked you to go down there, Johnny. The police arriving had nothing to do with me.'

'And Schenck's death? Also nothing to do with you?'

'What do you take me for?' he said, spreading his hands. 'I'm a lawyer, not an assassin. My concern was to get my son out of there, and then if possible expose the man by legal means. That's my speciality. I don't have a gun, or any other weapon. I work in the courtroom.'

'And what about Bruno?'

'What about him?'

'It must have occurred to you that he'll be a suspect.'

He paused, as though to turn over this new possibility in his mind.

'Maybe he will. Maybe we all will. We'll just have to take it as it comes. I'm very sorry you feel the way you do; that you suspect me of having tried to frame you, which I promise you is something that doesn't happen in real life, and would be far too unreliable and difficult a way to settle scores. You've been a very good employee here, but if you want to go after all this, I'll understand, and I'll make a settlement. Maybe six months' money, or something.' He sighed. 'I think we're gonna go anyway, get Bruno away from here.'

'I'm sorry,' I said. 'It's been a bad day, and I shouldn't accuse you of that, and I don't. It's just been hard to take, that's all.'

'Harder for Bruno,' he said, and I thought: and Natalie?

I shut the door behind me, numbed. I could have slept where I stood. But I forced myself to do one thing: at last I got my two suitcases out and threw my possessions into them. I was going to leave at dawn, and do what I could with what I had.

I lay down, and only seconds later, it seemed, I felt something, and I opened my eyes. But I was hardly conscious, and so tired I couldn't summon the energy to move. Natalie was sitting on the bed, and the light was on. Her eyes were wet.

'Johnny,' she whispered. 'Johnny.'

She reached out tentatively towards my head, and tried to stroke my hair. In my stupor I was at first indifferent, then I turned my head to avoid her hand. She was talking.

'I can never explain it to you, I know that. He had a hold on me, he was . . . he was a powerful man, and I needed that, and I knew he could help me. He tempted me with how he could.

'Johnny, I've got to know what you told Horst. Please tell me, I know you can never forgive me, but please tell me.'

I stayed silent.

'You must think it's pretty callous, getting Bruno to take it, but I couldn't stop Max. He knew he could do what he liked with Bruno, and he didn't think Bruno would come to any harm. He told me it would help cure him. I didn't mean any of this to happen.'

'No,' I murmured.

'I had nothing,' she said. 'I had nothing. Bruno got everything. That made me so angry, but I didn't mean anything like this to happen.' Still I stayed silent.

'Johnny, please. I'm scared now. I'm so scared. What's going to happen?'

'I don't know.'

'You've got to tell me something. What does Horst know?'

I was silent.

'Johnny, please. What does he know?'

After a while I said this:

'He doesn't know anything. I haven't told him or anyone else anything about you.'

She threw herself down so that her face rested on my hip. She felt for my hand through the sheet. She was kissing the sheet. She raised her head and whispered, 'I loved you. I love you.'

And I said, 'Go away, please.'

She became very still, and stayed that way for some time. Then she whispered, 'I'm sorry.'

Then she got up and left.

Chapter Eighteen

SOME TIME LATER I felt myself being shaken, and, still half in a dream, I thought: She's come back. This time I'll forgive her, whatever she has done. I twisted around in the bed, and mumbled her name.

Then I was shaken again, and I realized that nobody was touching me, that whoever was shaking me was shaking the bed, kicking the bed, in fact; kicking it hard so that my head was suddenly jolted against the frame.

And then a sneering voice said, 'Wakey-wakey. It is your girlfriend.'

It was Yari. He kicked the bed again, and then changed his tone.

'Hey, get up. I haven't got all fucking day.'

I sat up and he watched me, grinning.

'Jesus,' I murmured. I felt dreadful; feeble and exhausted.

'Come on.'

He frightened me, and I thanked God that he worked for Horst, and Horst was on my side. What he had done to Schenck was what frightened me. I knew now what he was capable of.

He left the room and I swivelled myself out of bed. My limbs felt heavy as lead, and every one of them ached. I got dressed, washed my face in cold water, and brushed my hair. Then I went downstairs. It was quarter to six, and I was nervous, early-morning nervous, a sensation I remembered from the beginnings of ill-prepared military exercises, punishing training routines. Horst and Yari's presence couldn't be good for anyone. There must be trouble in store.

It was like being in a strange place, the house unfamiliar in the brightening grey light before the sun, the sprinklers hissing in the garden. The living room was full of pale figures. Horst lay on the sofa. Marenkian stood by the window. Yari stood behind, near the fireplace. Bruno and Natalie were next to Marenkian, as if for protection. Their faces were closed up with sleep.

Had the gate not been broken it would have been impossible for them to get in. But perhaps there had been nothing forced about their entry. Perhaps Marenkian had invited them.

I said, 'Morning, Horst,' then, getting no reply. 'Would people like some coffee?'

There was a pause before Marenkian said, 'Yes, please, Johnny. Coffee all round.'

So I went through into the kitchen, leaving the door open, and made coffee. There was hardly any talk while I wasn't in the room. Just a few short, murmured exchanges.

I took the coffee through and served it, then started back to the kitchen. I was going to try to be a servant, nothing more.

But it was too late for that. On my way back across the room Marenkian said, 'Johnny, where are you going?'

'Just back into the kitchen. Would you like me to stay?'

'Yari didn't get you out of bed to make coffee. Sit down, please. Horst is here so we can get a few things settled.'

I sat down.

'Max Schenck was killed last night. Johnny found him, so he's done us another small service in letting us know. Now it seems that Max Schenck was in possession of property belonging to me. I have to tell you that this property is worthless without certain other documents that relate to it. So the property enshrined in those documents, among them certain investments of Horst's, is intact.'

'I'm not so goddam confident about that, Marenkian. I thought that one of your strengths was your total confidentiality. Whereas this information is flying about the whole of Nice.'

'I'd hardly say that, Horst.'

'Schenck, Bruno, now Johnny. Every one of those companies is to be dissolved, goddam. You've compromised yourself as much as me, you asshole. And what would Agostini say if he knew, huh? And all the others?'

'Why don't you tell me something I don't know?' Marenkian's temperature was rising a little. 'These things aren't readily comprehensible unless you explain them. Let's not make things worse.' I knew what he was saying, as they both glanced at me, and I stared at my feet, as if body language could say: *Look, I don't understand any of this. I haven't made any connections. I don't want to understand.*

'Do you know how much trouble you and your stupid family have caused me? Do you know?'

'I am aware of your problems, and I will reimburse your expenses.'

'You will do more than that. Do you think I care about the money?' After a pause, Horst said: 'What do you think this kind of thing does for my reputation, huh?'

'Perhaps I could remind you that we would now be in possession of our property if Max Schenck hadn't been killed. Did that occur to you?'

Horst grunted and continued to pace the room.

'Are you telling me that Schenck got this on his own?' he said eventually. He came to rest in front of Bruno, who seemed hardly able to bear looking at him. 'How do you think he got it, Bruno? Huh? Any ideas?'

'No,' Bruno whispered after a moment.

'You took it, didn't you?'

'I—'

'Did you think you could get away with stealing my money?'

'I didn't – I didn't know what he was doing.'

'Don't give me that shit, boy. You made a fucking bad mistake.'

'Horst,' I said, very respectfully, just to see, 'I don't think it was Bruno's idea at all. I think he was used and misled. I don't think he's responsible for it.'

Horst turned and looked at me. He was livid.

'You,' he shouted. 'You fucking shut up. You are the most stupid of all of these.'

Yari grinned at me. Bruno looked at his feet, Natalie stared out of the window. Horst shoved his hands in his pockets, paced across the room, then came back to Bruno.

'And then you killed the man. Always a risk for a head shrinker, huh, that one of his patients might go mad and kill him.'

Marenkian intervened. 'That's enough, Horst. Don't try throwing your weight around here.'

'Who the fuck are you?' growled the Russian.

'Shut up, Yari,' Horst said, and there was silence, and it was suddenly quite clear who was in charge. Marenkian looked at Yari as though he were noting him down. It was not a look I would have liked to receive.

'Come down to my office now,' he said, 'and we'll settle this.'

'OK,' Horst said immediately. 'And Yari can look after the young people.'

We sat morosely in our various corners of the room for several minutes, until Bruno turned to Natalie.

'What do you know about this?' he whispered.

'Nothing,' she said.

'Come on, don't give me that shit. I know you've seen him.'

'Shut up, Bruno, for Christ's sake,' she hissed.

'Yeah, shut up,' Yari said, which seemed to me pretty moronic, given that he had the opportunity of learning, more or less, what was going on.

'You just tell me where the fucking book is.'

'What book?'

'Dad's blue book.'

'I haven't got it,' she said. 'Bruno, please.'

Then Yari walked over to where Bruno sat and grabbed his face, turning it up to him, squeezing hard.

'I told you to shut the fuck up.' He palmed him back. Bruno swayed, blinked and rubbed his cheeks, and his face filled with fury. But Yari reached into the back of his trousers, under the leather jacket he was wearing, pulled out a battered old pistol, and clicked off the safety catch. Bruno looked at it. I thought for a moment that he was going to have a go at Yari just the same, but he mastered himself. Then Yari laughed a little.

Natalie turned and looked out of the window. So Yari had killed Schenck, and here I was in a room with him, and a gun which he happened to be holding. It was all utterly implausible. A gun? This was a Provençal farmhouse deeply to die for. I was a cavalry officer. This only happened in the movies. But I thought I knew what was coming; Marenkian had tried it last night. It would tie up their loose ends nicely.

I decided to test my theory. I walked over and picked up the coffee jug, then went towards the kitchen.

'Where you think you are going?' Yari said.

'I'm just going to make some more coffee.'

'Uh-uh,' he said, shaking his head.

'It's only into the kitchen. You can come if you like.'

'Sit.'

'Come on, Yari. We're on the same side.'

'Sit fucking down.'

So I sat fucking down. Bruno stole a look at me, then

looked away. I could hardly believe they were going to try it. My imagination was in the habit of working overtime – could theirs be too?

Twenty minutes later – I looked at my watch at the end of practically every one of them – they came walking back up the path.

'Yari,' Horst said sharply, 'come here.'

Yari got up and trotted towards him, like a fiercely loyal fighting dog.

'Got to keep an eye on these,' he said, with a jerk of his thumb.

'OK,' Horst said.

Marenkian stepped into the room. He said, 'I'll handle it.'

Yari looked questioningly at Horst, who nodded; then he handed the gun to Marenkian. Outside, Horst whispered to Yari, who listened intently, his eyes screwed up, nodding from time to time. With a growing disbelief I watched the gun. Who was being guarded now?

Then they played the hand.

Horst strolled back in, followed by Yari.

Bruno stood up and said plaintively to Marenkian:

'What's going on? What's happening?'

'It's been settled. Don't get involved.' Marenkian said it in a dry tone, as you might say 'Pass the butter, will you?'

Horst was watching me, a little smile on his face. Yari walked over and sat beside me on the sofa. Something was forming around me. Then Horst came and sat on the other side of me, and Marenkian on the coffee table facing me.

Then Horst gripped my upper arm and said, 'So, Johnny, why don't you tell us what *you* were doing in the house of Max Schenck?'

'I took Bruno there.' *Perhaps they're refining the story, for the police.*

'No, not then. The other time.'

'There hasn't been another time.' I was impatient with them. *You can't be about to try this?*

'Come on, you've been in his house lots of times.'

'I haven't. I've been in his house that once.'

'Ah, you are so stupid,' Horst said.

Then Marenkian began to speak, quietly and venomously.

'Who the hell do you think you are? You come in here and you're trusted. You betray that trust. You get this family into this kind of trouble, and then you expect us to help you out?'

'What? I don't understand what you're talking about.'

'You don't understand?' he shouted. 'Do you expect me to let my son go to jail to protect you?'

Silence.

'I – I don't expect anything. I'm not involved in this.'

'Snooping around here. Reporting back on what you could find out. Selling information. I should beat your crummy little head in.'

'I admit,' I said slowly, 'I admit I took money from Horst. But you don't need to help me. I can just go, now, and you won't owe me anything.'

'Oh, he can just go!' Horst said sarcastically. 'He can just go! That is very good of him.'

'When he's done what he did,' Marenkian said, 'he expects us to let him go.'

'Hey, hold on a minute. What are you trying to do? I didn't have anything to do with Schenck's death. Yari has to answer for that.'

Yari hit me hard on the side of the head, so that I fell back against Horst, who said: 'Be careful.'

'Hey, sorry, Horst.' Then – as I came up for air, half deafened – 'Don't speak that kind of crap.' A ringing started in my ear, and I felt dazed.

'But really, what he's been interested in all along is money, right?' said Horst.

'Selling just about anything.'

'Yeah.'

Then Bruno stood up, looked at me, and said, 'Hey, just what are you doing here? You can't pin this on Johnny.'

'You stay out of this, and you shut up,' Marenkian said.

'No way are you doing that.'

Marenkian stood up and strode over to him.

'Listen to me. If this doesn't happen this way, you're gonna carry the can, OK? Do you understand?'

'That doesn't mean you can do this. I didn't do anything to Max, anyway. Why does anyone have to carry the can?' But he turned away, and stared sullenly out of the window.

There was silence for a moment, and then I breathed hard, and said, 'Look, this is ridiculous. You can't do this. You'll never be believed. I had no motive. I was nowhere near the place. There would be no proof whatsoever.'

Then Marenkian came over to me and put his face close to mine. It was a face different to the one I knew. It was raw and enraged. His skin seemed to have changed colour, his physiognomy its shape.

He whisper-growled, 'What gives you the right to screw my daughter? In my house! Do you think I don't know what goes on here?'

Natalie's head hung low.

'We were in love,' I said quietly.

'In love?' he shouted. 'Don't be ridiculous.'

'And when you found out—' Horst began, and was interrupted by Marenkian.

'And when you found out the kind of *whore* she is, that Schenck was getting it too—'

'That's right,' said Horst. 'I remember you telling me—'

'I didn't tell you that, Horst. I didn't—'

'Come on, Johnny, let's not have any lying now.'

'You lost your temper,' Marenkian went on.

'This is ridiculous.'

'And you took the car.'

'What?'

'You were so angry that you crashed the car into the gates. I remember talking to you just before you went. You were drunk and you were in a savage mood.'

'Oh, for God's sake, just let me go,' I said, and started to stand up.

Yari stood up too, and pushed me down. 'Siddown,' he said.

'No, I fucking won't,' I said, and stood up again. 'You people listen to me. You people are bloody mad if you think you can do this to me. It's a complete fantasy.' They stared at me. I thought for a second I might be reaching them. 'I mean, come on. You can't possibly expect people to believe this,' I said, my hands spread in front of me.

Then I saw, in the corner of my eye, Horst's meaningful look at Yari. And Yari swung his fist, his shoulder behind it, into my solar plexus.

It took me a while to recover from that blow. I was winded, and I lay on the sofa coughing and gagging my way out of it, my eyes streaming.

'You crashed the car into the gates,' Marenkian said quietly and deliberately. 'I was surprised. I wondered what the hell was going on. So did Bruno. So did Natalie.'

Then Natalie said, very quietly, 'You can count me out of this.'

'What did you say?'

'I said you can count me out of this.'

Perhaps if both of them refused to cooperate in this it would fall to pieces. It was absurd in conception, and yet it was somehow convincing, and I knew they were serious. They were going to try it.

Marenkian continued, in a grey, matter-of-fact voice,

'Count you out of it, shit. You're in it. I gave you everything. And if you can't give this little bit back to me, after all *you've* done, then there's a ticket to Colombia for you – one way. *And* for you,' he said, turning to Bruno. 'We have people out there who'll make goddam sure you go back into the gutter you came out of.' Then he turned back to me, completely calm.

'You came back here and tried to slip into the house, didn't you? You were traumatized. But I saw the blood on your T-shirt, the shirt you then burned. It's still sitting out there in the grate. Did you know that the presence of blood can be detected from ashes? You had evidently been in some kind of fight. Your knuckles were broken. Later I asked you to collect medicines from Schenck. You objected violently. You refused, and wouldn't say why. Eventually I ordered you to go.'

'Come on, Marenkian, you know this isn't going to work. Why are you doing it? Bruno didn't kill Schenck.'

'There's a lot of evidence to be accounted for, Johnny. The Range Rover was at the crime scene at the time of the murder. Maybe it was seen. Maybe a young man was seen getting out. Let's not go into it further.'

'It won't work. It won't stick.'

'There'll be a lot of circumstantial evidence against you, Johnny, and a lot of testimony. We'll have witnesses – you know that? We'll have people who saw you going in. Passers-by. Maybe the people who live next door. Don't you under-stand? This is part of my job.' He laughed suddenly, and I think it was the first time I had ever heard him laugh. 'You hated Schenck. You threatened him. He was your rival. You went down there and you beat him to hell.'

'Come on—'

'Don't hand me that, boy. I'll see justice done. When you came back you refused to talk to anyone. You went straight to bed. Your T-shirt was covered in blood, literally soaked in it, and we wondered what the hell you had done. After you had tried to burn it, I recovered the remains and put them away. You weren't very thorough.'

'And of course I knew that you had been hanging around Schenck's house, watching, waiting, perhaps planning what you were going to do. I remember you telling me what you thought of the bastard,' Horst said.

'Understandable, given the way Max Schenck had of humiliating you. There were arguments. He didn't treat people with respect. He took the girl you were in love with,' Marenkian continued quietly.

'No,' I said. 'I'm not going to do it. You want me to admit it, don't you? Well I'm not going to.'

'Listen, boy,' Marenkian said. 'Take it from me, there's a good case against you. You wouldn't have a chance of beating it. The authorities here have a very strong dislike of this kind of incident. The police always like a culprit, a quick culprit. A British drifter is ideal. They don't like the Brits down here any more. Do you think most murder cases are open and shut? With the evidence we give them, they'll have as good a case as they're gonna get anywhere. And we have friends. Friends who can smooth it out. Our friends can get us a result, Johnny. Don't try and buck it. It won't work.'

He turned away for a moment and there was silence.

Then Horst started. 'OK, Johnny, let's be businesslike about this. You wanted a job, right? You wanted to earn some money. Here it is. An unusual kind of job, certainly, but good money, very good money. OK, I'll be honest. I'll be objective. Monsieur Marenkian and I don't want people looking around our business here, disrupting all our lives. Or the lives of our clients. And so Monsieur Marenkian is willing to pay you, pay you a great deal of money to admit to this crime. Fifteen thousand dollars a year for the period of your prison term. Prison is not so bad when you've got the right friends, you know – and when you've got a lot of money.'

'And a bad place when you've got no friends,' Marenkian said. 'And a *real* bad place when you've got enemies. We have friends who can be good friends or bad enemies – in jail. We just say the word.'

Fifteen thousand dollars! Fifteen thousand. What a bloody insult.

'After all, it was a crime of passion, wasn't it, John?' Horst remarked to Marenkian, as if discussing an event of the distant past. 'And the French are still quite lenient on this, yes?'

'If you have a good lawyer,' Marenkian replied, 'it is a plea in mitigation. It would mean five years actually served, with good behaviour.'

'Good character references, all the help he could want from his employers, even after what he had done. It's charming, you know. Five years, Johnny. Seventy-five thousand dollars. Not bad, yeah?'

They both looked at me.

'No, I can't do this. No way.' Now I had to do the right thing. They had played their hand. It was not a very good hand, but they had played it very well.

'Just think about this, Johnny,' Marenkian said. 'If you deny this, with the weight of evidence against you, statements against you from everyone involved in the case, the police—'

'The laboratory doctor—' Horst interrupted.

'With that weight of evidence against you, do you really think you've got a chance? Do you really believe you've got a chance? Take my word for it, boy. Take my word for it. Not an ice cube in hell's chance. Go along with it, and life will be good to you. Turn down the chance we're giving you, and things are going to look very bad.'

The chance we're giving you! I was disappointed in Horst,

but not surprised. I hadn't expected anything more of him. I don't suppose I had the right to expect much from Marenkian.

It wasn't time yet. My first move would be to wait. I would lead with something low.

I would go along with it.

'Come on, Johnny,' Horst said. 'Now is your last chance.'

'OK, Horst,' Marenkian said. 'Let's just get on with it.'

Horst continued to look at me. And I said, 'OK, OK. I'll do it.'

There was a silence in the room, and a tension, and the three of them stared at me. None of them grinned now.

Then Marenkian turned to Bruno, and said, 'Come on. Get him round the neck.'

'What are you doing? I've said I'd go along with it.'

Bruno stood gazing dumbly at Marenkian, while Yari said, 'Got a bit of wood?'

'Find something in the kitchen,' Marenkian replied, and then shouted at Bruno. 'Come on, get him round the neck.'

Bruno moved slowly towards me, and Yari came back from the kitchen with a wooden meat tenderizer.

'What are you doing?' They continued to ignore me. What were they going to do to me now? Damaging me couldn't be in their interests. I had agreed, hadn't I?

Yari looked at Bruno and said casually, 'Not round the neck. Get his left hand.'

Bruno came and sat beside me on the sofa. I tried to catch his eye, but he wouldn't look at me. I even said, 'Bruno', but he just stared at my left hand, the one that his two great paws gripped so tightly round the wrist. Yari crouched down in front of me and put the meat tenderizer down on the floor. Then he drew on a pair of battered leather gloves and picked it up again. Horst gripped my other hand.

'Don't worry, Johnny,' he said. 'We are just going to graze your knuckles a bit.'

'I – my knuckles are already cut – on the left hand. Look,' I said.

'That's good,' he replied, then he forced my right hand onto the table top and held it there. Yari contemplated the tenderizer for a moment. Then he brought it down on my knuckles in a kind of oblique motion. The first time he drew no blood. The second, when he struck harder, he succeeded. He made a little pocket of scuffed-up skin. Behind it a large bubble of dark blood welled up, and then collapsed and seeped gently down between my fingers. There was no pain. He did it again.

Then for some reason – and I'm sure it wasn't the blood – I felt very ill. There was a loud noise in my head, and my skin felt hot and cold. I passed out.

It was like plunging into dark water, with the rushing sound in one's ears that you can just hear when you make a deep dive. Then a dream, with dark figures rushing past me in the night – disembodied voices, shouts. Then I rose near to the surface, and I could look through the water to see faces staring down at me, faces I didn't recognize, and voices speaking, although I couldn't make out anything of what they were saying.

So that when somebody placed something in my hand I could not identify what it was, or why it was there.

Then it was removed, I was left alone, and consciousness slowly returned. Or perhaps it was not so slow in returning. The truth was that I didn't want it to return. I ended up lying on the sofa, awake, feeling weak and sick, my eyes shut.

Then Marenkian pushed my shoulder, and said, 'Come on, you're awake. Sit up.'

I obeyed, defeated.

Yari said, 'What do I do with this?'

He held in his hand a socket wrench, chrome plated, which looked at first sight as if it was covered with rust. Then it became obvious that the dark red was blood. There was some brighter red on it: my blood. I realized with a shock that it must be what he had used on Schenck.

'Bury it the other side of the pool,' Marenkian replied. 'Just put it down for now and get him into the cellar.' Yari came over and took me by the upper arm, pulling me up off the sofa. Then he marched me to the cellar door.

'Come on,' I said. 'You don't need to lock me in anywhere.'

'All part of the job, Johnny,' Horst said as they hustled me across the room.

'Right,' Marenkian said. 'You're doing fine.'

'For Christ's sake,' I said, as they got me to the door.

But they opened it, removed the key from the inside, pushed me in, shut the door, and then locked it.

'Hey!' I shouted. 'Hey! Come on!'

There was no response.

Chapter Nineteen

DABREMIGNE STANDS up and gathers his robes triumphantly around his paunch. The idiot doesn't know why this is happening, but he's going to enjoy it, and if by some chance he doesn't enjoy it he's going to look as though he is.

'The defence would like to recall Mademoiselle Natalie Marenkian.'

The president looks haughty. It must be you, I think. You corrupt little monk, steering it all the right way.

'What is the purpose of her appearing a second time?'

'She wishes to give new testimony which has a bearing on the case.'

He turns to the clerk of the court. 'Is Mademoiselle Marenkian in the witness room?'

'She is, Monsieur le Président.'

'Very good,' he murmurs, then adds in a louder voice, 'Call Natalie Marenkian.'

She's led in, then takes herself to the witness stand. This time she looks different: dressed in white at her first appearance she dazzled with restrained glamour; dressed in black now she seems smaller, more human, more like the girl next door. In fact her original costume was smart and expensive, whereas this is cheap and poorly cut.

The president is not going to give her an easy time: he'll want to be seen to be performing his duty. The procedural questions are repeated.

'You have new testimony to give which bears a relation to this case.'

'Yes, Monsieur le Président.'

'State your testimony.'

A pause.

'On the afternoon of November the sixteenth' – she speaks almost in a whisper – 'I was with John Denner.'

'Speak up.'

But he heard, and so did everyone else. That rustle of sighs you hear in films ripples across the court.

'On the afternoon of November the sixteenth I was with John Denner.'

I can see her shake, even though she braces herself against the rail.

'Between which hours were you with him?'

'Between the hours of two thirty and six thirty. Then at the house between six thirty and ten.'

'In fact, therefore, at the time of the murder?'

'Yes.'

'Where were you at this time?'

'We drove to Nice. We walked from one end of the Promenade des Anglais to the other, then we drove to Saint-Paul, and we sat in the car.'

'How did you travel?'

'We drove in the Range Rover. He scraped it against the gates because he was worried that my father would see us together.'

'You were in the Range Rover when he crashed it?'

'Yes.'

'Were you not seen?'

'I was hiding.'

'Did you stop to eat, or for a drink?'

'No.'

'Did you meet anyone else?'

'No, monsieur.'

'That is to say, Mademoiselle Marenkian, is there anyone else who can confirm your story?'

'No.'

He pauses for a long moment, then looks up at her.

'Have you heard of the crime of perjury?'

'Yes,' she replies very quietly.

'Are you aware that it is a serious crime, and that you can be imprisoned for several years?'

'I was not aware of that.'

'It is my duty to warn you that if you give false testimony you will be punished under the law. You may be acting out of pity for the accused, or even for sentimental reasons. I will now give you the opportunity to tell the court that this testimony is false, that you invented this alibi for Monsieur Denner, and you will not be punished. If you persist in your testimony you may be arrested and charged. Do you understand?'

'Yes.'

Another, longer pause.

'Did you invent the testimony that you were with John Denner on the afternoon of the sixteenth of November?'

'No, monsieur.'

'Was your earlier testimony therefore false?'

'No, monsieur.'

'Yesterday you did not reveal that you were with Monsieur Denner at the time of the crime. Therefore you lied.'

'Yes, monsieur. I regret that I lied.'

'It is possible therefore that you will be charged with perjury. Does the prosecution have any questions?'

The prosecutor is red with anger, but he composes himself before he addresses Natalie.

'So, you claim you were with Denner while your lover was being murdered,' he says, his voice dripping with contempt.

'Yes.'

'Why did you lie to the court?'

She pauses. She seems on the verge of tears.

'Because I was ashamed,' she whispers.

'You were ashamed?'

She looks up, tears are running from her eyes.

'I was ashamed that I was with him when somebody was doing what they were doing to Max.'

'Were you Denner's lover?'

'No.'

'Then what were you doing, spending an afternoon with him in secret?'

'I was trying to make him see that I couldn't be his lover, and that he had interpreted our friendship wrongly.'

He puffs himself up into incredulity.

'You are telling the court that you spent an afternoon in secret with a man who was not your lover, telling him that he couldn't be your lover?'

'Yes.'

'And that nobody saw you?'

'I was trying to keep it secret that I was seeing him. My father would have been very angry if he had found out.'

The prosecutor's eyes flash and he frowns. It all makes unexpected sense.

'And you claim that this took what – six hours? Eight hours even?'

'We talked about other things.'

'Why are you protecting Denner?'

'I wouldn't want to see him go to jail for a crime he didn't commit.'

This has been an exceptionally long set of questions for one of the lawyers; it's the president who normally asks the questions, and he is looking impatient. And so, with a scowl, the prosecutor holds his fire.

'No more questions.'

The president nods to the lawyers for Schenck's family, but

they don't have anything to add. He looks to Dabremigne, who stands up.

'Monsieur le Président, in the light of this new evidence, which demonstrates beyond any doubt that John Denner could not have committed the murder of Max Schenck, I move that the case be dismissed and the trial brought to a close immediately, and that John Denner be freed immediately.'

The president puts his hands over his microphone and confers briefly with the two acolytes. Then he speaks.

'The judgement of this court is that the case will continue to be heard, and that the second testimony of Natalie Marenkian will be considered along with the first, and that the jury will reach a conclusion.'

Then he addresses Natalie. 'Mademoiselle Marenkian, you are released, but not definitively, and you will stay in the courtroom pending the necessity for further questioning, or to answer the charge of perjury. The court will decide whether such a charge is to be made following the court's decision in the case of Monsieur Denner.'

Then he turns to me.

'Monsieur Denner, please stand up. Tell me, please, why you did not reveal to the court that you were with Natalie Marenkian on the afternoon of the murder.'

I draw a deep breath.

'I hoped that she would reveal it to the court herself. But I also didn't wish to involve her in any scandal.'

'Are you, or have you at any time been, the lover of Natalie Marenkian?'

'No.'

'Is there any sentimental relationship between you?'

'No, monsieur.'

A long pause.

'You may sit down.'

*

I switched the cellar lights on. I didn't know how long I would have to wait and I would need to time my move to a nicety. I was fairly certain I would be able to hear Horst's car leave, and I could only hope the police wouldn't come too soon afterwards. It seemed certain that Horst and Yari *would* leave before the law arrived.

The waiting was torture, of course, but I disciplined myself, sitting at the bottom of the stone steps. I had to be patient, I told myself. Marenkian might swallow the hook, but Yari never would – nor Horst, in all probability.

About half an hour passed, then it was time. Time at last to play my hand. They might be experts; I might be a novice; but I held the aces. I wasn't going to be bluffed.

'Marenkian!' I shouted. 'MARENKIAN.'

Silence. I shouted his name again, and banged on the inside of the door. Had they *all* left? I banged again and, just as I took a breath, his dry voice sounded through the wood.

'Shut up in there or I'll shut you up.'

'I need to talk to you.'

'No talking.'

'Come on, Marenkian. It's important.'

'No talking,' he said again, and I heard his retreating footsteps on the terracotta.

'MARENKIAN. YOUR WINE. I'M GOING TO SMASH YOUR CLARETS.'

I ran down the steps to the nearest bottles. It wouldn't matter what they were.

'LA LAGUNE, EIGHTY-FOUR. COME ON.' I picked up a bottle and threw it against the wall. That would give him pause.

'ANOTHER ONE . . .' and I repeated the exercise.

'MONTROSE, EIGHTY-TWO. COME ON.' I smashed it. Then the bolt rattled and he was standing at the top of the stairs, gun in hand.

'Get up here. You're going in a goddam cupboard.'

'Wait.'

'Move it.'

'Last night I removed all the bearer share certificates from rue Pilatte.'

He stopped for the shortest moment.

'Yeah? I just have to make a phone call and those companies are worthless. The money will just disappear down the wire. Thanks for letting me know. Now, get—'

'Bollocks, Marenkian. Don't try and bluff me. You and Horst and your blabbermouth family have given me all I need to clean you out. I've got the blue notebook too. I've got the key to your network.'

'No, you have not got that notebook.'

'In a safe place, Marenkian. A blue leather notebook.'

'In five minutes, Johnny, that information will be out of date and totally worthless. And if I need any of those bearer shares, I'm going to beat the location out of you, boy.'

'Try it.'

'In fifteen seconds I'm going to shoot you through the foot. Do you know how incredibly painful that is? Do you know that it's impossible to rebuild the foot? That you'll limp for the rest of your life?'

He does need them.

'Listen, Marenkian.'

'And I'll tell you something else. You're going to live to regret taking those. Once you're convicted, when you're in jail, people will come and find you in the night. I don't even like to think what they'll do to you.' He waved the gun. 'Now, give – where are they? Five seconds.'

'I have evidence incriminating Bruno in the Schenck murder.'

'As you said yourself, Bruno didn't commit that murder.'

'I have a letter he wrote to Schenck. I was given this letter to deliver to Schenck the day before he was killed.'

Marenkian went very still.

'Now, I don't know just exactly what Bruno did in Baltimore, but he threatened to do it again to Max Schenck.'

'Well, I hate to disappoint you, Johnny, but that's just Bruno's hysteria. He was up on a drugs charge in Baltimore.'

'Is that so? Well, you may be telling the truth, Marenkian, but I doubt it. That letter is on its way to a contact in the UK, and the matter will be investigated and handed to the authorities here.'

'Johnny, you're wasting your time.'

'What did he do? Did he kill someone? "Give the notebook back, Max," he said in the letter. "If you don't give the notebook back I'm going to do what I did in Baltimore." Who did he kill, eh? He's got a previous record, then. And if suspicion falls on him, you can forget about your evidence, and his, and Natalie's. This whole thing will fall apart. And then, once I've cooperated with the police, it'll just be a question of whether Bruno is picked up, or Yari.'

He stared at me very intently for a moment, then turned on his heel without a word, sprang up the stairs, and went out, locking the door behind him. A few minutes passed and he was back. He pushed Bruno in front of him as they came down the steps. I opened a bottle of Black Label and swigged from it.

'Describe this letter,' Marenkian said.

'It says: "Max, you've made a bad mistake now. You know what I did in Baltimore. Unless I get the notebook back I'm going to do it again, to you. Don't think I can't, so just give me the notebook back, *today*. I'm coming to see you, and I'll want it then. Or else."'

Bruno didn't even speak, and he didn't look at me once. He just nodded at his father.

'Leave us alone now,' snapped Marenkian.

Bruno turned and went, and for a little while Marenkian and I stood facing each other.

'So let me go.'

'No, I can't do that.'

'You don't have a choice.'

'My standing,' he said slowly and, God, he was calm, 'wouldn't allow me to do that. It would make it difficult to deal with Horst, for instance. And there are risks on your side. You might not even get the letter admitted as evidence. And I wasn't bluffing when I told you I had friends in the police force and the judiciary. Evidence has been suppressed. Things have happened to people in police cells.'

'Come on, Marenkian. That's bullshit.'

'It's a risk. And I work in a risk business. And I have very good contacts.'

'Take the risk, then.'

'OK, Johnny, I'll be straight with you. I can't be seen to let you go now. Not while Horst and Yari are around to know it, and to let other people know. In a few months' time Horst and Yari won't matter any more. But they matter now. And if there's a protracted police investigation I have a lot to lose. So do they. Maybe more than what your letter can lose me. The police will turn up links between all of us, and will start nosing into my business, and the businesses of my colleagues and my clients. I can't allow that to happen.'

'That is going to happen if they get the letter.'

'Maybe. But there's something else, you see. If I let you go, who becomes the chief suspect? Even though he didn't do it: Bruno, letter or no letter. The authorities here will uncover what happened in Baltimore anyway. It'll be a matter of routine.'

'What *did* happen in Baltimore?'

Marenkian was silent for a moment.

'He pushed his girlfriend off a building, and she was killed.'

Silence for a moment.

'So, no, Johnny, I can't let you go.'

'Come on, Marenkian. You're just trying to bluff it. You can't take that kind of risk with the rest of your son's life.'

'But I can do a deal with you.'

'What deal?'

'You do stand trial for Schenck's murder.'

'No way.'

'Listen,' he said. 'Listen to me. You stand trial, but you're never convicted. We rig it. Listen. You go on trial. The evidence in the case is heard and shown; attributed to you. It's your T-shirt, your fingerprints in the car, your fingerprints in Schenck's house. All the evidence points in your direction, but it's all circumstantial. Then, late in the case, when your links to this evidence have been established – it's been established that it's your T-shirt, for example – a new piece of evidence emerges that absolves you of blame, that forces an acquittal. That says: sure, it was his T-shirt, but the blood on it was innocent.'

'What kind of evidence?'

'An alibi, Johnny. It can be done, with the right planning, and a little assistance I can arrange.'

'So you're saying—' I said slowly, 'you're saying that the evidence that links Bruno to the case will be associated with the case against me. Like it's my T-shirt, not Bruno's. And when the case against me collapses, the evidence is . . .' I searched for the word.

'Neutralized. It wouldn't exist for another case. It would never stand up.'

'That's a hell of a risk for me to take. But, come on, tell me about this alibi.'

'Natalie.'

'Natalie wouldn't do that.'

'Natalie will do just exactly what I tell her to do. In every detail.'

'You can't guarantee any of this. How do I know you're going to keep your side of the bargain? How do I know she's really going to change her testimony?'

'Well, you can't be sure, can you? But it's the best I have to offer. Believe me, I can make it work. Oh, and I'd produce somebody to back it up, some place you had lunch, or something. And someone in the process would help us along.'

'Sorry?'

'Someone in the judiciary, Johnny. I told you I have good contacts.'

'It's a hell of a risk. I could take my chances and fight you on this. You'll have to give me an incentive.'

'Fifty thousand dollars.'

'Just let me go now. I'll give you the letter and you won't owe me a thing.'

'No. It's the deal or nothing.'

'Fifty thousand isn't enough. This could take a year to come to trial. I want much more than fifty.'

'A hundred.'

'Five hundred.'

After some time we came to terms. Then we started the delicate, slow business of constructing the story. We couldn't make any mistakes.

They came for me, after the right hints had been dropped in the right places, a day later, and I went without a murmur.

Chapter Twenty

THE PROSECUTOR has been speaking for some time, pulling his ermine around him as he builds to a climax, then dramatically casting it aside for effect. He dwells lovingly on Schenck's injuries, on the savagery with which they were inflicted. And he reminds the jury of the accumulated circumstantial evidence: my interest in Natalie; my enquiries into Marenkian's finances; my fury at the discovery of her affair with Schenck, witnessed by the bearded neighbour; my taking the Range Rover and crashing the gates, my cut knuckles, bloodied T-shirt. He ridicules my explanations; it is absurdly improbable that I had a fight with a passing motorist, completely impossible that such an encounter should put so much blood on the T-shirt. He is of the old school, this prosecutor: he should have been on the stage with his thundering denunciations, his spills-and-thrills oration.

'So here is a young Englishman who is well known as a womanizer, and not only as a womanizer but as the particularly despicable kind of man who lives off women. Unfortunately we regularly do get spongers and parasites of this kind on the Côte d'Azur: men who hang around rich women and try to seduce them. Men whose ultimate aim, of course, is to take all that these women have.

'Denner had found just such a girl in England, but then he was arrested for drug running, and her father paid him off. Yes, ladies and gentlemen, her father paid him to go away and leave their family alone. Because Denner is the kind of man who can make a girl do almost anything once he has his hands on her. Oh, yes, ladies and gentlemen, as we will see.

'Now he's in close contact with a girl who has everything he's looking for. Imagine! He's down on his luck, he has no money, and instead of being a wealthy army officer, he is a mere servant with no money. But living in the house in which he serves is Natalie Marenkian. Her father is a highly successful, specialized lawyer, so she is potentially very rich. Not only that, she is beautiful and accomplished. And she seems to like him. A wonderful chance for him, ladies and gentlemen. And not only a wonderful chance,' he growls, his eyes bulging and his voice swooping, 'but his last chance! His last chance to hit the big time. To get back everything he has lost.

'And we know, ladies and gentlemen, from what she herself has told us, that there is more between them than simply the relationship of a servant and an employer. Which woman goes driving in the hills on her own with a servant? Or even with a friend? *Non! Je dis non!* Natalie Marenkian claims that she went into the hills with him to tell him she couldn't be his lover. The kind of claim women often make when – excuse me – they are about to go up the stairs! "I had to be alone with him to tell him that I couldn't be alone with him"! *Bien!*

'So things are going very well with him, according to his plan – and I don't deny there may have been some very real sentiment there. Perhaps, even, they may have fallen in love. We will never know the truth. But what we do know, and we know with no doubt because we heard it from an independent witness who has given evidence in this court and will not lie – what we do know is that Denner found out that Dr Schenck was the lover of Natalie Marenkian, and that in his rage at this discovery he swore to kill him.

'Imagine, ladies and gentlemen, what Denner's feelings were when he discovered that all his plans and ambitions were to come to nothing. His rage was not something we can picture. We know that he has a criminal past, and we know that he had hated Dr Schenck before ever he knew that the doctor was Natalie Marenkian's lover. So he went back to Dr Schenck's house after the humiliation he had received. You will remember the testimony of Monsieur Marenkian, a highly skilled and intelligent lawyer. He saw Denner take the car and crash it; more importantly he saw subsequently the large bloodstain on Denner's shirt, the T-shirt that he later tried to burn. You will remember the testimony of Monsieur Delbos, the neighbour of Dr Schenck, who heard Denner threatening the doctor's life. And, finally and conclusively, you will remember the evidence of the expert witness who clearly identified Denner's thumb-print on the socket wrench used to beat Dr Schenck so savagely to death.'

He pauses, turns away from the jury and then turns back, his voice raised to a fresh pitch, a look of pantomime disbelief on his face.

'And today, ladies and gentlemen, a surprise. Natalie Marenkian, the body of her old lover hardly cold, has got a new one. A young lover this time. She says she had a secret meeting with him. Well, how many other secret meetings did she have? When does anyone have secret meetings with people who aren't their lovers? Naturally she denies it. Naturally she doesn't want you to know that she is Denner's lover. For then you wouldn't believe the alibi she has provided for him. And naturally she is ashamed.

'You might ask yourselves, ladies and gentlemen, whether she is the sort of woman you would be inclined to believe in any circumstances. In her own father's house she gives herself first, in secret, to her father's friend, a man twice her age. Then she associates herself, at the same time, with the servant in that house. She is obviously in the regular habit of lying to her father. And she has lied to this court; there is no doubt about that. The only question is when did she lie. Did she lie when she said nothing, the first time she gave testimony; or did she lie when she came back to give an alibi to the man with whom she is on intimate terms? An alibi that nobody else can support.'

The atmosphere in the court has stiffened slightly, and it seems to me, without any doubt, that he is overplaying his hand. Natalie put dew in the jury's eyes, and they don't like this old queen wiping it out.

'There is a very clear case, ladies and gentlemen, supported by a wealth of evidence, that Denner murdered Max Schenck in cold blood. And there is only one piece of testimony, brought at the last moment by an unreliable witness with whom he is on intimate terms, to suggest that he may not have done. It is a desperate attempt to pervert the course of justice. To that evidence I say: no, I don't believe it. No sensible person could do anything other than set it aside, and find Denner guilty of murder. And then sentence him to life imprisonment.'

He swivels on his heel and sits down.

One year, three months, six days.

That's not bad, for an acquittal in France. It was strange being behind the wheel of a car again, savouring again the colour, the wide open space, the richness of everything after those drab greys and greens. It was the same story all over again, but a lifetime seemed to have passed, and I wasn't the same man who had walked from a prison into the sunlight once before. Then it had been my first time, and in a way I really had been an innocent, the victim of an unfortunate accident. I could hardly call myself an innocent now. I was guilty, although not of the crime for which I had been tried. I was guilty of certain criminal offences, of course: perverting the course of justice, perjury, blackmail. But had I not committed them, I would have gone to the wall. I had been obliged to protect myself.

Instead of feeling triumphant, though, as I drove into the hills for my one and only meeting with Marenkian, I felt tired and seedy. I had chosen to follow a certain road, and it was not a very clean or honest one. It would be a long haul back to the crossroads if I wanted to change my mind. But I didn't want to change my mind. I wanted to exact from Marenkian what was my due. My due for spending another year of my life in jail. My due for the four and a quarter hours the jury took.

I was confident that he wouldn't mess me around, at least in part because of the treatment I had received inside. Over the first couple of days several individuals had introduced themselves to me: a senior warder who vouched for my safety and had me transferred to a two-man rather than three-man cell; a small, genial inmate with the strange nickname of Coco, who offered simply to be my friend; and a gigantic, taciturn inmate named André who said he would show me the ropes. Eating dinner with Coco and André conferred immediate celebrity status, and from that meal on nobody in the place showed me the least sign of disrespect. I was able to renew my acquaintance with speed and cocaine, and I gave myself some of the purest, meanest hangovers of my life with the pastis they made. So there was no doubt at all about Marenkian's weight, or his intentions.

It took me a little while to find the place he had specified for our meeting; discretion was needed now. It was a longer drive out of Nice, up into the drier, higher hills behind Vence and Grasse. There is little development up there; little of anything. So the first time I drove past the track with the chain across it I missed it.

The house at the end was something quite extraordinary. It was built in what might once have been a shallow quarry, so that you couldn't know it was there until you descended the hill to the front of the horseshoe. It was hooded by a dark tiled roof like a monk's cowl, projecting far over the plate-glass windows of the front, so that its rooms were in deep shade. A large swimming pool glinted in the sun; people flying into Nice would perhaps see a tiny opal in the sand. Marenkian stood inside the plate glass, in an enormous empty room floored with dark wood; a little concert hall in the hills.

'Hello, John,' I said. *I'm not your servant any more.*

There was the ghost of a smile in his eyes.

'You look like an Englishman. Pale like you've just arrived out of some foggy day.'

'Let's hope it's tanning weather out there.'

'The rainy season, I'm afraid. But you needn't worry. It just rains for about an hour at four o'clock, then life goes on. Have you brought them with you?'

'It wasn't part of our agreement that I should bring anything with me.'

'Sure. You'll take them with you to Panama.'

'So you can snatch them in the terminal? Come on, John. I've had a year to think about this. So the certificates are all somewhere safe, ready to be picked up when I get there. A year and a quarter. That's six months longer than we thought.'

'And you want more money?'

'A bit more. I only want what I'm owed. I'm not trying to screw anyone down. Four hundred.'

'It's a deal,' he said, somewhat to my surprise. 'Here's some spare change,' he said, and pulled an envelope from his pocket. 'It's enough to get you to Panama. You know the score when you get there. Pan-American Banking Trust. Pablo Enrile Barbena. You introduce yourself, you produce the letter and the bearer shares. And in exchange you'll get – what you're owed.'

'They never followed it up, did they?'

'Not really. The official line was that owing to a miscarriage of justice the culprit got away with it. The culprit being you. The *juge d'instruction* wasn't interested in an alternative. He couldn't have made it stick.'

'Tell me,' I said to him. 'How much of this was planned? I know that Horst was working for you all along.' I stopped.

'*Do* you know that?' he replied. 'I don't. Horst was looking out for himself. When the cards were dealt he saw where his interests lay. You see' – he spoke slowly, almost dreamily – 'people think there's some kind of strategy, some big plan. But it's not like that. It's like a poker game, maybe. You wouldn't say: "Tonight I'm gonna go all the way each time I get a straight." If you did, you'd lose. You watch the cards, you watch the players, you think, and you make your move.'

'But if Horst was working for you, why did he keep that from me?'

'What makes you think Horst was working for me?'

'Jean-Robert Sospine. The French boy Yari beat up; the old woman's grandson. Your employee; Horst's driver.'

He held out the envelope.

'That was observant of you, Johnny. Now you understand the need for discretion.'

I said one more thing.

'If you have hard feelings, don't forget what you tried to do to me. You never talked to Schenck that night. Horst reported in, didn't he, that Yari had gone a bit too far in trying to extract information from Schenck.'

'True.'

'And Horst had this touching loyalty to Yari. So you had to go to all that trouble to protect him.'

'Yari was a powerful man in Moscow.'

'Was?'

296 ◄ William Hutchison

'You've changed, Johnny, and now you're living life a little. But when you get to Panama, don't make the wrong move. This time you got lucky.'

I couldn't summon a cliché worthy of the occasion, so I just took the envelope and said, 'Thanks, John. You can rely on me.'

We looked at each other for a moment in the shadows of the big, empty room – a very cold moment, and I knew that I was nothing to him but an irritation, and that I had indeed been very lucky. Then behind him there was a click. I looked, and at the open doorway at the far end Bruno stood alone. Marenkian didn't turn.

Bruno's presence was curiously and disturbingly eloquent. What would he be now? What could he do? I knew this would be the last time I saw him, and that I would always picture him standing for the rest of his life alone in that empty, shaded room. It was a sad picture. And, as if it were only a picture, or that he were standing the other side of a glass wall, I felt that I couldn't speak to him or acknowledge him in any way.

So I turned my back and walked out, my footsteps reverberating on the polished wood.

'I thought it might amuse you,' she said.

'Pin-up looks, eh?' I handed her back the cutting. 'You can't believe everything you read, can you?'

'Did he warn you off?'

'No, he didn't, actually.' There were the ruins of some small building, a miniature lighthouse perhaps, on the rocks near where we sat. Inland, only the high walls of the very expensive residences on the Cap. As far as I could see there was nobody to watch us. 'I would imagine he thought that unnecessary.'

She looked at me sadly. 'You're still angry with me.'

'I'm not sure if I am, actually.'

'I took a big risk for you.'

'No, you didn't.'

'Johnny, I could have gone to jail. You heard what the judge said about perjury.'

'Yes, my dear, but you didn't do it for me. You did it on your father's orders.'

'Well . . . OK. But I wanted to do it for you, too.'

'Cheap credit, eh?'

'*That's* cheap.'

'OK, it is. Why not? I feel cheap.'

'You've changed, you know that?'

'I dare say I have. Who wouldn't?'

'You used to be an idealist: very fresh, and a little naïve.'

'And now I'm a hard case.'

'I wouldn't say that. You're not quite so soft.'

God damn her, she got at me. I had arrived at that little outcrop on the coast as cold as a stone, and I wished my heart were made of stone so that it could withstand her.

'You know,' I said sarcastically, 'it gave me pleasure to think, while I was in prison, that I had allowed you to play a meaningful part in your father's business. You were very good in the courtroom. I particularly liked the way you were all rich and upper-class the first time you appeared, so the ordinary folk on the jury wouldn't trust you, then all poor the second, like some peasant in her Sunday best.'

'Going to a baptism.'

'Yes, exactly.'

'That was Marenkian. He coached us in everything, chose the clothes, wanted to see my make-up.'

'He's good, isn't he?'

'He's done it before.'

'And has he rewarded your performance with a slice of his cake?'

She was silent for a moment, a sour look on her face.

'Even less likely than before.'

I curled my lip. I wasn't going to tell her I was sorry, even if I was.

'Really?'

'Yeah. You see, Bruno's come out of this smelling of roses. It's been made known in certain circles that he killed Max. And that's been very good for his credibility. And the absence of Max has improved his recovery beyond recognition.'

'How could you have done that? I know he's not your blood brother, but to stand by and watch what Schenck was doing—'

'I didn't *know* what Max was doing. Everybody including Marenkian – including Bruno – believed that Max was doing the right thing. The way Max put it to me was that he could help me at the same time as helping Bruno by removing the malignant influence of Marenkian, who was destroying him. Claiming that Bruno's confusion and everything were just temporary problems. Anyway, I couldn't have influenced him.'

'Well, I suppose that's about it,' I said. The late afternoon sun had turned the water to a sheet of gold.

'What's he paying you?'

'Enough.' I didn't want to tell her.

'Half a million's my guess.' Bitch. She saw it in my face. 'Chickenfeed. Nothing. You know how much money there is in his business? Half a million dollars is a flea bite, a drop of piss. And you're gonna go chasing all over the world for that piece of nothing, feeling all sexy about it.'

'I'm getting more than that,' I said. I hated her, not least because she had made sure I wouldn't feel good about it again.

'You've got him by the balls. You could collect ten, twenty million out of this.'

'Come on.'

'He's worth a hundred. You could be set up, for life. And what are you doing? You're accepting a tip. Ten dollars for Johnny.' Her voice was full of contempt.

'It's something, Natalie. It's what's due to me.'

She came close to me, her eyes fixed on mine, and her voice was almost a whisper.

'You've got the shares. I've got the notebook.' She stared at me.

'I know,' I said quietly. 'I know you've got the bloody notebook. Why else would Schenck have sat there and let them smash his head in?'

'It was an accident that he was killed.'

'It was because he wouldn't tell them where it was.'

'Sorry, Johnny, but you're wrong. I know that it was Yari running out of control. He got angry and took a swing, and that was it. Max would have told them. But he didn't get a chance. You don't believe me? Try looking Yari up. He's in the bottom of some hole – and that's why.'

Then she came even closer, and I could suddenly smell her, and I gritted my teeth.

'For once in your life,' she whispered, 'you have a chance. You have the kind of chance that only comes once. Once only. You've got to take it. We put the notebook and the shares together and we have the key. Don't you see? The shares on their own are useless, because it's impossible to know where the companies are located. So is the notebook. But together, then you have my father's money and the money of all his clients. Hundreds of millions. I mean it.'

'What if he's moved the funds around?'

'Johnny, he can't without the shares. His business has been paralysed for a year. Take the chance,' she shouted.

'Oh, God,' I shouted back, and wheeled away. I had thought I was going to find some peace. But I had come here to meet her, hadn't I? And whatever I might be busy telling myself, I didn't want to leave without her. I wanted her to proposition me.

'He sent you down to Schenck's house. He tried to frame

you for a murder. Come on! What kind of man are you? Take me with you. I'll be anything you want. And we'll take that fucking money.'

I turned to her, out of my mind, knowing what I was doing. I almost ran to the driver's door.

'Come on, then. Get in the car. Get in the car!'

She snatched up her bag and jumped in the passenger seat, and I drove. We stopped at some lights, and I looked behind, to the slim leather briefcase on the back seat. I had lied to Marenkian about the documents, of course; I had picked them up at the Carlton before driving to the Cap. I glanced at her, then pulled the briefcase over and slipped it into the pocket beside me. It was just a little too close to those light little fingers of hers.

I shook my head at myself. What kind of glutton for punishment am I? Then I glanced at her again, and she was grinning. I looked at her rosy lips and her sharp white teeth and I thought: What the hell, we deserve each other. We'll probably go down together. They'll probably find us, and she'll probably leave me to my fate. Or one day I'll wake up and find that she's taken off with the money.

I looked across at her and grinned back.

'Let's find a hotel.'

45

986P